An oath to uphold, a tragedy to avenge

HANK
HANEGRAAFF

SIGMUND
BROUWER

THE LAST TEMPLE

TYNDALE HOUSE PUBLISHERS, INC.
CAROL STREAM, ILLINOIS

Visit Tyndale online at www.tyndale.com.

For more information and resources, visit Hank Hanegraaff's Christian Research Institute online at www.equip.org.

Find Sigmund Brouwer online at www.sigmundbrouwer.com.

TYNDALE and Tyndale's quill logo are registered trademarks of Tyndale House Publishers, Inc.

The Last Temple

Library of Congress Cataloging-in-Publication Data

Hanegraaff, Hank.
  The last temple / Hank Hanegraaff, Sigmund Brouwer.
    p. cm. — (The last disciple ; 3)
    ISBN 978-0-8423-8446-9 (sc)
    1. Bible. N.T. Revelation XIII—History of Biblical events—Fiction. 2. Rome—History—Civil War, 68-69—Fiction. 3. Church history—Primitive and early church, ca. 30-600—Fiction. 4. Rome—History—Nero, 54-68—Fiction. 5. End of the world—Fiction. I. Brouwer, Sigmund, date. II. Title.
    PS3608.A714L376 2012
    813'.6—dc23   2012008612

Printed in the United States of America

18   17   16   15   14   13   12
7   6   5   4   3   2   1

To my daughter Elise Hanegraaff.
Brilliant and beautiful, she relentlessly
explores the world through the power of story.

Calendar Notes

THE ROMANS DIVIDED the day into twelve hours. The first hour, *hora prima,* began at sunrise, approximately 6 a.m. The twelfth hour, *hora duodecima,* ended at sunset, approximately 6 p.m.

hora prima	first hour	6–7 a.m.
hora secunda	second hour	7–8 a.m.
hora tertiana	third hour	8–9 a.m.
hora quarta	fourth hour	9–10 a.m.
hora quinta	fifth hour	10–11 a.m.
hora sexta	sixth hour	11 a.m.–12 p.m.
hora septina	seventh hour	12–1 p.m.
hora octava	eighth hour	1–2 p.m.
hora nonana	ninth hour	2–3 p.m.
hora decima	tenth hour	3–4 p.m.
hora undecima	eleventh hour	4–5 p.m.
hora duodecima	twelfth hour	5–6 p.m.

The New Testament refers to hours in a similar way. Thus, when we read in Luke 23:44, "It was now about the sixth hour, and darkness came over the whole land until the ninth hour," we understand that this period of time was from the hour before noon to approximately 3 p.m.

The Romans divided the night into eight watches.

Watches before midnight: *Vespera, Prima fax, Concubia, Intempesta.*

Watches after midnight: *Inclinatio, Gallicinium, Conticinium, Diluculum.*

The Romans' days of the week were Sun, Moon, Mars, Mercury, Jupiter, Venus, and Saturn.

The months of the Hebrew calendar are Nisan, Iyar, Sivan, Tammuz, Av, Elul, Tishri, Heshvan, Kislev, Tevet, Shevat, Adar I, and Adar II.

3RD WALL

2ND WALL

Hippicus

Antonia
Tower

Courtyard

Holy of Holies

Temple

Upper City

Temple Mount

Lower City

Camp of the
Tenth Legion on
the Mount of Olives

JERUSALEM
✠
AD 70

Dramatis Personae

Alypia: Widow of Lucius Bellator; former lover of Maglorius; stepmother of Valeria and Quintus

Amaris: Wife of Simeon Ben-Aryeh

Annas the Younger: Former high priest

Atronius Pavo: Captain of the ship that carried John and Vitas to Alexandria

Bernice: Queen of the Jews; sister of Agrippa II

Caius Sennius Ruso: Wealthy senator; friend of John

Chayim: Son of Simeon Ben-Aryeh

Dolabella: Wife of Gnaea Lartius Helva

Gaius Calpurnius Piso: Plotted to kill Nero

Gaius Cestius Gallus: Governor of Syria

Gaius Ofonius Tigellinus: Prefect of the Praetorian Guard; member of Nero's inner circle

Gallus Sergius Damian: Slave hunter; brother of Vitas

Gallus Sergius Vitas: Famed general of the Roman army; former member of Nero's inner circle; husband of Sophia; brother of Damian

Gessius Florus: Former Roman procurator of Judea

Gnaea Lartius Helva: Fiscal procurator of Judea

Helius: Nero's secretary; member of Nero's inner circle

Hezron: Famed rabbi in Rome; father of Leah

Jerome: Slave of Damian

John, son of Zebedee: Last disciple of Jesus of Nazareth

John of Gischala: Leader of the Jewish Zealots in Jerusalem

Joseph Ben-Matthias: Prominent citizen in upper city Jerusalem

Leah: Daughter of Hezron and a follower of the Christos

Maglorius: Former gladiator; former servant in the Bellator household

Marcus Antonius Julianus: Roman procurator of Judea

Marcus Cocceius Nerva: Roman senator opposed to Nero

Nero Claudius Caesar Augustus Germanicus: Roman emperor; persecutor of the followers of the Christos

Quintus Valerius Messalina: Ten-year-old son of Lucius Bellator

Simeon Ben-Aryeh: Member of the Sanhedrin; escaped Jerusalem; fugitive of Rome with Sophia

Simon Ben-Gioras: Leader of a Jewish faction in Jerusalem

Sophia: Wife of Vitas; fugitive of Rome with Ben-Aryeh; a follower of the Christos

Sporus: Nero's young lover

Titus Flavius Vespasianus: Son of Vespasian; general of the Roman legions besieging Jerusalem

Valeria Messalina: Daughter of Lucius Bellator

CAESAREA

Province of Judea

The beast was given a mouth to utter proud words and blasphemies and to exercise his authority for forty-two months. He opened his mouth to blaspheme God, and to slander his name and his dwelling place and those who live in heaven. He was given power to make war against the saints and to conquer them. And he was given authority over every tribe, people, language and nation. All inhabitants of the earth will worship the beast—all whose names have not been written in the book of life belonging to the Lamb that was slain from the creation of the world.

REVELATION 13:5-8

From the Revelation, given to John on the island of Patmos in AD 63

❧ SUN ❧

HORA QUARTA

THE CROWDED MARKET SQUARE of Caesarea, in a city that was solidly a Roman possession, should not have been a place of danger. But a good soldier should always remain watchful. So later, in the early hours of the following dawn—before the first hammer blows descended on his helpless body as a result of his carelessness—Gallus Sergius Vitas would look back on what had happened and realize he had made his first mistake when he allowed irritation to overcome his habitual watchfulness.

He could not excuse the lapse, even though there were plenty of reasons to justify his irritation. Not the least were the fresh tattoo marks on his forehead that identified him as a slave, a criminal punished with bondage—a possession of the Beast named Nero. With these markings came a copper band on Vitas's wrist and the rough tunic of the new class of society to which he now belonged.

Since arriving in Caesarea months earlier, Vitas had posed as a slave to his brother, Damian, because that was his best protection as a fugitive from Nero. His tattoos were not from ink but from a paste made of the powdered leaves of the henna plant. They would not remain permanently. While the false markings were a symbol of hope, signifying Vitas's expectation that someday he would no longer be a fugitive but a free man again, in his heart Vitas felt this hope was a mere pretense. Each morning was an event that dulled his soul, for waking brought with it the ache that never seemed to lessen—knowledge of his wife's death.

Only recently, Damian had proposed that since Vitas was already perceived as a slave, there would be no harm in carrying the deception a step further. He had convinced Vitas to allow himself to be sold into servitude to the household of Gnaea Lartius Helva, the fiscal procurator of Judea. Damian, a slave hunter who had engaged Vitas to join Helva's household and spy on a domestic situation, had promised him it was only a temporary situation.

Vitas should have known better. Once he had agreed—with reluctance—to assume an identity as a slave named Novellus, Damian had promptly left for Jerusalem to find an old friend—Maglorius, who had been a renowned gladiator in Rome. Vitas guessed that Damian now probably spent his evenings on silk in Jerusalem, while Vitas slept on a filthy straw mattress each night, sharing cramped quarters—and fleas—with two other men who had not bathed in weeks, if not months. Vitas itched in places he'd never itched before, and for every flea he caught on his body and pinched with grim delight between the nails of his thumb and forefinger, there were scores more to replace it.

These were minor irritations, however; after he had survived a campaign in Britannia, nothing seemed worth complaint.

Just before the disastrous events in the Caesarean market unfolded, Vitas's major source of irritation was the woman his new master had assigned him to guard. Helva's wife, Dolabella. The mistress of the house rotated her bodyguards and, it was rumored, occasionally subjected them to her lascivious whims. But because her retinue numbered a dozen, she had yet to turn her attentions fully to Vitas.

Vitas had observed her closely and did not like what he saw. She was the sort of woman who relied heavily on her looks and was at an age where she had realized her looks would not remain eternal. For this day's visit to the governor, she had dyed her hair a blonde that verged on orange, donned the most luxurious clothing possible, and draped herself with pounds of jewelry, then set out to enjoy a stroll through the market, grandly pretending she was just another Roman citizen.

In the marketplace, Vitas walked behind her with another slave, a monstrous mute named Jerome, at his right side, and two other slaves at his left. Like Vitas, Jerome had been assigned to this deception by Damian; unlike Vitas, Jerome truly was a slave and had belonged to Damian for years.

Dolabella's husband, Helva, hurrying ahead because of an urgent summons from the governor, was accompanied by half a dozen soldiers. Caesarea was not an area of unrest like Jerusalem, and the soldiers were mainly a show of prestige. The group formed a wedge that shoved aside the people at the entrance to the market.

As they made progress through the market, a trumpet sounded three times. Vitas had his mind on the synagogue beyond the market, and the noise of the trumpet barely registered on his consciousness. The smells of the market, however, were difficult to ignore.

The morning was ripe. In all senses. Perhaps in the hills, where an aqueduct fed water to Caesarea from Mount Carmel across the fertile plains, the growing strength of the sun would be welcome, as a breeze moved among the green vines. Here, in the market, where the buildings trapped the heat and the smells, the mixture of camel dung and fish and fly-speckled goat carcasses was strong enough to overpower even Dolabella's perfume.

She stopped abruptly, pushing aside a boy who was waving a branch above a skinned lamb to keep it clear of flies.

"I want that!" she shouted at her husband.

Helva stopped too. He had to raise his voice above the noise of the market. "The governor expects us. We can't be late."

"That porcelain dish!" She pointed past the boy at an old woman in a formless dark dress, rocking back and forth on her heels in front of a set of plates and cups arranged on an old blanket. "I want it."

"We must keep moving," her husband answered.

"Then you keep moving," she said. "I want this, and I want it now. Continue without me, and I will catch up."

She did not say "*we* will catch up," although Vitas and Jerome and the two other slaves assigned to attend her made it a group of five. Slaves were objects; it would be ridiculous for their mistress to speak as if they were somehow with her.

Helva gave a wave of frustration, his face displaying a universal look of impatience and helpless exasperation. Then he walked away, flanked by his soldiers.

"How much?" Dolabella demanded of the old woman.

The old woman's reply was barely audible as she named a price.

"What?" Hands on her hips, Dolabella projected outrage. "Robbery."

Unlike most slaves, Vitas had a sense of the value of fine objects. In another lifetime, he'd accumulated more than his share, only to have his entire estate confiscated by Nero. He knew the old woman's request was anything but robbery.

"It is the last of our household," the woman said. "I need the money to—"

"Save your lies," Dolabella snapped at the old woman, then cocked her head. "Your accent. You're a Jew. Here, in the market. I should have you arrested."

"My entire family was killed during the riots," the old woman said. "My home taken. Please. This is all that I could rescue. I need to sell it to survive."

The riots had taken place months ago, in the fall, just before Vitas had arrived in Caesarea with Damian and Jerome. Vitas well knew what had happened. A dispute between Greeks and Jews over a building project near the synagogue had festered, then erupted because of the former governor's incompetence and greed. Twenty thousand Jews had been slaughtered in the city, triggering rebellion all across Judea. Jerusalem had rebelled against Rome and was in the hands of the Jews. Then came the formal declaration of the empire's war against Judea. Rome had two legions in Ptolemais.

Vitas had heard that the Fifteenth Legion was on the way from Alexandria to add to the buildup of military power; the news reminded him of all he had lost through Nero's persecution.

"I said, save your lies. This is my offer." Dolabella named a sum that was one-tenth of what the old woman had requested. Then Dolabella noticed that Vitas was frowning. "Is this your business?" she demanded.

Vitas stared at the ground. He should not have given any indication that he'd been listening. But seeing the old woman had awakened what was never far from his thoughts. Memories of his wife. A Jew. Murdered by Nero. If only his estate were all that Nero had taken from Vitas.

A blow struck his face. Dolabella had slapped him. "I asked you a question!"

Vitas lifted his eyes again to Dolabella, whose cheeks were tightened with rage, exposing the wrinkles at the corners of her eyes that she was so desperate to hide with makeup.

"It is not my business," Vitas said.

"Make sure it remains that way." Dolabella leaned forward, grabbed the old woman's hair, and yanked her to her feet. "Jew, perhaps you should just give me the dishes. I won't tell the authorities about you."

Vitas stepped forward and grasped Dolabella's wrist. "Let go of this poor woman."

"What? You defy me? I shall have you crucified."

Vitas doubted that. The household had paid too much to acquire him and Jerome. Helva would not allow execution. Vitas did expect punishment for this, but he guessed it would be a token effort to satisfy Dolabella's pride.

"Let go," Vitas repeated to Dolabella. "Now."

She must have seen the cold resolution in his eyes. Heard in his voice the iron of a man long accustomed to giving orders.

She dropped the old woman's wrist and glared at Vitas.

This, Vitas realized later, became the moment where irritation overshadowed his military-trained watchfulness. Vitas had some coins hidden in his belt. He smiled at Dolabella as he dug out the coins. Easily a month's wages for a laborer.

Later, thinking about these events before he faced death for his role in them, Vitas would wonder if his impulse came from a sense of justice, from sympathy for the old woman built on the love he had for his dead wife—who had also suffered because of her Jewish identity—or from the satisfaction of defying Dolabella. Whatever the answer, later he would tell himself he should have been more aware of the impending danger.

Somehow the mood in the market had shifted, quieted. While he noted it, he did not act upon it. Instead, he remained focused on what was directly in front of him. Vitas gave the coins to the old woman. "Hold on to your porcelain," he said. "And may God be with you."

Dolabella slapped Vitas again. "On your knees," she spat. She snarled at all of her bodyguard slaves. "Each of you. On your knees with him. A lesson will be taught here."

Still standing, Vitas glimpsed motion over Dolabella's shoulder, and he looked past the woman.

A transport man had been trying to move a herd of camels away from a silk vendor's stall, each animal tethered to the next. But there was smoke. Of torches. And . . .

Another slap across his face. "On your knees," Dolabella shouted.

Vitas felt a hand on his waist. Jerome, already kneeling, was trying to pull him down.

But Vitas had greater concerns. Someone had thrown oil across the backs of the camels. Others, armed with the torches, were lighting the soaked camels, turning them into living firebrands. In seconds, the huge beasts had begun to plunge up and down in panic, breaking free of the tethers and crashing among the people of the crowded market.

HORA QUINTA

SCREAMS ROSE IN REACTION to the mayhem. Vitas pushed Dolabella backward, toward the market stalls.

"You filthy—" Her hand rose in an arc to slap him yet again, but this time, Vitas lifted his own forearm in a lightning-swift move of self-defense and blocked the blow with his wrist, stunning her into silence. He rammed a shoulder into her belly and rose with her over his back, carrying her with his right arm.

His path to safety, however, was blocked by the old Jewish woman. He crouched and grabbed the old woman's wrist, pulling her to her feet. He was just about to attempt to lift her with his other arm when Jerome moved him aside and pulled the old woman into his arms. He rushed ahead of Vitas with the fragile woman and set her in a stall, beneath a table covered with copper pots and pans.

Vitas rushed in the same direction with Dolabella and, with no effort at gentleness, tossed her beneath the table. As both men backed away from the table, Jerome grabbed the overhang of the stall and pulled it down, bringing the front half of the entire structure over the table. It was the best protection they could offer as they turned back to the market. Even with half a dozen soldiers, Gnaea Lartius Helva was vulnerable. Gone berserk, camels were nearly unstoppable.

Yet that wasn't the danger.

Vitas was taller than most, and he saw it unfolding. Against the flow of the stampede of people fleeing the camels, men in long robes, perhaps twenty of them, advanced. Vitas saw a flash of steel in sunlight. A short dagger.

Sicarii. A planned assassination.

These extreme Jewish Zealots were known to conceal their *sicae*, or small daggers, beneath their cloaks to stab their enemies—Romans or Roman sympathizers, the Herodians, or wealthy Jews who embraced Roman rule—then lament with those around them to blend into the crowd.

In Caesarea, because of the rebellion, no longer were crowds allowed to assemble for events or holidays. Lighting camels on fire was a brazen tactic, and they could have only one target in mind: Gnaea Lartius Helva, the fiscal procurator of Judea.

Protecting Helva was more than duty for Vitas and Jerome and the other bodyguards. It was literally life or death—not only for Helva, but for his slaves. Allowing an owner to be murdered meant punishment by death for all the slaves in the household.

As Vitas sprinted forward, he saw one soldier go down. Then another. And another. The Sicarii swarmed in deadly precision, taking down the ring of men around Helva.

A camel plunged toward Vitas. He dodged, feeling the bulk of the camel's body brush against him and the heat of the unquenchable fire on the camel's hide.

When he looked again, Helva was down.

Knowing Jerome was beside him and knowing the mute's intelligence and ability to assess a situation, Vitas stopped and held up a commanding hand, for a moment becoming the Vitas of old. This sense of authority was second nature to him, something he'd had to set aside after the copper band had been put on his wrist and the mark on his forehead.

"Too late," Vitas said tersely to Jerome. "We've failed."

Vitas understood too well the implications. They had not only failed, but failed spectacularly. As fiscal procurator of Judea, now including Galilee and Samaria, Gnaea Lartius Helva had been one of the highest-ranking officials in the province, with only the procurator Marcus Antonius Julianus—governor of Judea—having more authority. Even so, Helva did not report to Julianus but directly to Nero. That the second-highest official in the land had been assassinated was disastrous enough. To give the triumph to the Jews was double disaster. It would only add to their sense of invulnerability that had grown in the weeks after routing Gaius Cestius Gallus and chasing him and his army back to Syria.

Vitas put his hand on Jerome's shoulder. The man had a blocky head with ragged hair and could not speak, his tongue having been cut out in his childhood. Vitas knew this because Jerome, too, had been sold by Damian to Helva.

"My friend," Vitas said, looking upward into the large man's face, "we should take care of ourselves now. We need to run and find a place to hide until Damian returns tomorrow to vouch for us. In this chaos, it's our opportunity. Follow me."

He turned, expecting Jerome to instantly obey. But Jerome spun him around with a hand on his shoulder. As Vitas stumbled off balance, Jerome hammered him in the forehead with an elbow. An ox would stagger under a blow like this from Jerome; Vitas had no chance. He fell flat onto his back.

With fleeing people streaming around them as if they were boulders in the center of a river, Jerome dropped on top of Vitas, sitting across his chest, pinning both of Vitas's arms with his knees.

Vitas was too dazed to speak. Against the glare of the sun, he saw Jerome's arm rise, then slowly descend. Vitas felt a bite on his throat. He knew what it was. The sharpened edge of steel. He'd seen the knife in Jerome's hand.

It was an incomprehensible turn of events. Jerome had been Damian's slave for years. To turn against the master's brother was beyond belief.

Yet it was happening. And Vitas was powerless.

He closed his eyes, seeing the face of his dead wife, Sophia. If he was going to die, that was what he wanted to take with him. In this moment, he didn't need to pray that he would see her on the other side. That had been his prayer every night before sleep and every morning before rising from bed. If those pleas had not been heard in all the months since her death, a prayer in the confusion of the market stampede would not be heard either.

The pressure of the knife against his throat increased. Then stopped.

Vitas opened his eyes.

Jerome's face was expressionless.

This time, Vitas did not close his eyes. He would show no fear, let his steady gaze of silent condemnation be the last thing Jerome would see of him alive.

Again, the pressure of a sharp blade against his skin.

And again, just as suddenly, the pressure relieved.

Abruptly, Jerome slid off Vitas's chest. He reached down, grabbed Vitas by a wrist, and pulled him up as effortlessly as if Vitas were the old woman Jerome had just rescued.

With the noise and confusion around them, it seemed to Vitas as though the two of them were in a bubble of silence.

Vitas touched his neck, then pulled away his fingers. A brief glance showed blood.

Jerome reached forward and extended the knife, handle first. He pressed it into Vitas's hands. Then, with both of his large hands wrapped around the hands of Vitas, he pulled the knife forward so the point pressed into the softness just below Jerome's ribs.

Tears filled the eyes of the mute slave. He nodded. Death. This was the punishment for a slave who turned against his master.

In the silent space, Vitas could again find no comprehension for what was happening.

Jerome had taken perfect advantage of the chaos. As if he'd been waiting for a moment to kill Vitas. With one swipe of the knife, he could have left Vitas on the ground, life force gushing into the dirt. Jerome could have melted into the crowd, leaving Vitas behind as if Vitas were another victim of the Sicarii. For Jerome, escape would have been simple with so many ships in the harbor where a strong man could find employment and passage to a foreign country. A murder without any chance of recrimination.

Yet now, Jerome was offering his life. Waiting for Vitas to plunge the knife forward.

They stared at each other.

Then the bubble of silence was broken as Roman soldiers finally appeared and Dolabella began to screech for help. Within seconds, Vitas and Jerome had been arrested.

HORA NONANA

HOURS HAD PASSED since the mayhem in the market, and Vitas was alone in a garrison cell. Dirt floor. Rough stone walls. The smell of urine. He and Jerome had been seized immediately along with two other slaves, then thrown into separate cells.

He understood it was a standard interrogation technique. But he had not been interrogated yet. His only interruption was the delivery of a message from a scribe Damian had hired before leaving for Jerusalem.

The employment of this scribe was the one condition Vitas had set for agreeing to help Damian as a spy in the Helva household. Each Sabbath since his arrival in Caesarea the previous fall, Vitas had gone to the local Jewish synagogue. Although it had been destroyed during the riots and was now merely a shell of broken walls, duty and curiosity compelled Vitas to wait each Sabbath at what had once been the entrance.

All because of a portion of a letter that he'd found in his clothing during his escape from Rome and Nero, a letter in Hebrew, given to him by unknown benefactors.

You know the beast you must escape; the one with understanding will solve the number of this beast, for it is the number of a man. His number is 666. You have fled the city of this beast; from the sea it came and on the sea you go. North and west of the city of the second beast, find the first of five kings who have

fallen. (The sixth now reigns, and the seventh is yet to come.)
There will be two witnesses, killed yet brought alive. Find them
and rejoice with them; then take what is given.

Then go to the woman clothed in finest purple and scarlet
linens, decked out with gold and precious stones and pearls. She
is the one who slaughtered God's people all over the world. Find
the Synagogue of Satan, at the end of the Sabbath, and stand
at the gate closest to the den of robbers. Persevere and you will
find your reward.

Much of the coded letter—written in ambiguous Hebrew to
ensure Vitas's protectors would remain safe from Nero if the letter
fell into the wrong hands—did not make sense to Vitas. However,
he was in Caesarea because of what he had learned from a man
named John, the last surviving disciple of the person many claimed
was the Jewish Messiah, who had been crucified and, if his followers were to be believed, had risen from the dead.

John had been on the ship with Vitas, also escaping Rome. It
was said he'd been among twelve who witnessed miracles done by
the Christos and attested to the Resurrection. John had translated
the Hebrew and explained much of the ambiguity, proving to Vitas
it was no coincidence he and John had been put on the same ship.

Nero was the first beast; Jerusalem was the second. North and
west of Jerusalem was Caesarea, built by Herod the Great and
named after Caesar Augustus. But Augustus himself had taken the
name of Caesar from the first king of Rome, Julius Caesar. Nero,
the sixth, now ruled the Roman world.

What Vitas could not make sense of was the reference in the
letter to two witnesses, "killed yet brought alive."

He understood, again with assistance from John, that in the
Revelation, the mention of the two witnesses was a figurative reference to the long-dead Jewish prophets Moses and Elijah—who
represented the law and the prophets and ultimately the Christos,
who John had explained was the perfect Prophet and High Priest.

As literary figures, these witnesses represented the entire line of
Hebrew history testifying against Israel and warning of God's
imminent judgment on Jerusalem.

Vitas had kept silent during John's explanation of this. He didn't
want to become argumentative by challenging John, but Vitas
could not accept that the Christos had risen from the dead, and
he found it impossible to believe that Jerusalem would fall, as predicted by the Christos and in John's revelation. For Vitas, as a military man, had spent time in Jerusalem. It was such a secure fortress,
not even the mighty Romans could ever take it down. Therefore, to
Vitas, if that prophecy was wrong, anything else said about and by
the Christos must be suspect.

And it was irrelevant to Vitas. He wanted to know what the
"two witnesses" represented not in John's revelation but in the
coded Hebrew letter that had been left with him before his escape.

But nothing in the months since had helped him understand
the puzzle. What two witnesses, once dead, would be alive to him?

Nor did Vitas know why he needed to find the woman in finest purple—who John had explained was Jerusalem, given that the
slaughter of God's people all over the known world had resulted
from the Jewish religious establishment's years of persecuting followers of the Christos.

Vitas was uncertain whether the letter directed him to wait at
the synagogue of Caesarea or the synagogue of Jerusalem, and he
suspected this vagueness was deliberate, to protect the writer of the
letter from Nero if the emperor ever found the letter. As was common with writings of this kind, the arrangement of the instructions
did not necessarily have to be followed in a linear fashion.

With Jerusalem in the hands of rebels—something Damian was
willing to risk because he intended to be there for only a matter of
days—Vitas had employed someone in the city to go to the synagogue every Sabbath and make note of anything unusual at the end
of the day.

Here in Caesarea, Vitas had initially gone himself every week.

Once he knew he would be in the Helva household, Vitas had insisted that Damian send someone else every Sabbath—someone who believed Vitas was a slave named Novellus and who was instructed to bring any news directly to him.

The messenger had brought some writing on a scroll for Vitas in his jail cell, and he had been pondering it since.

An old man, a Jew, arrived and waited the entire Sabbath at the ruin of the synagogue. At dusk at the end of the Sabbath, I approached him to ask if he'd been given a message to go to the synagogue. He refused to identify himself and was agitated when I would not divulge why I had been waiting too.

What had Damian promised before leaving for Jerusalem? *"Don't worry, Brother. If nothing has happened yet on any of the previous Sabbaths, why would it happen now? Besides, it will only be a matter of days for you as Helva's slave. What else do you have to do here? Continue moping? Why not make yourself useful. We could use the money, after all, and my client is a fat goose waiting to be plucked."*

Damian's prediction had been proven wrong. It did happen now. An old man arrived and waited the entire Sabbath. A man Vitas could only believe had been looking for him.

Vitas had been banished from Rome, owing his life to a mystery he could not explain. Someone had put him on the boat with a coded letter to send him to Caesarea. Who had done this? Why?

The old man who had been at the synagogue might have the answers. But Vitas was in prison.

He heard a woman's voice as the far door to the hallway began to open.

Dolabella.

Vitas guessed his prospects were about to get worse.

HORA DECIMA

"THIS IS THE SLAVE. Novellus." Safe on the other side of the bars that held Vitas prisoner, Dolabella gave a theatrical shudder as she addressed the magistrate, a balding, skinny man wrapped in a toga. "He attacked me in the market. And the big mute one. They both assaulted me. The others failed in their duty to protect their master."

"As I have promised, the interrogator will see the mute next," the magistrate said. "No need to worry about it. You have so much else to deal with right now."

He spoke with the solicitousness owed to a very recently widowed woman who had inherited a large estate. He grasped Dolabella lightly by the elbow and turned her away as if the matter were complete.

"I am guilty," Vitas called out. "I assaulted this woman. I failed to protect her husband as a result."

The magistrate paused and frowned at the obviously unexpected statement. As a slave, Vitas's confession of assault against his owner was essentially a self-imposed death sentence.

"The other slaves," Vitas continued, "had been ordered to remain behind with the master's wife as he continued through the market. Furthermore, she had commanded them to get on their knees. They could not see the attack on the master nor get there in time. They are not responsible for his death."

"You think I can't see through your lies?" the magistrate said. "Your answer does not spare the others."

It was commonly believed in a case like this—when the slaves and their families would be held responsible for the death of a master—that slaves would lie to protect themselves. Therefore, an interrogator would only be satisfied with an answer if it came after hours of torture.

"The big one," Vitas said. "Because he is mute and illiterate. There is no way for him to answer an interrogator."

Nor, Vitas could not help but think, was there a way for Jerome to explain why he almost murdered Vitas, then changed his mind.

"The mute one assaulted me too," Dolabella said.

"Then," the magistrate said in a soothing voice to Dolabella, "we will assume he is guilty as well."

This was Vitas's opportunity to protest and explain that he was a Roman citizen. But to prove it would expose his identity, and without doubt news of his whereabouts would reach Nero, who believed that Gallus Sergius Vitas, a man once among Nero's innermost advisers, had died in the arena. Perhaps if Vitas was fortunate, after proving his citizenship and securing his freedom, yes, he could flee Caesarea to escape Nero, but that would mean he would lose the chance to find out whom he'd been set up to meet at the synagogue.

Instead, Vitas had no choice but to hide his citizenship and hope for the timely return of the one person he'd learned from experience was all too often unreliable. His brother, Damian.

To save the others from torture, Vitas would take full blame here and count on Damian's promised return the next day to explain that Helva himself had hired Vitas to be a spy, and the reasons for it. Although Helva was dead and could not confirm this, Damian had been shrewd enough to get a contract from him in writing. Furthermore, Helva had sealed the contract with molten wax and the stamp from his ring, leaving a raised surface on the wax seal.

"The mute is not guilty of anything except being in the wrong place at the wrong time," Vitas told the magistrate. "The attack was planned, not simply an assassination of opportunity."

"What?" The magistrate was startled.

"Find out who owns the camels," Vitas told the magistrate.

"What are you talking about?" The magistrate puffed his chest, posturing for the attractive widow.

"If you have any political ambition at all, find out who owns the camels that were crossing the market when the Sicarii attacked. Find out who arranged the transport of the goods on those camels. Take that information to the governor. Tell him the question about the camels comes from the slave named Novellus, who was sold to Helva by the Roman citizen Gallus Sergius Damian."

"Gallus Sergius Damian?" The magistrate laughed. "And to which brothel should we send the governor to look for Damian?"

"The governor will know what to do with that information," Vitas said. "And you will be rewarded for it."

"This is exactly the insolence and disobedience you would expect from a slave like this," Dolabella said. "Can't you see?" She slipped her arm around the magistrate's ribs and drew him close. "I should not have to endure this. Not when I'm so badly in need of comfort." She murmured something in the man's ear.

"Yes, yes," the magistrate said to her. He pointed at Vitas, using his free hand. "Tomorrow at dawn, you and the other slaves will be crucified."

❧ MOON ❧

HORA PRIMA

VITAS HAD NOT SLEPT for hours, knowing what was ahead. Soldiers had moved Vitas and Jerome and the other criminals to the public thoroughfare just outside Caesarea, where the frequent crucifixions were intended to serve as a display of the empire's power and a deterrent to further crime or sedition.

With the sun barely up, the soldiers approached. What Vitas had been dreading had arrived.

The sleepless early dawn had afforded Vitas too much time to think about his lapse in watchfulness. Too much time to consider how even if Damian returned to Caesarea this day as promised, it would be too late to save Vitas or Jerome from the hammer blows. It wasn't that Vitas doubted the sincerity of Damian's promise. While Damian wasn't fully dependable, long gone were the days of his wanton irresponsibility. A few years earlier—when Vitas and Maglorius had rescued him from certain death in the arena—Damian's close brush with mortality had sobered him. He'd discovered a talent as a slave hunter, and while it would have been impossible to repress Damian's charm, he had realized that accountability had its merits as another hunting tool. If Damian didn't return from Jerusalem as promised, it was likely because he was delayed by the political volatility of the region.

Vitas expected, then, that he would die on a cross.

He'd had time in the early hours to think about the irony. Sophia's fervent faith had come about because of the eyewitnesses'

27

accounts of the resurrection of the Christos after his crucifixion. There was so much that was appealing about Sophia's faith and how it gave her life purpose. Often in quiet moments, especially when mourning Sophia's death, Vitas wanted that same certainty of life beyond this life. Of any reason to worship the Christos, for Vitas, this was the greatest: to be reunited with Sophia after death.

But the two stumbling blocks to acceptance of the Christos were too great. How could Vitas believe a man was a prophet if he predicted the total destruction of Jerusalem within the lifetime of those who heard him, when it was so clearly impossible? And how could he believe that any man could return to life, especially after the hideously torturous death of crucifixion?

So here was the irony that Vitas had been unable to avoid during his sleepless early dawn. His only hope beyond death was to believe in and accept the Christos, who had died in the same horrible way Vitas was about to die.

Unless, by some miracle, Damian would arrive in time to take them down from their crosses while they were still alive.

Nearly a dozen crosses were already up from previous days, each with a sign describing the crime that had led to the punishment. Some crosses held men who had expired during the night. Others held criminals who had been there for up to three days, even four. Men died slowly on a cross, most often from dehydration.

Vitas had supervised an occasional crucifixion during his military time, and he knew that fighting the soldiers was not only useless but would result in more injury. Still, it took all his willpower not to jerk away and struggle as four of them pushed Vitas flat on a cross on the ground, his arms spread. He wore nothing but rags wrapped around his midsection. The hole for the base of the cross was a couple feet away. Once the impaling spikes secured him to the cross, the soldiers would heave his weight upward and slide the base of the cross into the hole, leaving his feet only inches off the ground.

A fifth soldier held a spike with tongs, the point of the spike centered in Vitas's left palm. The tongs were a safety measure. It was common for a hammer to miss the spike and smash a prisoner's fingers. No sense putting a soldier's hand in the same danger.

A sixth soldier lifted his hammer for the first blow. Vitas took a deep breath. In the hours alone in his cell, clinging to memories of his wife, Vitas had believed he'd prepared himself for the pain.

The hammer came down, ringing on the spike. Vitas flailed as the iron spike went through the center of his left palm. He bit completely through the strip of thick leather that the soldiers had provided him to clench between his teeth. The leather had not been provided out of mercy but because the soldiers were long weary of the screams that came with each hammer blow.

Pain shuddered through his entire body. This was infinitely beyond the dread he'd already suffered. Ahead were two or three spikes for each hand, then spikes through his anklebones. How could he endure it? Or the hours of agony ahead in the sun? What insane impulse had led him to defy Dolabella in the market?

Another spike placed against his palm, held by the tongs.

Another swift upward motion of the hammer.

"Stop!" The order came from the centurion.

Damian, Vitas thought, sagging in relief. His brother had returned in time. Or nearly in time. While the first spike had not gone through any of the bones in his hand, it was going to leave a nasty hole.

"No more spikes," the centurion said, standing above Vitas and the soldiers who crouched over him. "No spikes for him or the mute one. Ropes instead."

Vitas slumped. Damian had not arrived. The crucifixion would proceed.

The soldiers bound one of his wrists, then the other, to the horizontal beam of the cross.

They pounded spikes into the vertical beam, near the base, where the spikes should have gone through his ankles. They bent his legs sideways, so that when his feet were immobile, his thighs would cramp without any chance of respite. They bound his feet in such a way that the weight of his body on the spikes would make the iron bite cruelly into the arches of his feet.

When Vitas was in place, they lifted him and secured the base. Arms wide, his body weight held by the tight ropes around his wrists and by the one spike already in his hand, he pushed down with his feet to support himself. Within seconds, the spikes tore into his skin. To find relief from it, he sagged against the ropes bound tightly to his wrists, against the spike in the center of his palm, and new pain flared into the skin there. The weight of his body tore against his arm muscles.

That, however, wasn't the worst of it. Without his feet to support his weight, he was unable to expand his diaphragm with any effectiveness. Unable to draw even a quarter of a lungful of air, he began to suffocate. The sensation led him to unreasoning panic, and he pushed downward on his cramped legs, driving his torn feet into the spikes. He endured that pain as long as he could, then whimpered as he let his body hang from his arms again until suffocation drove him to push against his feet.

Flies settled on his face, darting to the moisture of his eyes. He blinked repeatedly, but the flies kept returning in swarms.

This was only the first five minutes of crucifixion.

HORA TERTIANA

THE SOLDIERS STEPPED away from the final victim but remained nearby, telling jokes as they threw dice, howling with laughter and pretended outrage at the results of each throw. They ignored the wailing of the mothers and daughters of the men on the crosses. Armed with swords and spears, they weren't worried about anyone, let alone women, trying to take down the criminals. The Romans did not care that families often gathered around those who were crucified; in fact, they often encouraged it. Seeing the agony of this torture up close, hearing the strained death rattles and the pleas for mercy, served to deter others who wished to avoid a similar fate.

The pain exhausted Vitas, and he dropped his head to his chest, ignoring the people who were walking into and out of Caesarea on this road. Time did not exist for him. A man could only acknowledge time when his mind was aware of hopes or dreads for the future, pleasures or regrets in the past. But the agony was so intense, it consumed all his senses and thoughts and kept him in the horrific present.

Vitas's head hung only a few feet off the ground, and he saw the movement as an old woman stepped up to him and touched one of his knees. She held a stick, a sponge, and a bucket.

It was the ancient Jew, the woman from the market. She reached up and ran gnarled fingers over the spike in his hand, not flinching from the congealed blood.

"The centurion promised they would not use spikes on your hands," she told Vitas. "I paid to use rope."

"You?" When he spoke to the woman, it came out as a croak.

"Because of your kindness," she said. "I was able to bribe him with the money you gave me in the market. I am sorry that even one spike pierced you."

"There is nothing to be done about it," Vitas said. Unless Damian appeared before Vitas succumbed to exhaustion and dehydration, Vitas was going to die. What did another injury matter, especially when his body was overwhelmed by other agonies? Even if the centurion commanded the spike be removed, the soldiers would likely break his fingers prying it out with a metal bar.

Vitas was looking at the bucket and the sponge and the stick. He was no coward, but he hoped she was about to offer a small mercy worth more to a man on a cross than a person could comprehend. Water. Perhaps more.

As if answering prayer, she dipped her sponge into the bucket and pushed it to his face on the short stick.

"Drink," she said. "I spent the remainder of the money on poppy tears, mixed with water and wine."

Vitas sucked at the sponge with greed. As a soldier in battle, when he'd required a surgeon to repair skin and muscle, he had never taken opiates. On the battlefield, he believed he needed a clear head at all times. Here, however, there was no reason not to drift along on the relief that would come with the opium. He was a dead man. Poppy tears were a gift beyond description.

"Tell me your name so that I can thank you properly," Vitas said.

"My name is Arella," she said. "But I'm the one who owes you. You defended me in the market. And gave me money. Men rarely show such kindness to an old woman."

"Arella," Vitas repeated. He groaned as he placed weight on his feet. But he needed a foundation to be able to draw breath, and he gasped for air when he was able to move his diaphragm. "I know some Hebrew. It means *angel*."

"You know Hebrew?"

"I was married to a Jewish woman."

"Yet you speak with the accent of a Roman."

"She was the best thing that happened to me." Vitas felt the tears well, then stream down his cheek. He wondered why he hated showing this weakness, even when he was as helpless as any man could be. "Please take care of the man beside me."

Arella shifted a step sideways and also offered the mixture of wine and poppy tears to Jerome, who gulped at the sponge with the same desperation Vitas had shown.

"She belongs in a brothel," Arella said, speaking to both of them. "The Roman with orange hair. Already it's whispered that she spent the night with a Greek, and her husband not yet cold. The Greek was there, you know, in the market."

All Vitas could manage were a few more croaked words. "You stayed?"

"No," she said. "The Greek pulled her out from the table. She kicked me as he helped her leave. He was there when she shouted for soldiers to arrest you."

The old woman pushed the sponge back up to Vitas. He could barely concentrate, and the poppy tears were beginning to dull his senses. He drank from the sponge again.

Soon, though not soon enough, his mind and body would no longer be connected. There was one thing he needed to know before he let himself go into a timeless void. Separated by soldiers, put into different jail cells, he had not had a moment to address his brother's slave.

"Jerome!" Vitas said.

On a cross barely a couple of feet away, joined by the intimacy of dying, the mute turned his head to look at Vitas.

"You meant to kill me in the market," Vitas said. "Yes?"

Vitas did not care that the old woman was listening.

Jerome strained to give a single *ungh* sound, the best he could muster, meaning *yes*.

Vitas often thought language was the single greatest thing that separated man from beast. Jerome could not speak, could not read or write. Because of it, the world had too often treated him like a beast.

"You changed your mind and spared me," Vitas said. "Yes?"

The answer was another strained *ungh*.

There was a way to communicate with Jerome, but it was slow and frustrating and not always fruitful. It was to ask a series of yes-or-no questions—the success depended highly on the agility of the questioner's mind.

"You had a good reason to kill me? Yes?"

"Ungh."

"If you could, would you tell me why?"

"Ungh. Ungh." No.

Another mystery that would not be solved before he died. Along with the letter that had sent him to Caesarea, the question of who had saved him from death in the arena in Rome and arranged his escape by ship with the disciple John, and the identity of the man who had just appeared at the synagogue this Sabbath, obviously looking for Vitas.

Vitas stared at the old woman and felt the tears glistening again in his eyes.

"May the remainder of your life be blessed," he said. "You have no idea how much mercy you've provided."

"I do," she said. "Two of my sons died to Roman crosses."

She dipped her sponge in the bucket again and pushed it up to Vitas.

HORA SEPTINA

THE SUN HAD MOVED beyond the midpoint of the day, a ferocious white ball of attack that pressed down on Vitas as he gasped for each new breath. Even with a cloth that the woman had draped over his face to offer shade and a privacy of sorts from the curious stares and occasional jeers of passersby, Vitas's lips had cracked into fissures because of his body's desperate need for water as it battled between suffocation and pain, exhausting him beyond his endurance. But Vitas was unaware of how he constantly swept his tongue across his lips in a useless effort, for the poppy tears had put him into pleasant dullness, where it seemed he had the freedom to rove through his mind, like a foreign visitor seeking idle amusement.

His awareness drifted away from the wailing cries of mothers tending to sons on nearby crosses and of little girls begging their fathers to come down and hold them.

Mercifully, he found himself no longer on a rough cross made of hewn wood, but in his childhood home at age twelve, climbing a tree in the villa's garden with his brother and trying to stop Damian from throwing oranges at slaves in a neighboring garden—oranges Damian had stolen from the kitchen and carried into the tree in a sack. He remembered his sense of outrage when he was caught in the tree, appearing as if he were joining Damian, and his anger that he had to share Damian's punishment.

In the hot sun, Vitas wept—not from pain, but from grief as his mind shifted from the villa to adulthood, where he strode through a battlefield in Britannia, the low green hills behind him in cold mist, the bodies of his soldiers scattered among the motionless women and children who had been slaughtered in ambush, his first and only son among them.

And as time shimmered like a distant mirage across the desert, he felt the joy of holding the hand of his wife, Sophia, sharing a flower-scented walk through the palace grounds of Nero, as they dreamed together of how they might raise their children.

Then moisture on his face pulled him back to a reality veiled with dull pain.

Arella had lifted the cloth from his head and pushed a sponge to his face again.

Yet as he lowered his head to the sponge, the delirium was so intense that he saw Sophia passing along the other side of the road, hemmed in by travelers, averting her face from the horrible spectacle of men impaled upon wood. It was only a glimpse of her face, but so real to him that he croaked in agony that struck his heart with far more force than anything the cross inflicted upon him.

Arella spoke. "Soon it can be over. Just give the word."

"I saw her!" Vitas uttered. It took willpower just to draw air into his lungs. "My wife. She was there. Not dead! Jerome. Did you—?"

He stopped. The question was useless, and he was wasting precious breath. Jerome's head was veiled too, with a small protective sheet that the soldiers had allowed Arella to place on him.

"My child, my child," Arella told Vitas. "You are dreaming. Drink."

He sucked at the sponge and, when finished, gasped for air. As the drug coursed through his body, a vision came to him, so utterly real that he smelled the blossoms and felt the softness of petals drifting over his face. A month after their marriage, Vitas had fallen asleep in the gardens of the estate in Rome. It was midafternoon. Slaves had served a light lunch of cheeses and wine, and he'd leaned against a tree, content—not from the afternoon sun, a perfect temperature on that day, nor the excellence of the cheeses, nor the satisfaction of being able to look around at property that belonged to him, but from the joy that filled him because of Sophia. She truly did complete him, and after far too many years as a soldier and a man alone, he was content to live a life utterly without adventure or excitement. How incredible, to wake each morning beside Sophia, to nuzzle her hair and whisper stories to make her laugh, knowing nothing more was expected of them throughout the day than a chance to stroll through the markets. With those images to comfort him, he'd drifted into sleep, only to be woken by a sensation softer even than Sophia's hair across his face, puzzled by the colors and sweet aroma until he realized she'd taken petals and was sprinkling them over his face to pull him out of sleep.

"Have you given it thought?" she asked. "The poison?"

So completely lost was Vitas in the memory that only after long moments did he realize where he was and that the old woman was talking about something she had promised earlier. To find poison.

It was a risky promise.

The soldiers who stood guard had not stopped the old woman from draping Vitas's head with a cloth, for the same reason that she—and others who came to gather around a husband or son or father dying a slow death—had been allowed to offer water from a bucket. The mercy it extended was also a form of torture. These ministrations lessened the discomfort, but at the same time they would lengthen his life. The victim's choice then was simply another form of torture. Die sooner with greater pain? Or ease the pain yet suffer it longer?

But Arella was offering suicide as an abrupt escape from the prolonged agony of crucifixion. If they caught her in the attempt, she too would be crucified.

The old woman's question brought to Vitas a knife's blade moment of clarity.

"Yes," he told her, still in agony over the deluded sighting of his wife and the searing memories of their last moments with Nero before Vitas's actions had condemned him and his wife to execution. He could not endure this much longer, and Damian might be another week. "I want this to end."

❧ MARS ❧

GALLICINIUM

BENEATH THE STARLIGHT, there was a change of guards at the beginning of the next watch. The replacement guards kicked at a couple of soldiers who were asleep on the ground.

There was nothing unusual about these soldiers and their sleep. As dusk fell, with a spectacular sunset over the Mediterranean that none of the dying men gave any notice, the soldiers had thrown dice to see which ones would remain attentive on the remote chance that there would be any rescue attempt.

Among the crucified there were no high-profile political prisoners likely to be rescued—just common highway brigands and ill-favored slaves. And because of the logistical difficulty of prying spikes away from wood, taking down a man ensured such a drawn-out process that even the most sleep-drugged soldier would be roused, especially with the screams of pain that would come from the rescued.

So the soldiers who lost the dice throws grumbled, then sat with their backs against the vertical beams of the crosses—soldiers on one side telling stories and eating breads, meats, and cheeses; dying men hanging from spikes on the other.

During the change of the guards, Vitas gradually became aware of his pain again.

The old woman was gone, chased away by the soldiers at dusk like all those around the crucified men. Some would return in the morning to take away their loved ones for burial; their vigils had ended in late afternoon, when those they tended to had succumbed to one more day's heat and finally, mercifully, had taken their last breaths. The effect of the poppy tears had worn off for Vitas, and in his agony, he felt his fingers curl against the spike that impaled his left hand. The ropes had rubbed his wrists and ankles raw; they oozed with pus and blood. His chest muscles felt torn from the weight of his body. Sand fleas tormented his skin. He was thirsty beyond any cruel sensation he had ever experienced. And he couldn't breathe.

He moaned as he pressed his weight down on the mangled arches of his feet. It was a sound lost among the moans of the other men on the crosses nearby.

Even Jerome, large and stoic, added to the chorus with the peculiar sounds forced from his throat.

Vitas stared ahead in the darkness. Wondering about the vision he'd seen of Sophia walking along the road. Wondering about the vision and waiting to die.

It was only the sixth watch.

✦ ✦ ✦

With the sun, the old woman returned as promised.

"More poppy tears," Arella said. She immediately offered up a sponge to Vitas.

"No," he said. "Please bring me water."

"Water alone?"

"No poppy tears. No wine. Just water."

He imagined the glorious taste of it, slaking his thirst, telling himself that the joy of this sensation would force him to forget his agony. It was a lie, but he did his best to believe it.

"I have what you asked for," the woman whispered. "In a powder. All I need to do is dip the sponge and sprinkle the powder. I was guaranteed that after the poppy tears dull your senses, you will die as painlessly and quickly as possible."

"Water," Vitas said. Each word passing through his throat felt like sand. "Just water."

"I have only one bucket," she said. "If I empty it to carry water, all the poppy tears I was able to purchase will be gone."

"Give what you can to Jerome," Vitas said. "Bring me back water."

"The poison?"

"Not yet. I've changed my mind."

"Please," the old woman said. "I watched my sons die. What you've experienced until now is nothing compared to the final agony. If I'd had any money then, I would have begged them to take poppy tears. I would have begged for the chance to end their lives myself."

"Water," Vitas said. He was exhausted, and breath was too precious to explain. Water first; then he would ask her his question.

She held the sponge up to Jerome.

The big slave shook his head, refusing.

"Take it!" Vitas snapped.

Jerome made the *ungh-ungh* sound.

Their eyes met.

Even though the slave could not speak, Vitas believed in that moment he understood that Jerome was still seeking redemption for placing a knife against Vitas's throat. A slave would not take comfort ahead of the master or the master's brother.

"Fools," the old woman said. "Both of you are fools."

Another man farther down spoke in a ragged voice. "I beg you, give it to me!"

Vitas nodded at the old woman. "Give the poppy tears to others. Then please hurry for water."

✟ ✟ ✟

It felt like days passed before the old woman returned with water, but the well was just down the road, and Vitas was able to watch her walk to it and back.

She offered the sponge again, and he wept at the taste of the water. Badly as he wanted more, he found the strength to turn his head away as she lifted it again.

"Some for Jerome." No matter what mystery had caused the

mute to first draw the knife, then offer it to Vitas, he had truly
been a good slave and a good man.

Jerome gasped as he drank from the sponge.

Small mercies meant so much. The two of them took turns
drinking until the bucket was empty.

"Now," Vitas said. He pushed away all the pain that screamed
at him from various points of his body. "Ask around. For a traveler.
A Jewish woman named Sophia who is married to a Roman named
Vitas. Bring her here."

"The woman of your poppy delusion? It's a fool's errand. For
you and for me."

During the long, horrible hours of the night, his mind clear,
Vitas had given it thought. In all likelihood, yes, his sighting of
Sophia had been a vision induced by the narcotics.

But what if it wasn't?

What if—against all odds—Sophia had survived the execution
ordered by Nero? After all, so had Vitas.

What if—and yes, it was delusional hope—she too had been
directed to Caesarea, as he had been?

It was certain that Vitas would die on this cross. He doubted he
could make it through another day in the scorching heat, even with
water. He doubted Damian would return.

If he was to die, and if there was only one chance in as many
stars as the sky held that he could speak to Sophia before he died,
he was prepared to face any amount of agony.

"Please," he said to the old woman. "Just ask."

Those were the last words he would remember speaking over
the next few hours before he lost consciousness and, with it, all
sensation of pain.

INTEMPESTA

VITAS WOKE IN A BED, confused by the cool darkness that surrounded him. It was so startling and in such contrast to the blazing heat and the overwhelming pain that had been his existence that it took long moments for his awareness to adjust to other sensations. His body rested on soft linens. His hand, where it had been impaled by a single spike, was bandaged. His feet, too, were gently tended with ointment and strips of cloth, and his skin had been oiled.

And his feet were shackled to a short length of chain. As were his wrists. Enough slack to move about, but still a prisoner.

In comparison to the way he'd been bound to beams of wood, this was glorious freedom. His last moments of consciousness before waking to this had been the inexorable agony of his body hanging on a cross, flies across his face, a tongue swollen with thirst.

And now he was here.

But where was here?

As his eyes adjusted to the dimness, Vitas realized he was in a small room. He swung his feet to the floor and gasped as he put weight on them, reminded of where the spikes had bit into his arches. He shuffled and tried a door, which gave slightly before stopping with a solidness that told him it was barred on the outside.

He explored the walls with slow sideways steps and almost stumbled over a small table. It held a jug of water, a bowl of oranges, and another bowl that contained, as he discovered with a tentative nibble, delicately spiced cooked strips of chicken. He sat on the edge of the bed and drank. Ripped apart the meat with his hands and devoured it. Pulled apart the oranges and had them as dessert.

So focused was he on satisfying his belly, it took a while to realize the fingers on his injured hand were not crushed or broken. He'd been removed from the cross in such a way that his hand had been protected from further injury.

Only the governor could have ordered this, so the real question was why.

Had Damian returned from Jerusalem in time? No, he decided, otherwise there would be no shackles. And Damian would have been waiting for him to wake, ready for Vitas to show proper gratitude at Damian's rescue, prepared to ignore any protest that it had been Damian's idiotic schemes that put Vitas on the cross in the first place.

So what reason or person had persuaded the governor to commute the death sentence?

A disturbing thought: perhaps it had not been commuted but only delayed. After all, Vitas did wear these shackles.

Before he could contemplate this for long, Vitas heard the bar sliding on the other side of the door.

Flickering torchlight outside the room gave him a brief view of the figure who entered, covered with a shroud.

"Who are you?" Vitas asked. "Where am I?"

"Understandable questions, both of them." A man's voice. "I am Joseph Ben-Matthias. You are under guard in a rich man's villa."

The man spoke Vitas's native Latin, but with a Jewish accent.

"Why am I here?" Vitas asked. "In this room and not on a cross?"

"We have little time. What should matter to you more is why I am here. If I am caught with you, I will be set up on a cross alongside your brother's mute slave."

Vitas had been alert from the moment the door creaked open, but this brought his senses to an intensified level.

His mind registered the fact that Jerome was still on a cross. But

Vitas pushed that aside. The mystery man in front of him knew the true identity of Vitas. And this meant . . .

"Does that suggest you need to listen?" the man asked. "Because I'm letting you know that I know who you are?"

Vitas shifted slightly, and the chains of his shackles betrayed him.

"I also know that those chains aren't enough to keep me safe from you. Trust that if I've risked my life to bribe a guard that I might speak to you, you need to hear what I have to say."

"Then speak," Vitas said. If this man knew about Vitas and Damian and Jerome, surely he was part of the mystery of those who had rescued Vitas from Nero and sent him away from Rome.

"The city of the Beast. And the city of the second beast. What are those cities?"

"Rome," Vitas said. "Jerusalem."

"I'm impressed," the man said. "I knew you had read the letter of John. This tells me that you have made efforts to understand it. Few in Rome have. I expected no less, however, given the message that brought you to Caesarea."

Yes, the man was part of it. Vitas's own stillness gave away the fierceness of his concentration on the man in front of him. Vitas could quote the entire message that had been on the scroll he'd been given at his escape from Rome.

You know the beast you must escape; the one with understanding will solve the number of this beast, for it is the number of a man. His number is 666. . . .

"I'm told," Ben-Matthias continued, "that John himself was on the ship that carried you away from your death sentence."

"You've succeeded in impressing me that you know enough about my situation. I'd like to know why."

"Do you believe the prophecies of the letter of Revelation? That Nero will die? That Jerusalem will fall? That the empire will face death throes and then survive?"

"You risk your life—if I am to believe you—to meet with me just to ask me that?"

"Will Jerusalem fall?" Ben-Matthias asked.

Vitas felt a degree of impatience. "Unlikely. No, impossible. To any casual observer of politics, yes, it's obvious that the Jews are a constant thorn in Rome's side, and yes, anyone could have easily predicted that eventually there would be rebellion. But one of the reasons the Jews have come to the point of rebellion is their unshakable belief that God will always protect Jerusalem and their sacred Temple." Vitas snorted. "But anyone in the world can tell you they don't need God's protection. Its heights and walls are impregnable; it has a ten-year food supply, unlimited water, and an entire populace willing to die to save the Temple. You said your time is short. Why waste time on the obvious? What do you want from me enough to bribe a guard and risk your life?"

Vitas had decided that might be his only leverage. He badly wanted the knowledge it seemed this man had. The source of the letter that had sent him to Caesarea. Indeed, perhaps even the reasons for the letter and the identities of the men who had rescued him from Nero and put him on the ship. Once he understood what the man in the shroud wanted, Vitas would negotiate.

"Once," Ben-Matthias said, "I too believed Jerusalem would not fall until the promised Messiah arrived. Now I'm not so sure. Perhaps this Jesus of Nazareth truly was the Messiah. The Christos. If so, the Temple will fall within this generation as he prophesied."

Normally, Vitas would have pressed forward with this direction of conversation. He'd experienced events that bordered on the supernatural, that had brought him to the point of uttering a belief in the Christos himself, but was still unsure whether it was something to make the foundation of his life. Romans, after all—especially Romans with his family background and former wealth—were more pragmatic than that. It was simple. The Temple would not fall or be destroyed.

But in this moment, with the urgency first expressed by the

man who called himself Ben-Matthias, and especially with the sense that finally, here were answers to the mystery, Vitas did not want to be distracted from what was important. So he held back from speaking and waited.

"Here is the irony," Ben-Matthias said.

Irony? Vitas wanted to reach forward and grab the man's throat and shake answers out of him.

"You would think I should have been convinced by the man's miracles. Instead it's the prophecy. If Jerusalem falls, then I will be convinced the Nazarene was who he said he was. And . . ." Ben-Matthias paused gravely. ". . . Although all around me disagree, I foresee that Jerusalem will fall."

"You said time was short," Vitas again pointed out.

"Do you want to understand why you are in Caesarea?" It was a rebuke.

Vitas accepted the rebuke in silence. He wanted few things more than this knowledge. Only to hold Sophia. But that was impossible. His mind clear of poppy tears and undistracted by the agony of crucifixion, he knew he'd been hallucinating on the cross when he'd dreamed of seeing her face among the passersby.

Ben-Matthias continued. "The Nazarene was the first to foresee that Jerusalem and the Temple would be destroyed, the first to understand how the arrogance and greed of its religious rulers would finally bring them at odds with Rome and, in so doing, bring the full force of the empire against it. While I see it now, few others do."

He took a breath, for he was speaking with passion. "The worst thing that could have happened to my people was victory. First in Jerusalem during the riots and then against Cestius, chasing the governor all the way to Syria. They believe God has begun to deliver them, preserving the Temple until the promised Messiah arrives. Except it is a messianic fever that history will prove wrong. They have not been to Rome as I have. They do not understand the difference between an incompetent governor like

Cestius with his small army and the might of a full legion. And now Rome has sent two legions. Two!"

Another pause, until Ben-Matthias began again, almost at a whisper.

"You, Vitas, do understand what is ahead for my people. If, against all odds, two legions fail, Rome will send two more. And two after that. Because Rome knows if it suffers defeat against the Jews, other peoples in the empire will rebel. Rome must always win."

"Yes," Vitas said with equal softness. "I do understand the might of a legion, and yes, Rome will not lose."

"You owe me your life," Ben-Matthias said. "Keep that in mind as you consider my request."

"You had me taken down from the cross?"

"Rescued from Nero. If the day comes that Jerusalem will fall, then honor your debt to me."

"You rescued me from Nero. In Rome. Why should I believe that?"

"'You have fled the city of this beast; from the sea it came and on the sea you go. North and west of the city of the second beast, find the first of five kings who have fallen.'" Ben-Matthias stopped briefly. "Heard enough? Or should I quote you the entire letter?"

"You were in Rome, then," Vitas said.

"No. I have friends in Rome. It was arranged. Ask no more about the arrangements. Men risked their lives to conspire against Nero."

"How am I to repay the debt?"

"You will know only if the day comes that it is necessary to ask repayment, and that request will be necessary only if the Temple does fall to Rome. If the Temple does not fall, you are not obliged to me for your life. Hold out your hand."

Vitas had a degree of suspicion but complied nonetheless, telling himself if the man had meant harm, it would have happened already.

He felt something cold and round pressed into his hand.

"Wear this around your neck, and keep it safe. If someone comes to you with its twin, you will know that I have sent him. And when that person sees you with the same token, he will know you are the one to trust with the obligations put upon you. Until then, keep this portion of our conversation secret. From everyone. Not even Bernice or Titus or Ruso should know of it."

"Ruso?"

"I suspect you'll meet him sooner or later. That is irrelevant. If someone has the matching token, you repay the debt. That is all that matters."

"Why not to you?"

"I am not a military man, but I have been chosen to lead the Jews. I doubt I will live to see whether the last Temple falls. So, if necessary, it will be someone in my place who approaches you about repaying the debt you owe."

"The letter directed me to the synagogue here in Caesarea," Vitas said. "If you know of the letter, you could have found me there any Sabbath. Why now?"

"That is not it," Ben-Matthias said. "You are to meet—"

The door opened with a suddenness that brought a draft into the room.

"Soldiers approach!" a warning voice hissed.

"Tell me who I am to meet at the synagogue!" Vitas said to prompt the man.

"This is more important for you now. Remember this name. For the governor, Julianus. Remember this: Glecko Partho. He was the one who threatened Helva."

"Tell me about the Sabbath and the synagogue!"

"Glecko Partho. With that name, you can spare bloodshed of my people."

That was all.

The shrouded figure fled the room. And the door shut upon Vitas, leaving him in silence and darkness again.

❧ MERCURY ❧

HORA TERTIANA

IN THE MORNING, after a simple but adequate breakfast, slaves came to clean and groom him and provide a freshly laundered tunic.

Still in shackles, he was led to a courtyard, where he recognized why he'd been made presentable. In the shade at the far end of the courtyard of the luxury villa was a dark-haired woman famed for her attractiveness, seated with Marcus Antonius Julianus, governor of Judea. When she rose and walked toward him with Julianus at her side, he immediately knew her.

This was Queen Bernice, great-granddaughter of Herod the Great. Her father, Herod Agrippa I, had been a friend of Emperor Claudius, and the Herodian dynasty was on good terms with the Romans. She'd been forced into marriage with her uncle—at only age thirteen—and, after becoming a childless widow, had moved back to the palace, where rumor held her brother treated her like a wife.

While it was a surprise to see her, it was not so surprising that she would be in the company of the governor.

Herod the Great had built Caesarea on the site of what had once been a Phoenician port, dredging a deep-sea harbor, then constructing an aqueduct, a hippodrome, and a magnificent amphitheater. The process had taken twelve years and countless thousands of workers. After completion, it was the grandest city in Palestine other than Jerusalem. Then Herod had dedicated the city to Caesar Augustus and changed the name from Straton's Tower.

Naturally, then, given that Herod had built the city, and with the Herodian dynasty owning opulent residences all across Judea, Bernice was known to frequent a royal residence in Caesarea, especially during the hottest months when the sea breeze made life more bearable.

She was not, however, simply a woman spoiled by upbringing, a lapdog for Roman overlords.

The summer before, she had surprised her people—and Rome. When Florus, the previous governor of Judea, had loosed his soldiers to slaughter citizens of Jerusalem, she'd risked her life to cross the city and publicly beg for mercy for the Jews.

There was more to her bravery, however, and none of her people knew the extent of what she had risked in an effort to protect them. After pleading with him had failed, she'd attempted to seduce Florus, intending to murder him. She had failed there too, and Florus had demanded a sword to kill her. Florus would have decapitated her on the spot but for the intervention of a delegate sent to Jerusalem by Nero: Gallus Sergius Vitas.

Vitas forced himself to match her expressionless gaze.

If she recognized and remembered Vitas as a Roman citizen, he would be freed from his role as a slave, freed from ever being returned to the torture of the cross. But Vitas would then become a different sort of prisoner. Chances were, Julianus had heard already how Vitas had defied Nero and been sentenced to death, for a Roman governor was a well-connected man, acutely aware of the politics of Rome and even more acutely aware of whom Nero favored and whom Nero condemned. Sending Vitas back to Nero would be a gift the emperor would never forget, and in so doing, Julianus would secure his future.

His life was in Bernice's hands. Maintaining a lack of expression, Vitas stared straight ahead, not daring to meet her eyes.

"Yes," Bernice told Julianus, "this is the slave from Helva's household."

Vitas relaxed, but only slightly. What business did the queen of the Jews and a Roman governor have with a slave condemned to crucifixion? Or if she did recognize him and was pretending otherwise, what business did she have by presenting him to the governor? Or dare Vitas hope the magistrate who had condemned him to the cross had actually delivered a message to the governor?

Julianus was a big man, barrel chested with thinning red hair and a sunburned face. His voice was oddly strained. Vitas knew the man had been a soldier once and had survived a fire, leaving him with the inside of his throat scarred and forever altering his vocal cords.

"I'm told that you have information about the assassination of the fiscal procurator," Julianus said. "That you overheard a conversation about the plot to kill him."

This explained it partially. The most pressing matter facing Julianus would certainly be the assassination of Gnaea Lartius Helva.

"You have investigated the owner of the camels?" Vitas said.

Julianus frowned. "Camels? You make no sense."

Vitas silently agreed but deemed it wise not to show his own confusion. Obviously Vitas had not been taken off the cross because of any message delivered to the governor by the magistrate.

Queen Bernice spoke. "I've been told this slave is aware of the name of the man who plotted the murder of the fiscal procurator. He overheard a conversation where the man threatened to kill Helva. A Greek."

Vitas glanced at her. She met his gaze and held it, then gave the slightest of nods. What had Joseph Ben-Matthias said the night before? *"For the governor, Julianus . . . Glecko Partho. With that name, you can spare bloodshed of my people."*

Vitas made the connection. Although it did not explain the token given to Vitas, it did explain the name that Ben-Matthias had given him. He and Queen Bernice both wanted to protect innocent Jews. Vitas didn't need to be told the danger ahead for Jews of the area, for he was a Roman and understood Roman ways. Dolabella's husband, the fiscal procurator, had been killed—apparently by Zealots. It was an assassination that would demand reprisals by

Rome, likely the deaths of hundreds more Jews, most of them crucified as punishment. It would not matter if these were Jews guilty
of the crime. This was how Rome dealt with insurgency.

Glecko Partho was not a Jewish name. It was now clear that uttering the man's name might deflect blame from the Jews, sparing them
from bloodshed.

"Yes," Vitas said, "I do have a name."

He saw Queen Bernice exhale as if she'd been holding her breath.

Vitas knew now that she did recognize him and did trust
him. All Vitas needed to do was tell the governor about his visitor the night before and expose this plot, and she would probably
be condemned to crucifixion along with the rest doomed by an
imminent reprisal.

But it didn't explain how she had found him, for Damian had
been very careful to ensure Vitas had been delivered to the fiscal
procurator as a slave. Nor did it explain how Ben-Matthias had
been sent to him the night before. And it certainly didn't explain
the letter the previous summer that had brought Vitas to Caesarea.
The letter that Ben-Matthias knew about too, from halfway across
the world.

"Out with it then," Julianus snapped. He briefly turned to
Queen Bernice. "I will not accept this slave's word for it, but it
will be enough to begin a thorough investigation. Slave, if you are
correct, then the Jewish families we've captured will be freed. I've
spared your life for this, and I'm not a patient man. Perhaps you
should be placed on a cross again."

Vitas thought of Jerome, still on the cross. And the otherworldly
suffering that each slow second brought for a man bound to the
beams of wood.

"No," Vitas said. "Not until the other slaves are taken from the
crosses. They are innocent of crimes against their master."

"Give me the name! I will have you whipped for insolence."

Vitas smiled. Not a warm smile. "After crucifixion, do you think
I really fear the whip?"

"Bah," the governor said. "Let the Jewish families die."

Julianus turned to walk away. Bernice's face showed horror.

Vitas spoke, and Julianus halted. "What do you expect will happen to you when Nero learns you are too incompetent or lazy to bring to justice a man who killed a high-ranking official, especially when this province has revolted against Rome? Word will get back to the emperor that you could have had the conspirator's name but chose not to pursue it. You know that Rome never shows weakness, yet here you walk away."

Julianus whirled and slapped Vitas across the face. "A slave will not speak to me in this manner."

Vitas tasted blood. "They will once you are held in the same prison cells with them. But you won't find it offensive then. You'll have other things to worry about as you wait for the beasts of the arena to entertain Nero by ripping you apart. I'm told he finds it amusing to watch a man try to stuff his entrails back inside his body."

Julianus slapped him again. And twice more.

But it became obvious almost immediately that the blows were strictly for appearance. The governor of Judea could not merely overlook insolence of this kind from a slave.

"Take the others off the crosses," Julianus snarled at nearby guards. "Immediately. Bring them here, dead or alive, so that this slave sees my orders have been followed. Once he sees that I have honored our agreement, bring him to me."

Julianus slapped Vitas across the face one more time. "If the name turns out to be nothing but a bluff, I will pull out your entrails myself."

HORA QUARTA

WITH JULIANUS GONE, Bernice dismissed her slaves so she and Vitas could sit in the shade without fear of having their conversation overheard. She had openly established in front of the governor a reason to speak with Vitas; there was no cause now to worry what the governor would think.

"Vitas," she said. "Welcome back from the dead."

"I have you to thank, is my guess," he said. "My last memory before waking last night is on the cross, fighting for consciousness."

She took his injured hand and examined it, although there was nothing to see of the wound because of the bandage that hid where the spike had pierced it.

"I can't imagine what that must have been like," she said softly, "the hammer coming down." She let go of the bandaged hand. "But I wasn't referring to the crucifixion. I am welcoming you back from your very public execution. In Rome. Titus told me that you attacked Nero and were condemned to the arena. He said you fought poorly and were booed when you died by the spear of a *retiarius*."

She had spoken in a teasing voice and now sat back with an expectant look on her face, waiting to be entertained by an account of an escape from Rome.

For Vitas, however, there was nothing in the retelling that would give him pleasure. He'd attacked Nero to protect Sophia from his advances. Not only had his defense of her failed; he'd later signed over all of his estate to save her life, only to be betrayed and learn that she'd been forced to commit suicide. As for how he had escaped death in the arena and who had arranged it, he had no information to offer Bernice. All he knew about it was the scroll that he'd been sent with onto a ship to Alexandria, the scroll that had led him to Caesarea and vigils each Sabbath at the synagogue.

"Titus," he said, smiling to hide from her the pain of those memories. "His stories are hardly ever to be believed."

Titus Flavius Vespasianus was the son of the famous general Vespasian and had carved out a respectable military career himself. Vitas and Titus had fought together in Britannia, where they'd forged a lifelong friendship. Both were highly connected in Rome. Titus had been brought up in the imperial court, a companion of Britannicus, and he moved in the highest circles, for Britannicus had been the heir apparent for emperor until he was killed by Nero. Only once had Titus spoken of Britannicus's final night to Vitas. Like Britannicus, Titus was barely into his teens when Britannicus's father, Emperor Claudius, had died. Barely months later, Nero, the stepbrother, arranged for poison, and Titus was there, reclining beside Britannicus when he died a horrible, shuddering death.

Titus's first wife had died of illness, and his second wife had been implicated in a failed murder conspiracy against Nero. Titus had not remarried.

Naturally, Vitas began to speculate about the relationship between Titus and the woman in front of him.

"Titus is well?" Vitas asked.

"I know what you're asking," she said, granting Vitas a half smile. "And the answer is yes, we are intimate. He wintered in Alexandria, where we met at various functions." She lost her smile. "At first, I thought it would be an advantage to strengthen my ties to Rome through him. The Herodians have become experts at it over the generations. It's how we keep our power. But it's become more than that. At least to me. And I want to believe it's the same for him. He sent me ahead from Alexandria by ship. As you might know, he was in Alexandria with the Fifteenth Legion and has begun to march to Judea to meet Vespasian at Ptolemais. But I doubt that is news to you."

"I've been here for months, posing as a slave on behalf of my brother, Damian. I've heard all the rumors."

"Did you intend to meet him as he passed by this city with his legion?"

"No. It would have put him in danger from Nero. If Titus knew I was alive, he would have been obligated to report it to Nero."

"He wouldn't tell Nero."

"I know," Vitas said. "So by visiting him, I would have made him guilty of treason to the emperor. I would not do that to him. He is too much of a friend. Now, I'm surprised to learn he is aware I did not die in the arena."

She arched an eyebrow.

Vitas obliged with an explanation. "Titus would not have insulted my final moments in the arena if he believed I had been slain."

"Yes," Bernice said, "Titus knows you are alive. It was no accident that I found you on the cross. Titus told me to look for you and your brother. When I arrived, I asked for Damian, only to discover he had sold his slaves to Helva and gone to Jerusalem."

"How did Titus know I was alive?"

If Titus had not learned about Vitas from Damian, and if Titus had sent Bernice to Caesarea to look for Vitas, then Titus had long ago known of the letter that had sent Vitas to Caesarea.

"Tell me first, why were you among Helva's slaves?" she countered.

"You know Damian is a slave hunter. He was hired by Helva, who wanted to find out which slave in the household was betraying him. Damian thought if I joined those slaves, I might find information of use to Helva."

"No information will be of any use to him now," she said. "And it nearly killed you. Naturally, when I asked of Helva, I heard of his assassination. That led me to the prison to look for his slaves, and from there to the crosses. If I had found you even an hour later, I believe it would have been too late."

"I'd rather know how Titus learned I was alive. From Damian?"

"You will need to ask Titus yourself. He is barely a day's march from here."

Vitas could be certain, then, of one thing. By sending Bernice to look for him, Titus had given her information that could result in the execution of both Titus and Vitas.

Vitas spoke his conclusion to her. "Titus must trust you a great deal. One word to Nero from you, and he and I are both dead, and you will have gained great favor with the emperor."

"Perhaps," she said. "But Titus knows how badly I want to protect my people. I will serve Titus, not only because of love, but because he is a general and the son of a general, the men who control the legions in Judea. I will do everything I can to influence what he does and how he treats my people."

"He has no choice but to fight this war," Vitas said.

"Don't treat me like a fool," she answered. "Of course he will fight ruthlessly to end the revolt. But some generals kill the women and children and the innocents. Others will stay the sword if possible. I want to ensure he stays the sword. He knows that's one of the reasons I am close to him."

Before his marriage to Sophia, Vitas promised her that he would use his influence with Nero to protect the Jews if possible. Neither of them could have guessed, however, how badly it would end.

"It's strange, in a way," Bernice went on, "with all that is happening around us, how tightly interwoven are the individuals who make the choices that affect how the revolt will go. And I am in the middle. Titus representing Rome on one side, and Joseph Ben-Matthias representing Jerusalem on the other."

"Joseph," Vitas repeated. "My visitor last night."

She nodded. "He is descended from the priests, a nobleman of great reputation in Jerusalem. After the riots of last fall, he was chosen to lead the revolt in the provinces. He accepted the mantle, despite his constant insistence that Judea cannot defeat Rome.

Yesterday, Joseph met with me secretly and suggested this method of appeasing the governor."

"You want to give the governor a scapegoat. And you believe it will be credible if it comes from a slave of Helva's household."

"Yes. Truthfully, the governor is fully aware that a slave facing crucifixion is not the most reliable of witnesses. The information only has to appear reliable. The governor is in a difficult position. He cannot let the assassination go unpunished, but by punishing Jews, he risks even greater insurgency from the locals."

She leaned forward. "I'm begging you. When the governor asks you for the name of the Greek, spare my people."

"This name," Vitas said. "Glecko Partho. How do you know he is the conspirator?"

"He was chosen because he is guilty enough of other vile things to the Jews. Better that he die so that others may be spared."

An answer both sufficiently ambiguous and sufficiently illuminating. But before he could ask anything else, they were interrupted by a messenger from Governor Julianus.

"The governor has changed his mind," said the messenger, a lanky man with hair shaved short. He was panting slightly. "You are to immediately accompany the soldiers out to the crosses. When the slaves of Helva have been taken down, he expects you will honor the agreement. I am to take the name back to him."

"Our conversation is not finished," Bernice told the messenger. "This slave will depart when I say so."

The iron of the nails of the special military sandals—*caligae*—of a half-dozen soldiers in armor made their intimidating clicking sound on cobblestone as they crossed the courtyard toward them.

"You are welcome to tell the soldiers that you intend to disobey the governor," the messenger said. "I have my orders and must follow them."

"Step back," Bernice commanded. The messenger's eyes widened. He, like Vitas, obviously had no idea that such a woman could project such ice-cold authority. "Speak to me with that tone again, and I shall have your tongue removed."

He stumbled backward.

Bernice leaned in toward Vitas and kept her voice low. "It would be useless to protest against these soldiers. We have much to discuss, but it would raise too many questions if I walked with you. For now, all you need do is give the governor the name. I will find you later, for I have an urgent message for you from Titus."

HORA QUINTA

THE SOLDIERS, carrying shields and swords, were so strong and fit that they marched at a pace few unburdened men could match. Vitas well remembered that pace from his own military days—and well remembered the authority of a sword. The swords were heavy enough and sharp enough to completely sever a man's arm from his body. The small daggers favored by the Sicarii were useless against such a weapon. And when soldiers crouched in defensive formation with shields raised, makeshift weapons had little effect.

The soldiers had removed the shackles from Vitas's feet but left his wrists bound by iron, so with great effort, Vitas barely kept pace. The arches of his feet were swollen. But pride kept him moving forward. Pride and the knowledge that if he lagged, he would be none-too-gently prodded with a sword.

They would reach the public execution site in five minutes. Traders wisely muted their curses to make way for the soldiers. Women and children ran to the side of the road. All stared at the passing soldiers. This, too, Vitas remembered well from his military days.

He wasted little thought on memories, however, as he marched step by painful step. Vitas was trying to make his decision. Would he divulge to the governor the name that Joseph and Queen Bernice had supplied?

Vitas could guess at what Joseph and Bernice had conspired, for giving the governor a name solved a great many political difficulties.

As Bernice had pointed out, without someone to blame for the assassination, Julianus would have no choice but to engage in horrendous retribution. Rome was not known for mercy. When its armies surrounded a city, the citizens who surrendered were treated with decency. But those who were defiant would be slaughtered, including the women and children. It was an effective carrot-and-stick strategy, made more effective by tales that circulated ahead of the Romans.

Here, Julianus knew if there was no retribution, it would embolden the revolt. Yet killing innocent Jews would stoke the flames of revolt higher. For him, it was a difficult situation.

The solution, then, was to have a slave identify a culprit, with few other questions asked. An execution, despite the hapless man's expected protests of innocence, would relieve Julianus of the need for wide-scale punishment. Peace, at least in Caesarea, would be kept, and a report to Rome would show that he'd taken necessary actions, which would keep his own political career secure.

What did it matter if one man died for a sin that he did not commit, when he deserved it for so many other crimes? Yet the last half of what Bernice had whispered haunted him. *"Better that he die so that others may be spared."*

Because of his familiarity with the letters of the followers of the Christos, Vitas knew that nearly a generation earlier, sentiment similar to this had sent another man to the cross. This one truly innocent. Condemned by Pontius Pilate.

If Glecko Partho had not conspired to have Helva assassinated, then no matter what else he had done, in this case he was an innocent man.

Vitas knew too well what it felt like to be innocent and condemned. Could Vitas inflict that on another man? Even to save his own life?

But could Vitas allow dozens, maybe hundreds, of women and children to die by the swords of Roman soldiers by denying that the Greek had conspired?

The choices were clear cut. A man who had vilely abused the Jews would die so that Vitas and women and children could live. Or Vitas would refuse to speak, condemning himself and the innocents.

It was a mercy of sorts when he arrived at the crosses where a matter of exquisite suspense and torture compelled him to set aside the decision. For he saw a bracelet like one he had once received from Sophia.

It was hanging around the wrist of Jerome, who was unconscious and near death on the cross.

HORA SEXTA

JEROME WAS UNRESPONSIVE on the cross, but his chest still moved as he drew rasping, irregular gasps of air.

Vitas was more focused, however, on the bracelet. A bracelet freshly woven from green grass.

It had no value to anyone else, or it most certainly would have been stolen by a passerby, darting in when the soldiers were distracted.

To Vitas, however, such a bracelet had once been priceless. Sophia had woven one for him as a simple wedding present, saying her love for him would endure as long as grass grew in the fields.

He was trying to understand the message. It could not be coincidence that the grass bracelet had been placed upon Jerome. Only Sophia—as far as he knew—shared this small secret.

Vitas cursed the fact that Jerome could not speak. What secrets did Jerome hold about the grass bracelet? Or had it been placed on him while he was unconscious?

The governor's messenger interrupted the whirlwind of thoughts that Vitas could not escape.

"Proceed as ordered," the messenger said to the soldiers.

Three soldiers moved forward, each withdrawing a sword that flashed in the sunlight. Each moved to one of the slaves on the crosses, and each touched the tip of his sword to the sides of the condemned, to the softness of flesh just below the ribs.

"Now," the messenger said with the officiousness of a man

suddenly granted unexpected power, "give me the name to deliver to the governor."

"This was not the agreement," Vitas said. "The men are to be taken down first."

The messenger pointed at the slave on the far left and gave a nod of command. The man appeared dead.

Without expression, the soldier shoved the tip of his sword into the soft flesh; water poured from the man's side, confirming he was dead.

An unexpected memory came to Vitas of the letters written by men who had traveled with the Christos and reported his death on the cross. There, too, soldiers had pierced his side. The Jews would not permit a man to be on the cross on the Sabbath. To hasten death, some would have their legs broken and, with nothing to support their weight, would begin to suffocate, their shattered tibias just adding to the final minutes of suffering.

But for soldiers, it was still work to lift a hammer and smash the legs. Much easier to confirm a man was dead with the sword. When fluid poured out, it was a sign that yes, the victim had suffocated to death.

This image struck Vitas; it was the reason followers of the Christos had made a point to report it. For readers of the letters, there could be no doubt. The Christos had truly died on the cross. His resurrection on the third day afterward could not be attributed to a man pulled alive from the cross, only to revive later in the cool depths of the tomb.

"That's one," the messenger replied with prim satisfaction. "Do you have the answer for the governor? Or shall I have the next one impaled."

The next slave was not dead. He croaked out an anguished protest.

"And when all are dead," the messenger continued to Vitas, "you will be up on a cross again. Unless you give me the name first. Then they will be taken down to honor the governor's bargain with you."

Others might yet be saved, including Jerome. And if Jerome was taken from the cross and revived, he might be able to lead Vitas to the person who had woven a grass bracelet and left it as a message for him.

"I have the name," Vitas said.

He would not be responsible for the death of a man innocent of Helva's murder. Nor would he take the burden of the families of Jews who would die unless Governor Julianus had someone else to take the blame.

So Vitas gave the name of the one person he knew would be safe from the governor's reach. A man whose ship Damian, Jerome, and Vitas had set fire to in Alexandria.

"Well?" the messenger said.

"His name is Atronius Pavo," Vitas said, giving a lie that would buy him time he desperately needed. "A ship's captain."

HORA SEPTINA

VITAS HAD BEEN RETURNED to the courtyard of the villa, where the governor now glared at Bernice. "I did not question too closely how you knew a slave had overheard someone threaten Helva the day before he was killed. Nor did I question too closely how you knew the killers were intent on appearing like Sicarii. Only because you had promised you would deliver the name of a man I could arrest immediately."

Julianus swept his hand dismissively in Vitas's direction. "Now this. I'm to look for a ship's captain?"

"This is obviously not an intelligent slave," Bernice said, her own glare at Vitas a reflection of the one the governor had directed at her. "I'm sure if he gives it any thought at all, he will recall exactly which Greek was so clear in his threats against Helva. My own guess is that it was a Greek with considerable debts to Helva and sufficient motivation to plan the elaborate murder."

She frowned deeply at Vitas. "Give it more thought."

He'd been forced back with the soldiers to repeat the name to the governor, who had immediately registered shock.

Obviously, he and Bernice had been complicit in the determination to make Glecko Partho a convenient scapegoat. Vitas wondered what Partho had done to earn the governor's enmity too.

"Well?" Bernice demanded.

"One of the crucified slaves was dead by the time we arrived,"

Vitas said. "I would like to be assured that one is still alive. The one named Jerome."

"You dare bargain again!" the governor thundered.

"Again?" Vitas said. "No, Excellency. I just can't imagine that a Roman governor would not honor an agreement. I did my part at the foot of the cross. Jerome was a witness too. Perhaps he could join us. Not only will it be helpful for our conversation, but it will prove the agreement has been fulfilled."

In irritation, the governor snapped his fingers, and a messenger scurried away.

While they waited, Bernice did not stop once in her fierce concentration of anger at Vitas.

He tried not to smile, thinking of his friend Titus with this woman.

Titus might rule a legion, but there was much to fear from Bernice.

✢ ✢ ✢

"Satisfied?" Bernice asked Vitas some time later. "He is obviously alive."

Jerome had been escorted into the courtyard. The lines on his face were deep and drawn.

"Yes," Vitas said. "There was a man who swore he would kill Helva. I was there with Jerome. We both heard the conversation, didn't we."

Vitas nodded at Jerome, who made his peculiar sound of agreement.

"What kind of answer is that?" the governor said.

"He is a mute," Vitas said. "That is the best he can do. It means he agrees."

"So you bring me a second witness who cannot speak, but you have no hesitation to translate on his behalf?"

"This man bragged to Helva that the murder would not appear as a murder," Vitas said. "Is this not correct, Jerome?"

Another mewling sound, the same as before.

"Someone who does business among the Jews," Vitas continued. "A Greek named Atronius Pavo."

Mewling again from Jerome.

Bernice could not help herself. "A Greek named Glecko Partho!"

"No," Vitas said. "Atronius Pavo. Isn't that correct, Jerome?"

The big man nodded his massive head.

Vitas was glad that Bernice was not armed with a dagger. Her eyes were already suggesting he was about to die.

"This gets us nowhere," the governor said, slamming his hand down. "How can I send soldiers to arrest a man of unknown history and residence?"

"Send me," Vitas said. "I would recognize him. Later, in the market, I heard him discussing the hire of a camel driver with an old Jewish woman."

This gave the governor pause. It was obvious the man was calculating.

"Send me with soldiers," Vitas said, anticipating the governor would believe it was an escape attempt. "Wrists shackled, under guard. I'm sure I can find the old Jewish woman, and she will lead me to the camel driver. In turn that will lead me to the Greek ship's captain."

More silence. Vitas did not break it. He knew full well that the first to speak often lost the negotiation.

"I don't trust you," the governor told Vitas. "Your Latin is too polished. You have all your teeth. It suggests you were not born a slave but became one for a crime that likely involved deceit and treachery." The governor tapped his teeth. "Still, it would be practical to have the perpetrator of this crime flogged and executed."

He snapped his head into position, obviously at a decision. "You will go," he told Vitas. "The soldiers will take you as directed, in shackles, and they will have instructions to kill you at the slightest sign of treachery."

Julianus turned to Bernice. "And you will be his surety."

"Governor—"

"Not a word. You came to me offering a solution, which did not happen. You wanted to prevent bloodshed of your people, and you promised this slave would deliver the murderer. So I have decided. The slave will bring back a man to stand for the crime as you promised, or you will die in his place. There may be riots if families are killed in retribution for Helva's assassination, but I'm not so sure there will be protests if I choose you instead."

Vitas badly wanted just a little time with Jerome. In private. To ask about the grass bracelet. But it was not given.

One final statement to Vitas: "And you, slave, leave immediately. You have until dusk to bring in the man you insist murdered Helva. Or the queen of the Jews dies for her people."

HORA OCTAVA

VITAS FOUND THE ROPE that tied his ankles was not uncomfortable in any way. He could walk without tangling himself. If he tried to run, however, he would fall within two steps.

His wrists were likewise encumbered. His hands, in front of him, had ample movement but not enough to allow him to attack the two soldiers who stoically followed him into the slums of the Jewish community outside of Caesarea.

Not that Vitas had any intent of something so foolhardy. First, the soldiers were well armed. Second, Vitas was truly in pursuit of answers. He did not want to escape.

Governor Julianus had not been content to restrict the escort to Roman soldiers, however. There was a third man walking beside Vitas, a man who enjoyed talking.

"Remarkable, these Jews," the man was saying. Gneus Bucco, as he'd introduced himself upon his arrival with the soldiers, was a short, skinny man with a nose a little too long for his face. Young, but with pockmarked skin that took away any air of youthfulness. "They have been here months, but I see none of the garbage I'd expect. And already a semblance of order. Any other slum area would be infested with rats, but the Jews have done a commendable job of making it livable here. If only they weren't so stubborn about believing in one God."

As he had the entire journey, Vitas ignored the man.

Bucco was not dressed with any degree of luxury, but his fingernails were manicured, and the cut of his hair betrayed a higher position than most. Vitas guessed Bucco had chosen to dress in a manner that would not draw the attention of thieves.

It was unnecessary. With Roman soldiers—even an escort as small as two—they were immune from danger. It wasn't that the soldiers themselves would have been able to protect them from a gang of determined bandits or an angry crowd. It was the might of Rome that backed the soldiers: an attack on these two would be considered an attack on Rome itself.

The Jews were already afraid enough, considering the families that Julianus held hostage. They would not want to further provoke the governor.

This was one of the reasons Vitas, after further consideration, did not believe actual Sicarii had killed Helva. They were family men and knew the consequences. It was one thing to slip into a crowd and kill a Jew who was a Roman sympathizer. Quite another to challenge Roman officials, especially in light of all the other punishments already inflicted on the Jews in the previous six months.

"As I said: remarkable," Bucco prattled on. "These people do not behave as if they've been subjugated and beaten down in riots. It's almost as if they believe this defeat is only temporary."

Vitas had a destination and did not want to be distracted from it. This community of exiles was set half a mile outside of Caesarea—he'd walked past dying men on the crosses to get to it. At the first opportunity, he'd inquired about Arella, the old woman, and now he wanted to get there as fast as he could.

"Do you have an answer for that?" the chatty little man asked Vitas.

None that Vitas wanted to share.

As he continued to walk, Vitas thought of another time, reminded by the crowding of the hastily built stone walls of the small houses that were closer to huts, the obvious poverty of the children playing in the dust of the paths between the houses, the smells from cooking pots over open fires, and the upright, dignified strides of bearded men wearing shawls with tassels of religious significance.

Barely over a year earlier, he'd been in a similar slum outside the
walls of Jerusalem, among the stench of the tanners.

That day, tension had filled the air as surely as the heat of the
sun, tension that had broken into the screams of the dying when
Florus, the previous governor, had unleashed his soldiers.

But it wasn't the memory of the dying that took Vitas back; it
was the memory of his emotions. He'd been searching for a woman,
hoping to save her from the slaughter. He'd succeeded, found Sophia,
convinced her to marry him—only to deliver her to another beast of
Rome: Nero.

"Why this attitude among the Jews? This sense of specialness?
Are you even hearing me?" Bucco demanded.

Vitas let out a sigh. "Doing my best not to listen."

The little man squawked. Like a chicken indignant at the foot
that swept it aside.

"Let us not pretend," Vitas said. "You are along to spy for the
governor. I can't stop you from anything you choose to report, but
I don't owe you any conversation."

"Julianus said you weren't stupid," Bucco said.

"Suddenly I feel uplifted."

Bucco squinted. "Ah, sarcasm."

"Are we finished with this conversation?"

"Answer my question first. What possible reason could these
Jews have for believing that Rome will suffer defeat to them?"

"They wait for their Messiah," Vitas snapped. "Their God
has delivered them again and again from enemies as mighty as
Rome, preserving their people to ensure the Messiah will be
born among them."

"That does answer my question," Bucco said. He smirked.
"Not about the Jews. But about you. It tells me you are familiar
with these people."

Vitas was content to let Bucco think he had outsmarted
a lowly slave.

Especially because the stakes were so high.

Everything depended on what Arella might be able to tell him about the bracelet of grass that had been placed on Jerome's wrist.

At the end of the previous summer, Vitas had been in the bowels of the arena in Rome, enduring the smells of blood, vomit, and human waste as he waited in a cage to be released onto the sand to die in front of Nero.

Then, he had not been resigned to death; resignation would have meant his emotions were dead too. Instead, he'd been filled with enraged futility at the injustice of his imprisonment and overwhelming sorrow that his actions had condemned Sophia to an unknown fate.

But when he heard news of her death, he abandoned all hope of ever seeing her again, the loss like an abscess in his soul. Each morning, in that brief twilight between sleep and wakening, he'd reached for her, only to be devastated anew each time the truth dawned on him. Except for a curiosity he could not avoid about who had arranged his escape and what the letter meant, he'd truly become resigned to a state of emotional dullness.

The grass bracelet had changed that. With the rope still tied to his ankles to keep him from fleeing the escort of soldiers, Vitas shuffled into a makeshift hut built of dried-mud bricks and quivered with anticipation. His last request to Arella had been to look for Sophia. If she'd found Sophia and they'd returned to the crosses to discover Vitas had been taken down, that might be the explanation for the grass bracelet he'd found on Jerome.

Vitas was pretending—because of the governor's spy beside him—that Arella might have an answer to the whereabouts of Pavo, but what he really sought was a miracle.

That his beloved Sophia was alive.

From the outside, it was obvious the hut was but a single room. If Arella had found Sophia, she might be only a step away, the step through the doorway from sunshine into shadow.

But the hut was empty.

And the sensation of being crushed between two boulders was

enough disappointment to tell Vitas how much his fleeting hope had meant to him.

Especially when Bucco said in a cheerful voice, "If the old woman isn't here, she must be among the group the governor has set aside to be condemned for reprisal."

HORA NONANA

THE FAMILIES HAD been treated like cattle, herded into a compound on open ground and guarded by enough soldiers on the perimeter to discourage any rescue attempts.

Buckets of water had been placed in the center. The only possessions that the families had been allowed to take inside the compound were blankets, and Vitas saw that mothers were doing their best to shield the younger children from the sun. Some men paced. Others stood motionless, arms around their wives or children.

They could do nothing but wait, knowing their lives depended on the governor's decision, too keenly aware that if the governor decided to make an example of Roman power by executing them, each would be crucified. In other countries, Vitas had seen lines of crosses—one every five feet—that extended half a mile along a road, each victim crying out for help as death approached with excruciating slowness. It was an effective deterrent to future rebellions.

The compound was a semicircle, barely twenty-five paces across at its widest.

As Vitas scanned the families trapped inside, some stared back with open hostility and fear on their faces. To them, new soldiers had arrived. Did it mean the governor was proceeding with the retribution?

He saw Arella first.

And then . . .

Yes!

She was there. Sophia. Her head was up, and over Arella's shoulder, he could see her face turned sideways. She had not seen him yet. His ruse to find the old woman had been rewarded beyond the heights of any and all euphoria a man could experience.

He'd felt this before, too, on a day in Jerusalem after traveling the known world to search for her and finding her safe, but in the midst of a savage uprising that pitted Jews against Romans. On that day, he'd been able to stride forward and speak to her and resist the urge to sweep her into his arms. Now, to protect her, he wasn't even able to acknowledge her, an act of passivity made all the more difficult by his desire to shout with joy. It took all his strength not to betray the intensity of this sudden emotion. Not to croak out an exclamation of relief. Not to cry out questions.

How had she survived? What journeys had brought her here? Who had arranged it? All questions of vital importance, but all questions that Vitas must ignore. For the man beside him, Bucco, would pounce if he gained the slightest inkling how much this meant to Vitas.

"You!" Vitas yelled instead. "Old woman! Come here!"

The shout was a diversion to deliberately draw the crowd's attention. Among the rest of the surprised glances, Bucco wouldn't pick out a reaction from Sophia.

Arella merely frowned, puzzled. But Sophia gaped and stepped past Arella.

Their eyes met, and Vitas wanted to rush forward, leap past the guards, over the fence of the compound, and through the families, and pull her into his arms. Then he was staggered by a new observation. Sophia's belly was swollen with pregnancy. Months earlier, her face glowing, she'd informed him that he would be a father. But to see it now hit his heart, not his mind.

With great inner discipline, Vitas kept a stone face and gave the slightest shake of his head as their eyes remained on each other, hoping she would understand.

"That's the old woman we need," Vitas said to the soldiers with slightly less volume, pointing at Arella. "No one else."

Sophia heeded this additional warning and dropped her head, becoming a woman who did not want the attention of Roman soldiers.

His shout, however, had drawn someone else forward to stand beside Arella. A man who also gaped at Vitas.

"Another old Jew," Vitas said, lifting his shackled wrists in a dismissive action. "Don't let him become a distraction."

Far from being just another old Jew, this was a man Vitas knew well: Simeon Ben-Aryeh. They had first met here in Caesarea, almost a year ago, when Vitas had come to Judea to seek Sophia. Of high standing in the religious circles of the Temple, and ordered by Bernice to help Vitas, the man had been a reluctant, surly, resentful guide, a Jew who thoroughly hated all things Roman. He was now a fugitive from justice, long fled from Jerusalem for a crime he did not commit.

"I'll need to speak to the old woman alone," Vitas said to Bucco.

"That won't be permissible," Bucco answered. "I have specific orders from the governor."

"Then she won't speak freely."

"I'm sure she will," Bucco answered. "We could always put a knife to the throat of the daughter beside her."

Good that Bucco had made the assumption. Not so good that Bucco had identified a weakness, though Vitas was grateful that the little man had no sense of where the real weakness lay. Sophia had come back to life for him. Vitas would not let her slip away again.

"My name is Novellus, and I was a slave to Helva," Vitas said to Arella, calling out across the few paces between them. "I'm here because the governor wants answers to who killed Helva and how. I'm looking for a man named Atronius Pavo, and I've been told you might know where to find him. In the market, I overheard him once ask you where to hire a camel driver. If you tell me where he is, I'm sure all of you here will be safe. As will all the Jewish families held hostage by the governor. First, tell me the names of those two."

Meaning Ben-Aryeh and Sophia.

Each answered.

Nothing on Sophia's face betrayed the knowledge that Vitas was close enough to reach by extending her arms. Vitas felt like his legs were saplings shuddering in a breeze; he could hardly stand because of his relief and euphoria and the amazing surge of love that filled him. In his memories he had visited her often, recalling her beauty. But here, in front of him, the impact of how truly beautiful she was seemed like a physical blow and made a mockery of those memories.

He had to swallow twice to be able to speak.

"These names mean nothing to me," Vitas told Bucco. "I have not heard them in connection to the threats against Helva." He paused significantly. "But as the old woman will undoubtedly verify, a Greek asked her about camels. What do you know about the Greek? Where is he now? Is there a camel driver you sent him to? Or perhaps you gave him no answer at all, and this trip has been a waste of time."

It was a strong hint, and Arella took it.

"Bah," the old woman said. "Of course I remember. Some fool asked me about camels. But I didn't have an answer for him. So don't ask me where he is. Yes, you have wasted your time, because the only place you'll find an answer is in the market."

No. Anything but a waste of time. Arella was an intelligent woman and had responded perfectly. Vitas could have taken Bucco directly to the market to make inquiries about the camels, but this had been what Vitas wanted to accomplish.

To find out who had placed the grass bracelet on a crucified man.

Now that he'd learned the answer was as he hoped, he could go.

But he knew if he didn't find a guilty man by dusk, he might end up on the cross again, his crucifixion all the more agonizing because of the knowledge that Sophia was alive.

HORA DECIMA

THE MARKET BROUGHT the mixed smell of spices and offal, the sounds of grunting camels and shouted bartering.

Vitas found himself amazed at the vividness of each smell and sound. It was as if he had been freshly born and was rediscovering his world.

He knew it was joy. He did feel like a new man. Sophia—alive!

His elation was tempered, of course, by urgency . . . and also by a tinge of self-disgust.

Earlier, he had wrestled with the morality of sacrificing a criminal Greek as a scapegoat to save the families of Jews who were to be slaughtered as retribution for Helva's death. Now, when it was his own family at stake, he had to wonder: If he failed in his efforts today, would he let that innocent man die simply to save Sophia?

He tried to justify it.

Wouldn't any man—faced with choosing the death of his own son or daughter—give nod to a stranger's death if that would save the child?

Did nations not choose their finest young men and send them out in battle as soldiers so that the deaths of a few might preserve many?

As he moved through the bustle of the market, another thought occurred to him.

Despite the logic that a person should die to save many, could he as a father give up his own child to save a nation?

It led him to think of the Christos.

One to save many.

The Greek was not pure by any means and probably deserved death for any number of other reasons. Yet the Christos—according to reliable accounts by followers who knew him during his life and shared their knowledge through word and letter—had truly been not only an innocent man, but a man of love. A man who healed with a touch. If any man should ever have been lifted to a throne, not a cross, it should have been the Christos—who was also reported to have risen from the dead. But to Vitas, the one obviously flawed prediction by the Christos made everything else a lie. The Temple was not going to fall.

Vitas growled at himself. He needed a clear head to save Sophia, not one muddled with conundrums of philosophy.

Bucco glanced toward him. "Yes?"

Vitas realized his growl had been heard. "A pebble inside my sandal." He shook his foot as if to kick it loose.

"The smallest things," Bucco said, "are the ones that can trouble us the most."

More philosophy. Vitas did not need this.

He needed to find the camel driver, and one man could lead him there. The silk vendor who had bartered with the caravan, with a table out near some stacked amphorae filled with wine.

Now it was a matter of finding a way to force that man to give answers.

So Vitas told Bucco what was needed.

✝ ✝ ✝

Bucco stood in front of the silk vendor. His legs were spread and braced, his arms crossed, an aggressive stance that appeared ridiculous from such a small man. Ridiculous, but all the more intimidating for its ridiculousness.

Only a small man backed by Roman soldiers would assume this stance, and the swords of the soldiers behind Bucco gleamed in the sunlight.

The silk vendor remained behind his table stacked with rolls of the fine cloth.

"I am here on the governor's business," Bucco barked. "Out from behind there."

Vitas stood at a respectful distance from Bucco, head bowed and pretending disinterest. Yet he strained to hear the conversation above the noise of the market.

"You were here when the fiscal procurator was assassinated?" Bucco asked.

"I know nothing about it," the vendor said. He was tall and thin but had hunched in an impossible effort to make himself invisible.

"Of course you do," Bucco snapped. "Everybody does."

"What I meant was that I know nothing about the men involved."

"You presume that was to be my question?" Bucco studied the man. "To me, that alone suggests guilt."

"No!" A pause, then a rush to speak. "No! The governor's men have already questioned us. Again and again. To see if we could identify any of the attackers. So I presumed that once more he has sent someone for information." The vendor straightened slightly. "It was, of course, the Jews. As a Greek, I have no quarrel with Rome. I pay my temple fees and worship at the statue of Nero."

Bucco said nothing. Vitas was impressed. It was an intelligent way to get a man to speak, by letting him fill the silence.

"And aren't the Jews to pay?" the vendor asked. He reached beside him and nervously smoothed out the wrinkles in a roll of fabric on the table. "Just as well. They are troublemakers. The fewer of them the better. And who knows how many are spies for the rebels in the provinces."

"What I want from you," Bucco said, "is the name of the camel driver."

"Camel driver?"

"Who owned the camels that were sent stampeding through the market?"

All over again, Vitas saw it vividly in his mind: the great plunging beasts with oil on their hides, flames and black smoke rising to blue sky. He heard the screams of the camels, smelled the burning flesh.

"Do I have to explain?" Bucco said, then answered his own question. "A train of camels was passing through the market. Where is the owner now?"

"That is all you want to know? About the Nabataean?"

"Instead of wasting my time with a question, give me the answer. Who is the Nabataean, and where do I find him?"

Vitas found himself leaning forward. It was a slim hope, but all he had. He'd had hours to think about the assassination and how it had been planned. In the end, he believed it came down to one crucial starting point: the camels. If he was correct and this starting point could lead to an ending point, the local Jewish families would be spared impending slaughter. Bernice, too, would be spared execution. If his hunch was correct, upon Damian's return, Vitas would be freed from his role as a slave and reunited with Sophia. As for the mysterious visitor to his jail cell and the amulet that he was given, that would no longer matter. If Vitas survived this, he had no intention of involving himself in anything but a quiet domestic life with wife and child in a place far from Rome and Nero's spies.

The vendor's reply, however, crushed this small hope.

"I don't know the Nabataean's name," the vendor said. "And it doesn't matter. He is dead. Killed during the confusion in the market."

HORA UNDECIMA

"BACK TO THE QUEEN of the Jews," Bucco said with a shrug. He had little stake in the fate of the families who awaited death.

They were out of the market now. Vitas had not spoken a word in the five minutes since leaving the vendor.

"Not yet," Vitas answered.

"You order me?"

Eleven months ago—when Vitas had been among those in the emperor's inner circle, before Nero had taken his property and his wife and ordered his execution in the arena—the answer would have been yes.

In recent months—when Vitas believed all that was important to him had been taken away—he would have been too lethargic to bother caring.

Two days earlier, he'd been ready to accept suicide on the cross by drinking a potion.

But this morning, his life had been given back to him. Sophia was alive. And in danger of execution.

So Vitas had to stifle a natural impulse to behave as a landed Roman citizen with wealth and political power; he had to pretend he was merely a slave named Novellus, a disgraced Roman sold as punishment for a crime.

"I merely ask," Vitas said, "whether you have your eye set upon a greater role in Caesarea and perhaps someday back in Rome."

No answer. But Vitas didn't need it. Everything about this man screamed of the type of political worm Vitas knew too well.

"What harm is there in spending another half hour for an opportunity to position yourself solidly in the governor's favor?" Vitas asked. "Keep in mind that if the governor returns to Rome in good standing with Nero, it can only benefit the man who helped the governor quell an uprising in a difficult situation."

"Half an hour?" Bucco said. The bait had been taken and the hook set.

"Half an hour," Vitas repeated. He decided a little flattery would not hurt as a way to disguise the hook even more. "You can be a terrifying man when you desire, and I wonder if there are yet some people who might have an answer that you need."

✦ ✦ ✦

It was not difficult to find the Nabataeans, the tribal people who were slowly becoming less nomadic because of the protection of Rome. Over a century earlier, when Damascus had been the stage of a long struggle between warring Greek generals and the invading Roman forces, the citizens of that city had invited a Nabataean ruler, Aretas III, to be their protector, in essence making him king and slowly changing the status of Nabataeans from lowly caravan drivers who had roamed the desert to merchants, though still tribal in culture. In Damascus, where the Nabataeans poured their wealth into sumptuous houses, their lifestyles were opulent. But in the desert, they still lived in tents with divided walls as they skillfully navigated the cantankerous beasts of the desert along ancient caravan routes, depending on a water collection system known only to themselves.

The walk was a short one to the outskirts of Caesarea, where tents of the nomads billowed in the breeze that was growing with the rising heat of the day. Camels were staked to the ground, goats tethered to ropes.

Three robed men—short and stocky, with faces almost black from exposure to sun—stopped them at the camp's entrance.

"I've been sent by the governor," Bucco said with arrogance.

"I am here to see the widow of the man who died in the market during the stampede of the camels."

"She is grieving, protected by her sons," the man in the middle answered. The two others shifted to stand closer, presenting a united front.

"That doesn't matter to the governor," Bucco snorted. "Send her to me. Or escort me there."

"It matters to us."

Vitas leaned down to whisper to Bucco. "Nothing is of more importance to men of a tribe like this than honor. Nothing is worse to them than shame. It is how they've survived the desert. They will accept slaughter at Roman swords before the shame they would wear if they did not protect a brother's widow from the governor."

"What leverage do I have if I cannot threaten them with the governor's might?" Bucco growled, keeping a close eye on the men in front of him.

"Use their own swords against them," Vitas said.

"I don't understand."

"Perhaps I should speak with them."

"I thought you said I could be a terrifying man when needed."

"That is not what is needed now."

"You knew that all along, I suppose," Bucco said, not amused.

"We could walk back and report to the governor that you let a few Nabataeans stop you from rescuing him from this dire political situation," Vitas said quietly, keeping the conversation between himself and Bucco. "Or you could establish that you are still in authority and slap me across the back of the head, order me to my knees, and command me to speak to them."

"Happily," Bucco said.

Bucco's blow was as hard as Vitas had expected, and with pretended humiliation, he lowered himself to his knees, knowing how he appeared to the Nabataeans, with the rope around his wrists and ankles. He was a slave, a man of no value. The humiliation, however, was pretended because Vitas felt he had some control, and he was going to use it to full advantage to protect the woman—and the child—he loved.

From his knees, he spoke to the man in the middle.

"Your brother's death in the market was no accident," Vitas said. Whether or not the camel driver who had died was related by blood or by tribe, to the Nabataeans, the man was a brother. Either was of equal importance to these people. "The man who hired him gave orders to have your brother murdered. He's the same man who arranged for the camels to be set on fire."

In one sense, his accusation against the unknown man was a complete assumption. Vitas had no compunction about this degree of deceit, however. Not with what was at stake. But in another sense, Vitas spoke the truth. There could be no other explanation for the chain of events that had led to the assassination of Helva. It was no accident that the camels had been lit on fire and, undoubtedly, no accident that the one man able to identify who had hired him had died in the panic that followed.

Vitas also knew his accusation against the unknown man who had hired the camel driver now meant the man would be hunted without remorse and hunted until he was found, even if it took decades. There was a saying about these people. "I against my brother; my brothers and I against my cousins; then my cousins and I against strangers." Bringing the man to justice meant honor. Letting him escape meant shame.

"Ask among yourselves," Vitas said. "Find his identity and give it to us. It will put you in favor with Rome."

The man in the middle did not have to glance at his companions before answering with grim determination. "Wait here. It will be done."

HORA DUODECIMA

AN HOUR BEFORE SUNSET, Vitas and a ten-year-old boy followed Bucco and Bucco's retinue of twenty soldiers into the outer courtyard of the villa where Helva had lived. Vitas trailed the retinue into the house, watching with amusement as servants vainly tried to protest the intrusion. He noted with satisfaction that half of the soldiers dispersed throughout the massive villa, acting on previous instructions from the governor.

Vitas lowered his eyes and stayed behind Bucco's remaining soldiers, confident he was invisible to Dolabella as she marched toward them.

"This is an invasion!" Dolabella cried. "The governor will hear of this."

Bucco addressed Dolabella. "On behalf of the governor, I am investigating the death of your husband."

"I trust you have news for me, then. The Jews must pay for their atrocity."

"No news. Only questions."

"I don't like your tone."

"Is this how you would speak to the governor?" Bucco asked.

"You are not the governor."

"I've made it clear that I represent him. And my first question involves a slave who was in your employ—Novellus. I understand that when you and the magistrate began the initial interrogation,

Novellus suggested that you go to the governor with instructions to find out who had hired the camel driver."

Dolabella tossed her head. "Who told you this? The magistrate? If so, consider the source. He's been swooning around me, and I've spurned him publicly. Besides, why should it matter?"

"What matters is that neither you nor the magistrate passed along the information."

"If indeed that's what the slave said. He's been crucified, and you are clutching at hearsay. And you still haven't answered my question. Why should it matter?"

"Tell me," Bucco said, "the morning that Helva was killed, why was he in the marketplace?"

"He told me he had been called by the governor. There are a dozen servants who could confirm this, if only you asked them instead of bothering me."

"What's strange," Bucco went on, "is that the governor had not sent for your husband."

"Someone did," she said tartly. "It is not a concern to me."

"It's a concern to me," Bucco said. He raised his voice. "Novellus!"

Vitas stepped around the soldiers. He wasn't alone. He had the boy with him, a Nabataean.

Dolabella frowned as she recognized Vitas. "The magistrate . . ."

"Sentenced me to crucifixion," Vitas said. "Yet here I am. I, too, am curious why you wouldn't pass along my message to the governor. The diversion of camels was undoubtedly planned for when Helva was to pass through the market."

"I can hardly believe this," Dolabella said, drawing herself up with indignation, speaking to Bucco and pointing at Vitas. "This slave failed in his duty to protect my husband, and now he is part of your investigation for the governor?"

"No," Bucco said, "the boy is." Bucco turned to the boy and spoke softly. "Yes?"

"Yes," the boy said, nodding vigorously. "That's the woman

who met with my father's brother. She said she wanted him to drive some camels for her."

"I've never seen this boy before."

"He was working among the camels," Bucco said, "when you spoke to his uncle."

"Nonsense."

Hardly. And Vitas knew it. When the Nabataeans had brought him forward, the boy had described a woman whose hair was almost orange.

"You couldn't have done this alone," Bucco said. "I've been authorized by the governor to tell you he is prepared to let you draw a bath as an alternative to crucifixion. On the condition that you testify against the man who helped you murder your husband."

Draw a bath. Vitas closed his eyes briefly. It was how Nero had commanded Sophia to die. Suicide—slitting her wrists in a hot bath.

Vitas opened his eyes again, surprised at the silence. He'd expected a squawk, but instead Dolabella was gaping at Bucco with a mixture of outrage and fear.

Bucco pressed his advantage and cued the boy. "The trumpet."

"She asked him to release the camels at the sound of a trumpet," the boy answered. He was losing his shyness in the presence of the soldiers, speaking louder.

That's what had first struck Vitas as strange about the stampeding camels. The sound of trumpeting as Helva passed through the market.

Dolabella recovered her composure. "I know what is happening here. The governor wants a scapegoat to rescue his political situation. I'm a widow, far from Rome. So he sends you here to condemn me on the strength of the lies of a boy and a slave."

"He sent me here on more than that," Bucco said. "Soldiers are searching your house for a single earring with a large red ruby."

Dolabella brought a hand to her mouth as if to prevent all the air being sucked from her body as she visibly shrank in front of Vitas and the boy.

Bucco explained to Dolabella what all of them already knew. "You gave the boy's uncle one of the earrings and promised him the other if he accomplished the task. We found that earring among his possessions in his tent. Now we are looking here for the one that matches."

"Alexios," she said.

Bucco was puzzled. "Alexios?"

"That's the man you want. He was my lover and threatened to inform Helva if I didn't go to the camel driver. I had no idea what Alexios had planned to do, otherwise I never would have helped. He worked with some Sicarii who agreed to do the job. It served Alexios and the Sicarii. I had no choice in my involvement. You have to believe me. The governor has to believe me."

Bucco gave her a strange smile. "My advice is to draw your bath now. Save yourself the humiliation. And if it helps, take a flagon of wine with you. From what I've heard, the drunker you are, the less pain you will feel."

VESPERA

VITAS FACED JULIANUS AGAIN, still bound at the wrists and ankles. Behind the governor, other slaves were lighting oil lamps on a balcony where the governor sat in a chair woven from reeds and drank from a gold-rimmed goblet. The balcony afforded a view of the Mediterranean, and the sun was almost gone. Dusk served as a shield, hiding the red of the sunburn on Julianus's face.

"As you might know, already Alexios has been arrested and faced the red-hot tongs of torture," the governor told Vitas. "It didn't take long for him to break and give up the names of the others involved. We will have them all on crosses tomorrow." The governor shook his head. "Not only was he making a cuckold of Helva; he'd been embezzling from the man. Consider the irony. The fiscal procurator himself, clutching every denarius for Nero and letting his own cascade away to a thief."

Because Julianus had not asked a question, Vitas said nothing.

"You have saved Bernice's life," the governor continued. Odd, the strained voice that carried so much authority. "And you have served me well by eliminating this difficult political position. I'm sure the Jews who have been released would also feel gratitude toward you, but none will know of your role in this. You would do well to keep it that way—I have no intention of appearing like I needed the help of a slave. If the slightest whisper reaches me, I will put you on the cross again."

Vitas fought to hide his impatience. He did not want to be

here with the governor. Among the Jews who had been released was Sophia. She would not know yet all that had happened, only that Vitas was alive and not on a cross. He wanted to run full speed without stopping until he reached the settlement of the Jews and then shout her name until he found her.

But to all appearances, he was still a slave bound to the Helva estate.

"I have no intention of granting you anything in payment for this service," the governor continued. There was the slightest of slurs in his voice. Drinking wine on a breezy balcony with the orange of the sun on shimmering water was, after all, a relatively harmless pleasure. Or had the governor been drinking to steel himself to execute Bernice if Vitas failed? "Taking you down from the cross was enough already. And I'm not happy at the way you spoke to me in front of Bernice. I should have you whipped for it. So there you have it. By not whipping you, I have repaid you for your assistance. Besides that, other men in my position might have you killed merely to ensure your silence about all of this."

When Julianus stopped, the quiet became dangerous, as if the governor were daring Vitas to protest.

Instead, Vitas bowed his head.

"What's strange," Julianus said, "is somehow you seem familiar to me. Tell me, have we met?"

The first direct question of this audience.

"We have not," Vitas said truthfully. They had friends in common but had never been at a social occasion together.

The governor tossed back more wine. "No matter." A smacking of lips. "Bernice feels she does owe you."

Without warning, the governor laughed loudly. "But you may be out of the frying pan and into the fire. Dolabella as your mistress was one thing, for her reputation was rumored in all the streets of the city. Bernice, I daresay, may be another of the same stripe. She-wolves, both of them. And Bernice has purchased you. That's her thanks for saving your life. Keeping you from the slave auction with the rest of Helva's property."

In the light of the oil lamps, it appeared that Julianus was examining Vitas closely to see his reaction. If so, Vitas disappointed him, especially if the governor again expected Vitas to protest.

Vitas felt just the opposite—as though his heart were taking wing. Bernice was a secret ally who owed Vitas her life. Twice. He had no doubt that Bernice would grant his request for an armed escort to journey immediately through the darkness to the Jewish settlement.

"Bah," Julianus said. "Go. You'll be escorted to Bernice. And make a sacrifice of thanks at the statue of Nero that I don't have you whipped for insolence."

✢ ✢ ✢

Vitas felt slow torture as his fettered ankles shuffled through the streets to Queen Bernice's villa. Soldiers bearing swords and torches, one on each side, were there to ensure he did not attempt to escape.

The truth, of course, was that Vitas wanted nothing more than an audience with Bernice . . . and the subsequent swift trip to be reunited with Sophia.

Sophia!

Vitas was a man who held his emotions carefully, rarely trusting them himself, preferring to respond only after giving any matter a lot of thought. But tonight he wanted to burst into song.

Sophia was alive!

He ached to have his arms around her, to have her shuddering with relief in his embrace. He needed to get to Bernice much faster than these slow, awkward steps took him over the cobblestones.

"Can you feel it?" one soldier was saying to the other. "It's like the streets can breathe again."

"Had we crucified the Jews, it would have meant days of riots," the second answered. "Not even the legion of Titus would have prevented it."

"Titus. Now there's a commander to follow."

"Few better," the other said. "But give me Caesarea. I'm not anxious to be any deeper in the province. Give me guard duty anytime."

"You've heard the rumors, haven't you? I wouldn't be surprised if he's with Bernice right now."

Vitas finally spoke. "Titus has arrived with his legion?"

The first soldier slapped Vitas across the buttocks with the flat of his sword blade. "Shut up, slave. You're not part of this conversation."

It didn't matter that neither soldier gave Vitas an answer to his question.

Titus indeed awaited them at the villa, alone and pacing back and forth at the entrance.

"My friend," Titus said. He extended his arms and took slow, steady steps toward Vitas.

One of the soldiers lifted a sword in warning, stepped between them, and pointed it toward the general's chest. "Back away," he growled.

Titus smiled, amused. The light of the oil lamp showed his handsome, elegant features and hair that had been neatly—and expensively—trimmed. His toga spoke of wealth—spotless linen.

"You put me in a delicate situation," Titus said. "On one hand, I'm impressed at your sense of duty. On the other, however, I am the commander of the Fifteenth Legion, and I expect that you would put down the sword."

"Titus!" the second soldier exclaimed.

The first soldier spoke quickly. "Any man can claim to be Titus. And what reason would Titus have to call this slave a friend?"

Titus sighed. "You are delivering this slave to Bernice?"

"As commanded by the governor."

"And you will only release this man on the authority of Bernice."

"He is her slave."

"That is our difficulty, then," Titus said. "She sent me here to wait for this slave."

"You said *friend* earlier."

"Both," Titus said. "Let's be men of reason."

"No," the first soldier said. "If you are Titus, let's both be military men. I respect my orders. As should you."

The door behind them opened. Bernice stepped out with two male slaves behind her.

"You have delivered this man," Bernice said. "That should end the matter."

"Not quite," Titus told her. He spoke to the soldier who still held his sword at the ready. "Interested in joining the Fifteenth?"

"If you are Titus, the answer is yes."

"I'll arrange it with the governor. Tomorrow's password to get through the gates is 'eagles fly to victory.' Report to me at the camp at dawn, before the council meeting when the password changes. The legion will be on the march again as soon as camp breaks."

✢ ✢ ✢

Inside the doorway, Titus stepped back from Vitas. "You look like a man stepping foot outside of hades."

"Until today, I felt like that man," Vitas answered.

Titus laughed. Held out his arms.

Wrists still roped together, Vitas did the same.

Though Vitas's injuries were still raw, each man clasped the other's forearms and did not speak for long moments.

Titus broke from the clench first. "Let's get you out of these bonds and bathed and dressed properly. We have much to discuss." Titus glanced at Bernice, who nodded and retreated with her slaves, leaving Titus and Vitas alone just inside the doorway.

"It was you who saved me from the arena and sent me from Rome," Vitas said. "With that cryptic letter."

"Yes, I was among those who arranged it," Titus answered, pulling a short dagger from beneath his toga. "And that is much of what we have to discuss. But Vespasian expects no delay in the legion's march."

"That was the only answer I wanted for now," Vitas said. He held out his hands for Titus to cut the rope. "Instead of a bath, I'd prefer a sword and three hours of freedom."

"Time is short." Titus freed Vitas's wrists, then knelt to release his ankles.

"I owe you my life," Vitas said as Titus stood. "Understand, then, how important it is for me to leave immediately. It's Sophia. She's alive."

"If you know that, I presume she is in Caesarea as directed."

"Directed by you?"

"And the others. Bath first. Food. We will talk when you don't stink."

"No. I saw her today for the first time. And abandoned her. She has no idea if I'm alive or dead. Nothing matters more to me than finding her."

"Today was the first time you saw her?" Titus was surprised.

"Let me find her and return. Then you'll have your explanations."

"We'll find her together," Titus said. "It's night. And two swords are better than one."

"No," Vitas said. "You are too important to the empire. The Jews would be openly hostile. Who knows if among them is someone willing to risk crucifixion to kill you."

"They would not know who I am."

"You also risk your friends. If something happened to you—with me nearby—it would draw Nero's attention to this situation and those who conspired with you to set me free. We do not need to repeat the tragedy of Piso."

Titus's face clouded at the reference to the renowned Roman statesman. A little over two years previously, Gaius Calpurnius Piso set a plan into motion to have Nero assassinated, with the intent that the Praetorian Guard—the imperial bodyguards—would declare him emperor of Rome. Because of the growing discontent over Nero's excesses, prominent senators and equestrians supported the secret plot. When the plot was betrayed to Nero's secretary, the ensuing tortures revealed the conspirators, and nineteen prominent citizens were put to death, their properties confiscated by Nero. Among the executed were the uncle of Titus's wife at the time and the uncle's daughter. While Titus was now divorced, even two years was not enough time to entirely remove the stain of association.

Titus let out a long breath. "True enough. But do you remember Smyrna? Such a wonderful brawl you and I had in that tavern. I miss those days. Even now, I wanted to fight that soldier outside. I'm sure he saw this toga and mistook me for a soft man; it would have been wonderful to prove him wrong. A quick step inside the reach of his sword and a well-placed head butt was all that was required. But he was correct about military obligations. His to the governor, and mine to my title and my duties to Vespasian. A small adventure tonight to help my best friend would be a welcome diversion from my duties."

"Let me go alone and silently," Vitas said. "I'll avoid trouble. So will you."

Titus finally nodded. "If you won't risk my life, I won't let you risk yours," he answered. "I have a dozen soldiers who accompanied me here from the camp. I will send an escort with you, armed and carrying bright lamps. They will keep you safe on the road. Find Sophia and bring her here. Then we'll talk."

PRIMA FAX

IN THE WARM NIGHT AIR, Vitas heard the celebratory singing of hymns a few hundred yards before he reached the Jewish settlement. It only confirmed the decision he'd first made when he'd accepted the offer from Titus for an escort of soldiers.

"This is far enough," he said, stopping and holding up a hand.

"We have our orders to protect you," came an answer from the older soldier of the two.

"You have succeeded," Vitas said. "We are almost there. What's ahead of me will be safe enough. Please return to Titus and let him know it was my wish."

"We have our orders to protect you."

"Letting me proceed alone is the only and best way to protect me the final few paces. Listen to the singing. There are hundreds and hundreds of Jews gathered, and without doubt it's to celebrate that none were slaughtered in reprisal for the assassination of Helva. Am I safer walking among them unarmed to look for a friend? Or bursting into their presence with the same Roman military that might have put their women and children on crosses at the side of this road?"

"Point taken. We will wait here to escort you back when you are ready."

"Tell Titus instead that I will be at camp at dawn. I know the password to get through the gates."

"I understood from him that he wants you back tonight," the soldier answered.

"You've heard the rumors about him and Bernice," Vitas said. "And you escorted him to her villa. He has one night here in Caesarea before marching again with the Fifteenth. Are you sure he'll be disappointed if I don't return?"

"Once again, point taken."

✝ ✝ ✝

Vitas moved slowly among the men and women crowded near fires at the center of the Jewish settlement. The shadows made it difficult to see faces clearly. While he was careful to check each person, he did not expect to find Sophia dancing and singing among them. She was heavily pregnant, and he expected that she would be exhausted not only from the events and stress, but from the heat of the day.

He looked for those who were seated and saw the elderly Arella first. Then Ben-Aryeh. But not Sophia.

He tried to contain the surge of disappointment and rationalize his fears. If Sophia were in any danger at all, Ben-Aryeh would be helping her, not here.

Still, Vitas was anxious and could not help but hurry toward the old Jew.

"Vitas!" The old man sprang to his feet and engulfed Vitas in an embrace. "I told her you would find a way back to her."

"So much to talk about," Vitas said. "And so many questions. But later. Please, take me to her."

Ben-Aryeh grinned, his teeth gleaming in the firelight against the darkness of his beard. "Done." He began to lead Vitas away from the crowd.

Vitas took a couple steps to follow, then touched Ben-Aryeh's shoulder. "Wait."

Vitas turned back to Arella, who had not moved. "Come with us," he said.

"I know who you are and I know where you are going," she answered. "We left her resting."

"That's not what I meant," Vitas said. Life for a widowed elderly woman without sons or daughters was a perilous struggle. "Come with us. For what you have done to help, you must join our household."

He took her by the arm, and both of them followed Ben-Aryeh away from the fires and singing.

✦ ✦ ✦

She was asleep. On a mat in the hut that belonged to Arella.

With Ben-Aryeh and Arella waiting outside, Vitas held a lit candle and knelt beside his wife, the woman he loved and had believed was dead.

He listened to the slow, deep breaths that she took in her slumber.

Vitas did not believe in the gods of the Romans and wanted to believe in the God whom Sophia worshiped. He said a whispered prayer of gratitude, in the way he had learned from listening to her prayers. As he prayed, tears slid quietly down his face.

She was alive.

He set the candle down and leaned closer to take in the scent of her body.

She stirred. He moved away slightly, not wanting to startle her, and saw her lift a hand to her cheek, where a tear from his own eye had fallen upon her.

In the candlelight, he saw her smile. "You were in my dream," she said. "Tell me now that I'm awake."

"You are awake," he said. "And I am here."

"So long," she whispered. "And so many miles." She began to weep. "Hold me."

He did.

❧ JUPITER ❧

HORA SECUNDA

"EAGLES FLY TO VICTORY," Vitas told the guards at the camp's entrance.

The Fifteenth was essentially composed of infantry with some cavalry support—six thousand soldiers in all. The smell of the stables just inside the camp was comforting and familiar to Vitas; he had spent years in the military and knew the smells and sounds of living among horses.

The guards expected no attack—Vitas was obviously unarmed and alone—but neither relaxed the spears with which they blocked his access through a gap in the stockade fencing that surrounded the camp.

Vitas wasn't surprised at their discipline. First, it was expected of any Roman army. Large-scale discipline and organization was what made the Romans feared all across the world. Only the Romans would expect their soldiers to march twenty or thirty miles and then dig a ditch three feet wide and four feet deep to surround the camp. Only the Romans would put up the sharpened posts outward and upward at forty-five degrees to repel attackers around the entire perimeter, just for one night. Only the Romans would have three watches during the night, with a penalty of death for any sentry caught sleeping.

Second, this was the legion led by Titus, who was not yet thirty years old but had already earned a reputation for his military prowess. Were it not for the hereditary nature of succession, many would openly speculate that Titus would someday be emperor. As it was, Vitas had heard rumors of another revolt against Nero, and whispers already put Vespasian on the throne, which would someday bode well for Titus.

"Whom are you here to see?" the guard on the right asked.

No emotion in the question, no judgment. Entirely neutral. Another characteristic of the men who served Titus. They had no need to preen by bullying civilians.

"Titus."

"He's expecting you?"

"Yes," Vitas said.

"Wait for an escort." Not asking Vitas for proof demonstrated confidence. The guards fully expected that if Vitas were lying, Titus would dispense judgment and punishment. Their duty was not to interrogate Vitas, but to make sure that this strange slave could not wander camp at will, nor be a threat to Titus.

Vitas waited under their watchful eye, again comforted by the morning rituals. It was barely dawn, but already the camp was brisk with movement. It was set up in a large square to encompass all the tents. And since every legion's camp was set up identically, he could have walked blindfolded and found the general's quarters.

To each side of Vitas were stables, running lengthways along the perimeter of the camp, enclosing dozens of tents arranged in precise rows, each tent big enough to hold at least a century of men.

The main paths of a Roman camp were wide enough to allow for horse and wagon traffic, because except during the dark of night, it would always be busy with the movement of soldiers and suppliers. Via Principalis led straight ahead to the altar and camp headquarters and the general's quarters. Halfway through camp, Via Decumana was a ninety-degree turn one way, and Via Praetoria the other way.

When an escort of two soldiers arrived, they were informed of their task and led Vitas past the altar with fresh animal entrails spread on the ground around it. This legion had a proud history since its establishment over a hundred years earlier with the nickname Apollinaris—"devoted to Apollo." Daily, priests made sacrifices and read what the auspices portended for the day.

They reached the camp headquarters, a tent large enough to accommodate all the legion's centurions and the junior and senior tribunes.

Outside the tent, near the *aquilifer*—the standard bearer—with the golden eagle atop a long pole, Vitas waited with the soldiers who guarded him. He did not expect to hear a murmur of voices through the walls of the tent. Titus, like all other generals, would ensure only one person spoke at a time, and only at his invitation. This morning, Vitas guessed, there would not be much discussion. The legion was not preparing for battle but was on the march. The new password would be given to all the centurions to pass on to their men, discipline reports would be made, and scouts would offer what they had learned about the terrain ahead and how far the march would be until the next camp.

When the tent flap opened and men began to stream out, Vitas kept a bowed head. He and Titus were close enough to be brothers, but it would be a sign of disrespect to take advantage of that in front of the men Titus commanded, especially with the mark on his forehead that still identified Vitas as a slave of the empire.

Titus saw the escorts, stopped, and nodded before they had a chance to explain why the slave stood beside him. "Yes, I was expecting him. You may leave him with me."

HORA TERTIANA

"WITH YOUR LEGION joining the two under Vespasian in Ptolemais, it should be a short-lived rebellion," Vitas remarked as hundreds of soldiers scurried around them in their duties to take down camp and prepare to march. "Galilee will fall in weeks, if not days."

They stood outside the general's tent. None of the soldiers came within thirty feet, essentially giving them a private area in a vastly public place.

"Don't be surprised if it becomes months," Titus said.

"How many men could the Jews muster?" Vitas asked. "Ten thousand untrained and with few weapons? Against legions of seasoned veterans. And the royal troops of the Jewish king."

"These Jews are fanatics," Titus said. "You should know that as well as anybody."

"Fanatics of flesh and blood who die to spear and sword as any other mortal. With stories about them that become exaggerated as they multiply. *You* should know that as well as anybody."

"The stories serve Vespasian well. He's in no hurry to conquer Galilee, and it provides a good excuse to extend the campaign as long as possible. Until the Jews are defeated, Vespasian will be in command of three legions." Titus paused significantly. "After all, who knows what might happen in Rome?"

Vitas understood the implication immediately. A popular general might well be acclaimed emperor by his soldiers, and if he had enough of them, none would dare protest. But even a simple conversation about it was treasonous.

Titus laughed as if understanding those thoughts. "My involvement with helping you escape is already enough to mark me as a dead man if Nero discovers it. What is there to fear about this kind of speculation with you?"

"And you are wise enough not to speculate elsewhere? Not even with, for example, a devastatingly attractive woman who is queen of the land you plan to conquer?"

"The land has already been conquered. And as a descendant of Herod, she is Rome's designated authority here. My task is to reclaim it from the rebels, return it to her, and in so doing, return it to Rome. And there is no need to discuss what would be obvious to her. She is as shrewd at politics as anyone. Even if I did discuss it with her, I am at no more risk than before. She knows who you are and that you are hunted by Nero. That alone is enough to send me to the arena. Every day, my life is in her hands. But she sees a far greater prize."

"Her land returned? Or the trust of a future emperor?"

Titus became more serious. "All of that, perhaps. Or, difficult as you might find this to believe, it is also a matter of the heart. I have no intention of remarrying if it is to be a Roman. There is something about these Jewish women." A rueful smile. "Vitas, we should each know that as well as anybody. For you would not be here unless you had found Sophia and she was well. Otherwise, you would have sent a message and continued searching."

Vitas nodded and became equally serious. "Sophia is well. Last night, she told me about a letter that sent her to Caesarea, just as my letter directed me. Let me know your role in saving her life, for I believe I owe you everything I could ever offer, including my own life."

"Let it be said only that I was among those who made arrangements. Until we are safe from Nero, we must remember the fate of Piso and my ex-wife's uncle."

The fate of unsuccessful conspirators. The less each conspirator knew, the greater the safety of the others.

"Sophia understands our debt to you," Vitas said. "She also understands honor. I am at your command in any way that I can serve you. Either in my role as a slave or otherwise when this mark on my forehead disappears."

"I know you well," Titus said. "I know that you want nothing more than to be with Sophia. I also know she is heavy with child. I would not take you away from her."

Titus spoke the truth. Vitas longed for a quiet domestic life in some backwater of the empire, away from Nero, away from intrigue.

"We've made arrangements," Titus said. "You will stay hidden on an estate in Alexandria belonging to Queen Bernice. Enjoy life with your family."

Vitas had just been given everything he desired. But he could not in good conscience take it as it had been offered.

"There's an old Jewish woman. Would it be too much to make her part of the household in Alexandria?"

"Bernice will grant you whatever you want. She owes you her life from Jerusalem last summer, and now you've averted a slaughter of her people here in Caesarea."

"Thank you."

"I want you to be happy, my friend. But don't thank me. Someday, should Nero be gone, it will serve my father and me well to be known as your rescuers. After your time in Britannia, and after how Nero so unfairly took your estate, the name of Gallus Sergius Vitas still has substantial political currency, especially among the military. If there comes a time our family needs your public support, we would welcome it."

Another allusion that Vitas easily understood. A general with three legions was not a sure bet for emperor without the support of at least another three legions. Otherwise, legions went into battle against the others. Civil war.

"And Jerome?" Vitas said. "Could you send a message to Damian requesting I take him to Alexandria with me?"

That startled Titus. "You will be safe on her estate, trust me."

"There is more to it than that," Vitas said.

Titus waited to see if Vitas would explain, but Vitas held his silence.

"Take Jerome, then," Titus said. He put his hand on Vitas's shoulder and looked him straight in the face. "But there is no need to send a message to Damian. He found Maglorius in Jerusalem!"

"Maglorius!" Vitas's heart swelled yet again. First finding Sophia alive. Now discovering that Maglorius—an old friend who'd been lost in Jerusalem—had been found . . . "Damian told you this himself?"

"No," Titus said. "The children. Quintus and Valeria. Maglorius found and protected them during the uprisings in Jerusalem. He and Damian sent them here to Caesarea for my protection. They will join you tomorrow."

"Wonderful," Vitas said.

He saw a dark look cross Titus's face.

"What is it?" Vitas asked.

"In saving the two children," Titus answered, "Maglorius and Damian were captured in Jerusalem by Jewish rebels."

Vitas reacted immediately. "Then promise you will make sure Sophia is safe as you send her to Alexandria. I will go directly to Jerusalem."

"No," Titus said. "I'm sorry, my friend. Maglorius and Damian were executed."

June, AD 68
ROME
Capital of the Empire

I watched as he opened the sixth seal. There was a great earthquake. The sun turned black like sackcloth made of goat hair, the whole moon turned blood red, and the stars in the sky fell to earth, as late figs drop from a fig tree when shaken by a strong wind. The sky receded like a scroll, rolling up, and every mountain and island was removed from its place.

REVELATION 6:12-14

From the Revelation, given to John on the island of Patmos in AD 63

⚡ JUPITER ⚡

HORA TERTIANA

TWENTY-TWO MONTHS EARLIER, Vitas had been aboard a ship on the Tiber River to flee Rome in the middle of the night, sent by men he did not know, for reasons he did not know, to a destination he did not know—for twenty-two months earlier, Nero wanted Vitas dead.

Fleeing Nero, Vitas had given up everything that mattered. His pregnant wife, his freedom, his land, his honor.

Fleeing Nero, Vitas had journeyed to Alexandria, then Caesarea, and back to Alexandria.

In those twenty-two months, Rome's legions under Vespasian and Titus had officially entered into war with the Jews, crushing city after city, slaughtering Jews, and closing in on Jerusalem.

Jerusalem's political factions had begun to rebel against each other, fighting a separate war within the safety of the city walls, slaughtering tens of thousands more.

In Greece, Nero had continued to make the rounds of festivals, indulging his every whim in a fashion that suggested he was either oblivious to the growing discontent in Rome or determined to make himself oblivious. His personal degradations were so commonplace now that rarely did people find them scandalous, but in one of his more outrageous whims, he'd demanded a canal dug across the Corinthian isthmus. If completed, such a project would be a boon to shipping, but no other Caesar had attempted this impossible task. Nero believed, however, that for him as a god, nothing was impossible, and he began draining the imperial treasury at an even more alarming rate than before.

The empire had come perilously close to rebellion during Vitas's time of respite. In that twenty-two months, Vitas had been reunited with his wife, celebrated the birth of a son at the estate of Queen Bernice, and spent an anonymous idyllic year devoted to his small family. What had made their experience feel all the more idyllic was the fact that the rest of the world had been in turmoil.

In that twenty-two months, Vitas had enjoyed all that truly mattered—his wife and their newborn child, his freedom. Vitas did not need his land and wealth—Titus and Vespasian were his patrons. As for honor, there was no shame in having Nero as an enemy. In fact, given Nero's unstoppable megalomania, it was a matter of great shame to have him as a friend.

Vitas truly had all that a man needed on this earth. Of greater importance, he was fully aware that he had all he needed. He knew many restless men who believed that happiness was always around the next corner. Few men would have thought less of him for remaining in Alexandria with his family.

But few men were like Vitas, and the pangs of injustice gnawed at him.

Which was why Vitas was on the Tiber again, traveling upstream this time, returning to Rome, knowing that if Nero discovered he was still alive, he would once again lose all.

In a small boat behind him were two children he'd vowed to protect, and part of that protection meant they could not travel with him.

His dead brother's slave, Jerome, sat beside Vitas in the center of the craft, swaying as the water rippled beneath them.

From Alexandria, a ship carrying grain had taken them to Ostia at the mouth of the Tiber. Centuries of sediment had made passage up the Tiber impossible for larger crafts, so they now traveled on a ferry to go as far as the wharves lining the riverbank at the great city's Campus Martius.

Vitas was on the Tiber again because to stay in the safety of Alexandria as the empire crumbled would have been unbearable for him. His duty to Rome and his friendship with Titus bound Vitas to this task, just as his heart was bound to his family in Alexandria. Even if Vitas died in the next week in Rome, he'd been given nearly two more years of life, including the best and happiest year he'd experienced.

Risking his own life now for Titus was a small price to pay. Especially if it gave Vitas the one thing he did not possess—justice for the crimes Nero had committed against Vitas and Sophia, and justice upon Helius, the man who had plotted with Nero to condemn Vitas.

His intense desire for revenge was something he'd hidden from Sophia, and he felt no guilt about deceiving her. Vitas was not driven by rage at what Nero had done to him, but at what Nero had inflicted on Sophia.

All Vitas needed to do was remember the dinner party where Nero had beckoned for Sophia, determined not only to conquer her physically but to return to describe it. All Vitas needed to do was remember how Sophia had bowed her head, prepared to sacrifice herself to save Vitas. All Vitas needed to do was remember how he'd leaped at Nero in front of the horrified guests, ready to crush the emperor's windpipe with his bare hands.

If this wasn't enough to demand justice, there was Nero's command the next day for Sophia to commit suicide—and all that Sophia had been forced to endure in escaping Nero.

Yes, Vitas was in Rome. And either he would die. Or Nero would die.

It was definitely something he had hidden from his wife.

✦ ✦ ✦

Vitas remembered it well, delivering to the woman he loved the words he'd dreaded, though he knew he would eventually have to say them.

What made the recollection more poignant for him was the peace he recalled feeling in the garden in Alexandria, the perfume of the orange blossoms, the dappled shade of the leaves.

Tutillus was a precocious athlete. At fifteen months, he preferred running to walking, and he laughed in delight as he chased a butterfly, stumbling in a way that made it seem like every step would send him plunging into the soft grass.

Sophia, standing beside Vitas, had squeezed his hand as they shared the joy of watching their son. No words were needed. To any mother or father, there was nothing ordinary about the ordinary. Love swelled a soul, and love was unique, beyond comparison to anything of value in a man's life. Love for his woman, love for his children. This was what made life worth living.

Yet this great love and purpose, for Vitas, was always tinged with greater sorrow. Like the life of the butterfly that fluttered just beyond the reach of his laughing son, the love Vitas savored was doomed to be only a brief heartbeat against eternity. Vitas pondered what meaning could be found in lives that flitted away so easily.

Sophia squeezed Vitas's hand again, taking him away from the bittersweet reverie. "Tell me what you must tell me," she said. "I'd rather stroll this garden beside you without the clouds that darken your face."

He was startled, and she shook her head as if he were a naughty child.

"You think I can't tell when something troubles you?" Then a sad smile. "Of course, there is the fact that a letter arrived for you from Rome a few days ago. I've been waiting for you to tell me about it, and your silence has been worrying me. I'd rather hear now so we can enjoy the moments we have together."

"Titus needs my help." Vitas watched her face, waiting for a protest. For there were many, and all of them legitimate. Vitas had served the empire well. What more should be required of him?

"Our life here was and is not possible without Titus," Sophia said softly. She let go of his hand and reached up to stroke his face with the tips of her fingers. "When I think of what we almost lost, it brings me to the point of tears."

She pointed at Tutillus. "Without Titus, our baby would never have been born."

"Helping Titus will take me to Rome. Need I point out the risk?"

She shook her head. "Do what you must. Without those who helped us, we would have never had this year together. But this is more than bartering for time, choosing a death later for some time together now."

"You understand, then."

Another sad smile. "Yes, I understand. You live by a code, Vitas. It's a code held by men like Titus and Vespasian and the soldiers who served you. To turn your back now would be like fleeing in battle, and you could not live with yourself if that happened. Nor, I suppose, could you live long with me, for Tutillus and I would be a constant reminder that you had broken your code and diminished yourself." She drew Vitas toward her and placed her head on his chest.

Vitas allowed tears to fall on his cheeks. He'd wept at the birth of Tutillus. Joy. Now sorrow.

"I pray not for your safe return," Sophia said. "God's will shall be done."

He could tell by the sound of her voice that she was weeping too.

"Instead," she told him, "I pray that you, too, will someday trust in the Christos."

✛ ✛ ✛

Boat traffic grew busier as they approached the city. Vitas saw first the colonnades of the Porticus Argonautarum, commemorating Rome's naval victories a century earlier. Then the Pantheon, the temple for all the gods of Rome.

Vitas smiled sardonically to himself. Such a magnificent structure, the Pantheon. Yet he was beginning to understand that the true God had no need for this kind of show. Daily, he'd witnessed

Sophia beneath a tree in the garden with her head bowed in prayer, reaching out to the God of the Jews through the Christos, whom Sophia explained had given her freedom from temples and sacrifices by dying himself on a cross.

A sudden bump against the front of the boat took Vitas from his thoughts. He glanced down at the muddy water to see a floating corpse among all the other debris.

His smile and gentle memories of Sophia disappeared.

The body was that of an executed criminal—no doubt one who had been bound and strangled at the infamous Gemonian stairs of central Rome. Corpses were often left on the staircase for days in open view of the forum, scavenged by dogs, until eventually thrown into the Tiber. There was no method of death more dreadful or dishonorable for a Roman.

As the bloated body rolled under the boat, Vitas was fully aware of the likelihood that his return to Rome might result in that exact fate for him.

✠ ✠ ✠

Vitas instructed Jerome to wait in a tavern near the forum. Walking with the giant of a man drew too much attention, and Vitas needed anonymity for a while.

Vitas was not worried that Jerome might flee. In general, all slaves understood the folly of this, as a runaway slave would eventually be hunted down and executed, and his wife and children would suffer the same penalty.

Since that day in the marketplace of Caesarea, Vitas had every reason to believe he could trust Jerome with even his own life. Moreover, Jerome had been separated from his family for nearly two years and would not jeopardize a reunion with them.

Vitas kept his head down as he moved through the crowd. In numbers, there was safety. Rome held men from all parts of the world, and the tan that Vitas had acquired in Alexandria gave him the air of a foreigner.

Within minutes, he had reached the Curia Julia, where the Senate met, near the forum and the temple of Jupiter. He eased himself against a tavern wall and let the crowd flow around him as he waited for the senators to finish the day's business.

Huge buttresses adorned the Curia Julia. Its front wall was decorated with slabs of marble, but only the lower portion. The upper part was covered with stucco to imitate white marble blocks.

Vitas well knew the austere interior of the hall, brightened only by the opus sectile of the floor, a Roman art technique with materials cut and inlaid into the floor to make pictures or patterns. The squares were interlaid with images of cornucopias, all in reds and greens and purples. In contrast, the walls were veneered with marble that went two-thirds of the way up. Aside from the Altar of Victory, there was not much else except three broad steps that fitted five rows of chairs to accommodate about three hundred senators.

The Curia Julia had ample room. Almost a generation earlier, Augustus had reduced the size of the Senate from nine hundred to six hundred, but at any given time only a couple hundred were active.

In normal times, during Senate business, the emperor sat between two consuls, acting as the presiding officer.

These were not normal times. Otherwise, Vitas would still be in Alexandria.

Three months earlier, Gaius Iulius Vindex, the governor of Gaul, had rebelled against the tax policies of Nero, declaring his allegiance to Spain's governor, Servius Sulpicius Galba, and in essence had declared Galba the new emperor of Rome.

On one hand, it had been a bold move. If Galba had rejected the allegiance and remained loyal to Nero, Vindex's bid to overthrow the emperor would have ended immediately. But if Galba had added his legions to those of Vindex, the rebellion would have been difficult to stop.

On the other hand, both Galba and Vindex understood the dangers for any popular governor or general. While Vitas was still hiding in Caesarea, Nero, afraid of revolt, had summoned to Greece a popular general named Corbulo and invited this general to commit suicide. Instead of intimidating other generals, it had done the opposite.

Indeed, Galba had learned of earlier orders by Nero to have him assassinated and had accepted the title given to him by Vindex. A month later, the legions sent by Nero destroyed the army of Vindex, leaving Galba a decision to retreat or to attack Rome. Civil war had been narrowly averted, but the mood against Nero was such that the emperor dared not show himself in public and feared assassination traveling to the Curia Julia or even during a Senate meeting.

The recent upheaval had also changed life for Vitas. Vespasian was one of Rome's most popular generals, and he faced the same possible fate as Corbulo. Yet Vespasian could not return to Rome himself to reassure Nero of his loyalty, for Nero would surely see his arrival as an attempt to take power. Neither could Vespasian send Titus; Nero would see no distinction between a general and his son.

Vespasian and Titus needed someone they could trust to help them navigate the corridors of power in Rome, for these were times when an emperor might regain support and crush all insurrection— or times when a new emperor might be crowned.

Upon learning this, Vitas had seen his opportunity to serve Titus and had begun his own travels to the Curia Julia. This was a journey, then, where Vitas held not only the fate of his own family but also the fates of Vespasian and Titus.

Knowing what was at stake, Vitas could not help but glance beyond the Curia Julia, at the eastern side of the hill that overlooked the forum. There, in an unassuming building, the bureaucratic offices of the state were maintained, along with all official records of Rome, dating well back into the years of the Republic. It was a building used to store state archives—deeds, documentary laws, treaties, and decrees of the Senate.

The Tabularium.

Somewhere among the mountains of scrolls inside that building, Vitas had been told, was a single letter that inspired terror in Nero's court. And Vitas intended to uncover it.

HORA QUARTA

AS THE SENATORS FANNED OUT from the forum, Vitas immediately saw the man he was seeking.

Marcus Cocceius Nerva was a handsome, short, wiry man in his midthirties, with a square face and thick hair. He was from one of the most esteemed families of the empire, connected to the Augustan line of emperors through marriage and service.

Nerva was an adviser to Nero, part of the same inner circle Vitas had belonged to until the fateful night when Vitas had set prisoners free from unjust punishment by Nero.

The man walked with a confidence bestowed upon him by his lineage and position. Vitas began following and waited until Nerva entered a street that funneled the crowd into a compact mass, making it possible for Vitas to push through the people without making it obvious that he had targeted the man.

Showing that same confidence, Nerva didn't flinch with surprise or fear when Vitas came up behind him and spoke into his ear.

Vitas remained just behind Nerva's shoulder, jostling for position in the crowd. "Greetings from Vespasian," he said. "But keep walking as if I haven't spoken."

Nerva's pace didn't change, nor did he turn his head. Rome was such that intrigue was more common than pigeon droppings.

"Vespasian sends more than greetings," Vitas said. He named the tavern where Jerome was waiting. "If you are thirsty, the beer there is excellent."

Vitas dropped back before Nerva could turn to see his face, and the crowd filled the space between them.

The next hour would be dangerous.

As an adviser to Nero, Marcus Cocceius Nerva had been at the forefront of detecting and investigating the Pisonian conspiracy against Nero a few years earlier. For that, Nero had rewarded Nerva with triumphal honors—usually reserved for military victories—and given Nerva the right to have his statues placed throughout the imperial palace as a public reminder of Nerva's power and closeness to the emperor.

Nero wanted Vitas dead. And Vitas was about to put his life into the hands of one of the men closest to Nero.

✢ ✢ ✢

The smell of roasting pig in the tavern would have been pleasant, except the floor was dirt, and straw was used to soak up spilled beer that would have otherwise turned it into mud. Because the straw was changed so infrequently, the odor of rot overwhelmed the aroma of roasting meat.

Vitas stood alone in a corner, clutching a clay goblet of beer, half-full. The other half he'd dumped into the straw at his feet. He needed a clear head.

Waiting there gave him an advantage of sorts. Anyone entering from the full sunshine outside would take more than several moments to adjust to the relative darkness inside, while at the same time Vitas would clearly see each visitor's face.

Nerva arrived shortly, no longer wearing a senatorial toga. Still, his air of confidence marked him, and those who glanced up at his entrance quickly looked away, afraid to challenge him in the slightest way.

As Nerva scanned the room, Vitas gave the slightest of nods.

Instead of making his way directly to Vitas, Nerva first paid for a beer, then drank all of it where he stood.

While he drank, three large men entered the tavern and ordered beer of their own, then found an empty table in the center of the room.

He paid for a second beer before finally sauntering toward Vitas. Nerva leaned against the wall and pretended to lose himself in another couple chugs of beer.

He wiped his mouth and, looking ahead, not at Vitas, said, "Vitas, you lied. This beer is anything but excellent. But to a dead man, I suppose anything would taste wonderful. Shame that Vespasian has sent you. You would be worth a considerable amount to bring before Nero."

While Nerva had said little, he'd spoken much. First, he wasn't asking any questions about how Vitas had escaped the arena when all believed he was dead. Nerva was too smart for that and would want no involvement in the events. Nerva also acknowledged that Vitas had put him in a position of choosing between Nero and Vespasian and that, for now, he would not be calling for the three bodyguards who had followed him inside.

"How is Domitian these days?" Vitas asked.

"Subtle," Nerva laughed. "And by that, I mean not subtle at all. I don't need the reminder of my promise to Vespasian regarding his son, and I thought I'd made it plain—in my own much more subtle way—that I'm in no hurry to rush from this tavern to turn you over to Nero."

"Actually," Vitas said, "I wasn't trying to make a point. It's the first question that Vespasian instructed me to ask. He's a tough old general but loves his sons as much as any man can."

Nerva laughed again, with a trace of ruefulness. "Let me blame the times. Too much intrigue. Too many conversations of trying to hear intent, not words."

"Of course," Vitas said. "I suspect this conversation will be one of them. Domitian?"

"He fares well," Nerva said. "I gave Vespasian the vow that I would treat Domitian as my own son, and I've kept careful watch. Not that Domitian needs it. He's as aware as anyone how precarious it is to be the son of the empire's most popular war hero and commander."

"And you're aware of how precarious it is to be known as Domitian's guardian while Vespasian is in Judea?" Vitas asked.

"Don't paint me as too noble. I'm aware of the immense political currency for taking that risk. It does not hurt to have a man of Vespasian's power—and potential power—as an ally."

Again, little said but much spoken, underscoring Nerva's reputation as a skilled diplomat and strategist.

Nerva allowed a few moments, and when Vitas said nothing, he pushed harder. "It obviously does not hurt you either, putting Vespasian in your debt by risking your life with an appearance not only in Rome, but with me."

"While I have no intention of sharing it, I think you'd be surprised at my motivation. I promise it is not political currency. Remember, there was a time when you and I worked together at the palace. I had as much political currency as any man in Rome, and I walked away from it."

"Ironically, it now gives you even more currency, for it marks you as a man who can be trusted—and there are too few of those in Rome." Nerva took another gulp of beer. "You said you suspected this conversation would be one of trying to hear intent, not words, and already I've begun down that road. Let's save time and speak plainly. I'm committing treason simply by not calling for the nearest imperial guards to have you arrested. If you are here on behalf of Vespasian, he too has committed treason by shielding you from Nero, and the implications are manifold and staggering, especially given what has happened with the rebellions of Vindex and Galba."

"Even there you read too much into it. I am not here on Vespasian's behalf to begin a bid for the throne. While Nero is emperor, Domitian is vulnerable here in Rome. Vespasian's first concern is to protect his son. Vespasian wants you to ensure that his name is not put forth for consideration as a successor and that it becomes common knowledge that Vespasian will not declare his legions against Nero under any circumstances. In so doing, Domitian will be protected."

Nerva gave Vitas a thoughtful stare. "Vespasian is a shrewd man and chose well to allow you to speak for him, for Vespasian knows if those words came from anyone but Gallus Sergius Vitas, I would not believe them. It is a dangerous game you have entered on his behalf, Vitas. Especially with Vespasian making it clear he will not declare against Nero. When you are discovered here, as you surely will be, you have little leverage to protect your life."

"I'm aware of the dangers here," Vitas answered and said nothing more.

Nerva let a small smile play across his face. "If Vespasian will not set his legions against Nero, is he willing to pit them against another general on Nero's behalf?"

"Vespasian anticipated that question from you. I have been instructed to tell you that he is not willing to make enemies on either side of this revolt."

"Vespasian's second concern?" Nerva asked. "You mentioned his first concern is the life of his son. The word *first* implies that he has a second concern. Or more."

"Tell me," Vitas said, "would you agree that emperors can now be made outside of Rome?"

"Yes," Nerva responded without hesitation.

It was a significant question and a significant answer. To this point, an emperor designated his heir. But with legions away from Rome for years and giving more loyalty to their general than to the emperor, the true power had shifted from bureaucracy to military.

"Vespasian realizes this too. His second concern is the empire, and he fears that if Nero is deposed, generals will battle each other to be declared emperor and civil war will tear it apart."

"It is a valid fear," Nerva said. "Far too valid. Both the threat of civil war and Nero's difficult position. After months of indifference, Nero has finally woken to the dangers. Even when word of Vindex's revolt first reached Rome, Nero simply went to the gymnasium to

watch the athletics. He fainted dead away when he heard that Galba
had joined the revolt but, a day later, was hosting extravagant ban-
quets again. He believes the worst is over. But I've seen what is happening on the streets, and he's lost his support from where it matters
most: the populace. Nero was brilliant in keeping the masses happy.
He plundered the estates of the rich after ordering their suicides but
always provided grain and games for the poor."

Nerva shook his head. "He's lost his touch with them, however.
Nero's been profiteering in grain during this shortage. Word got out
that a ship came in from Alexandria—not with grain, but loaded
with sand for imperial wrestlers. He is universally loathed."

"Yet," Vitas said, "I understand that, after the defeat of Vindex,
Galba is considering suicide. Nero has not necessarily lost the
throne, has he."

"It depends on what happens here in Rome over the next few
days," Nerva said.

"Do you have a prediction?"

Nerva gave an enigmatic smile. "I haven't rushed to call for
imperial guards, have I?"

Titus and Vespasian had gambled Vitas's life on this: that it wasn't
clear if Nero would survive and that Nerva wouldn't choose a side
unless he knew which would prevail.

Vitas wasn't surprised when Nerva asked, "Does Vespasian have
a prediction on what will happen to Nero?"

"While Nero is emperor, Vespasian will continue his unshakable
loyalty. I have been instructed to stress that if Nero loses the throne,
Vespasian has no intention of using his legions to fight any other generals to gain the throne for himself. Vespasian does not want civil war."

"Thank you," Nerva said. "As I get a chance to make this clear
in my circles, it will have a calming influence. While naturally I am
curious as to how it is you are alive, no one will learn it from me. We
both know Nero would have his guards turn over every cobblestone
in the city to find you, for your survival is yet more proof of defiance
against him."

"I am grateful," Vitas said.

"It's I who may owe you," Nerva continued. "Soon it may become politically expedient to bring you forth in front of certain men. You are one of our war heroes, and Nero's injustice against you and your family still outrages many. To have them hear from you what Vespasian has declared will have much more power than if I say it without declaring the source."

And perhaps tilt the votes against Nero. But Vitas decided not to express the obvious. As Nerva said, Vitas was playing a dangerous game, when a slight tilting in either direction would have such dire consequences.

"That possibility has not escaped Vespasian," Vitas said instead. "Vespasian trusts that you will know the time and place, if it becomes necessary."

"Do you trust me?"

"It doesn't matter. I trust Vespasian."

"See there? The fact that you would risk your life for Vespasian will speak volumes for the truth of your message from him."

"There is more to it than that," Vitas said. "I want something too."

"Good," Nerva answered. "I like it when a man is obliged to me. What is it?"

For a moment, Vitas was back in his cell below the arena, where he had been waiting to die until a man he did not know appeared and whispered a message: *There is an obscure matter that Tiberius once brought to Senate vote. You will find it somewhere in the archives. It will be marked with a number. . . . Remember this, for the life of your family may depend on it someday. . . . It is the number of the Beast. Six hundred and sixty-six.*

"I want something from the Senate archives," Vitas said.

"Just tell me where to look."

"I don't know yet. But when I do, I'll get word to you."

"And how do I get word to you if I need your help?" Nerva asked.

"Address a letter to a woman named Sophia, and leave the time and place as if it is a secret romantic meeting. I'll come here at noon each day to see if it is waiting for me, and if I can't make it, I'll send my slave."

"Would he be the monstrous man on the opposite side of the tavern who has been watching my own three men as if he were a hungry lion and they were condemned prisoners in the arena?"

Vitas did not smile at the attempted joke. "You don't miss a thing, do you?"

"And neither do you," Nerva answered. "By the gods, I would have needed a dozen men against him, had I actually decided to turn you over to Nero."

HORA SEXTA

SINCE VITAS WAS a fugitive and unable to inherit, at his brother's death, Damian's villa had been transferred to the name of Titus, who ran the estate in absentia. This essentially meant arrangements among the slaves were unchanged, including the presence of Jerome's family.

There was a risk that Helius and Tigellinus—two men happy to serve any whim of Nero's and given great power accordingly—might have someone watching the villa for Jerome's return, but only a slight risk. The slave had departed Rome many months ago, and there was no reason to expect him now.

Until they reached the cross street to this estate, Vitas had never seen Jerome moving at a pace faster than a brisk walk. He smiled as the big, ugly man began to trot, not even looking backward to see if Vitas and the children were keeping pace.

Valeria and Quintus had been born into nobility, their father a wealthy Roman living in Jerusalem. He'd been murdered at the beginning of the Jewish revolt a few years earlier, and they'd managed to survive life on the streets. As a result, they were no longer the pampered children they'd been when Vitas first met them. Instead they were tough and wary and self-confident.

Quintus was small for a ten-year-old and looked like no threat to anybody, but in Alexandria, Vitas had witnessed him fight two boys at once, both of them several years older.

Valeria had grown into a beautiful young woman, and someday, if she and Quintus could claim the estate that their stepmother had stolen from them after the murder of their father, she would marry into the Roman nobility where she'd begun her life. Thinking about that, Vitas could only feel sorry for any future husband who might expect her to be a passive and pretty decoration.

Like Vitas, both were wearing clothes that marked them as residents of the slums, because as with Vitas, it was important that no one in Rome realize they had returned.

As Jerome increased the gap ahead and moved from a trot to a sprint, Vitas smiled. The man was about to be reunited with his family.

At the gate that led to the villa, Vitas spoke to Quintus and Valeria. "Any questions before we say good-bye?"

"None," Quintus said stoutly and proudly. He was a little warrior, and he knew what was at stake. Both were to join Jerome's family for the next few days, and both were to be vigilant for any spies in the household.

"Then good-bye," Vitas answered with a lightheartedness he did not feel.

Quintus and Valeria could have stayed safely in Alexandria but refused. They wanted to face their treacherous stepmother.

Valeria merely smiled a mysterious smile that Vitas knew would frustrate and hypnotize all future suitors.

"Don't worry," Quintus said. "I'll take good care of Jerome."

Vitas didn't point out that Jerome probably had the strength to crush a man's skull in one bare hand.

The brother and sister pushed through the gate without any hesitation.

In the background, Vitas heard children squeal in delight.

Jerome was home.

✦ ✦ ✦

Vitas stood at the gate to a magnificent villa on the Capitoline Hill. It had taken him over an hour of walking to get there. He was dressed as a common worker and carried bundles of wood, making him reasonably unnoticed.

Vitas knocked on the gate, and within moments, a slave on the other side slid back the covering of a small opening at eye level. Vitas spoke to the pair of eyes on the other side. "'Go to the woman clothed in finest purple and scarlet linens, decked out with gold and precious stones and pearls.'"

"Wait," came the voice.

Vitas heard a faint slap of leather on stone as the slave hurried away.

He waited. Despite his simple disguise of worker's clothing, Vitas felt exposed.

Half a mile away, if they'd had the ability to fly as crows, Vitas could have reached the imperial residence. There'd been a time when Vitas was a welcome visitor there. Now, if Nero learned of his presence in Rome, it would be death at the Gemonian stairs, not only for Vitas, but for any citizen who sheltered him.

Vitas tried to project an outer calm as he waited.

Someone returned and looked through the opening. "Repeat yourself."

"'Go to the woman clothed in finest purple and scarlet linens, decked out with gold and precious stones and pearls,'" Vitas said, quoting from the letter that had been with him on his escape from Rome.

"'She is the one who slaughtered God's people all over the world,'" came the reply from inside.

The passwords alluded to the letter of Revelation. The religious establishment of Jerusalem was the harlot of this letter; Jerusalem, the woman in finest purple, had literally slaughtered the Christos and had continued this persecution against his followers in all the lands. According to the letter, the city was calling down judgment upon itself, judgment that would lead to the utter destruction of the sacred Temple.

While Vitas, of course, was skeptical of the prophecy's accuracy, he still took comfort from the passwords. It would be safe to enter.

No one had intercepted the letter from Titus that instructed Senator Ruso, the man on the other side of the gate, to expect Vitas.

He also relaxed because the choice of passwords told him the stranger on the other side of the door was a follower of the Christos and, because of persecution by the Beast of Rome and the woman in purple, was undoubtedly a person of caution.

For now, Vitas was still safe from Nero.

✦ ✦ ✦

Vitas followed Caius Sennius Ruso through an atrium into the *tablinum*, where family records were traditionally stored. They continued through a dining room and past the kitchen, where slaves laughed as they worked.

Vitas took this as a good sign. Happy slaves were an indication of a kind and respected master.

Ruso led him past a library—another indication of Ruso's wealth—then outside to seats in a shaded garden protected by high walls, where a pitcher of freshly squeezed grape juice was waiting.

Ruso poured the juice into goblets, and Vitas sipped appreciatively.

Each studied the other.

Ruso was of medium height and middle-aged. His hair had probably once been dark red but was fading, both in color and thickness. But he was a man in trim shape, unlike many of his gluttonous peers who, it was said, dug their own graves with their spoons.

"I expected you to be accompanied by the bodyguard belonging to your brother, Damian."

"I travel as I see fit."

"You are aware," Ruso said without severity, "that as a bounty hunter, Damian is in pursuit of a man I protected from Nero."

"The man who escaped Rome with me. John, son of Zebedee, the last disciple of the Christos and author of a letter known as the Revelation."

"Titus could not have known. I did not identify to him the

man I wanted on the ship with you. All Titus knew was that a Jew would be there to translate the letter given you and that it was necessary to give you a code letter in case you or the letter fell into the wrong hands."

This meeting had been arranged by Titus, so it was natural for Ruso to ask that indirect question.

"Since John was with me as I fled Rome," Vitas said, "and since John was the person who translated the letter sent with me, I don't think it's a stretch to conclude that you are a link between John and me."

Ruso sighed and leaned forward. "I've received a letter from John; he is well. For how long, however? Your brother, after all, is famous in Rome for never losing his bounty. Most believe he hasn't returned because he is still on the trail."

Vitas waited a few respectful moments of silence before speaking. "Damian was put to death in Jerusalem. John does not have to fear pursuit from my brother."

Ruso matched the silence before saying, "You have my full sympathy, Vitas. We live in perilous times." He paused before continuing. "I'm also aware of how perilous it is for you here in Rome."

It was an unspoken question, and Vitas answered it. "I am here because of my obligation to you and Titus. I will also confess that I badly miss my wife and child and want to return to Alexandria. Let me know what you want from me so that I can fulfill that obligation as soon as possible."

"Direct to business then," Ruso said. "I have a slave waiting to take you to the person you need to see next. First, though, Titus's letter hinted at news about the campaign in Judea that he did not want to commit to parchment."

"Judea goes well for Rome," Vitas replied. "I would guess you've already heard about the fall of the last rebel city outside Jerusalem."

"Gischala."

"And before that, Taricheae, Tiberias, and Joppa."

Ruso nodded. "Each Jewish city folding as easily as the one

previous, if you consider slaughtering all the young men in each city an easy task."

"While the Jews have my sympathy," Vitas said, "leaders in rebel cities well know the consequences of holding out against Rome."

Ruso sighed. "If only Jotapata had not been so successful against Vespasian. The other city leaders would not have been so bold. Titus suggested you would tell me more about Jotapata."

"Two months of valiant defense against an entire legion, and even then it would have been longer had the city not been betrayed by someone inside the walls." Vitas gave Ruso a careful look. "But all of this anyone in Rome knows already. You want specific information, don't you? Information not available to all of Rome. About one Jew in particular."

"Joseph Ben-Matthias," Ruso said.

Because Ben-Matthias had spoken of Ruso in Caesarea, Vitas had been expecting this answer, but it did nothing to slake his curiosity. Joseph Ben-Matthias was the Jew who had risked his life to visit Vitas in prison just after Vitas had been taken down from crucifixion, the Jew who had given Vitas a token along with a request that he might someday be called upon to fulfill.

Titus had also spoken to Vitas of Ben-Matthias, apparently unaware of the token and of that secret meeting.

"Yes," Vitas acknowledged, "Titus did specify to pass along news about the man. How do you know him or know of him?"

Ruso shook his head, indicating he would not answer. "In Rome, secrets are a way of life. I expect that naturally you would withhold some things, as in return, you would expect the same of me. Some secrets are too important, don't you agree?"

"We are at an impasse, then," Vitas said. "I'm not interested in delivering to you anything from Titus unless I know more about the man."

"Despite your obligation to Titus?"

"My obligation is to ensure the well-being of Titus," Vitas said. "I cannot do this to the best of my ability if I don't understand the role that Ben-Matthias has in all of this. Especially if I don't know his relationship with you."

Ruso shook his head again. "I do not see it that way. I cannot betray certain confidences."

"You. Queen Bernice of the Jews. Ben-Matthias. And Titus, the son who serves his father, Vespasian, Rome's greatest living general. The four of you have placed me in the middle of something. Do you really expect that I will blindly proceed? Start by telling me how Ben-Matthias is connected to Rome. And to my escape from Rome."

Ruso stood and slowly paced back and forth. Vitas did not speak. Finally Ruso seemed to arrive at a decision that allowed him to sit again. He leaned forward, elbows on knees, fists together beneath his chin. "It will betray no confidence to tell you Ben-Matthias is a remarkable man. First by lineage. His mother descended from royalty under the former ruling Hasmoneans of the Jews, and through his father, he is descended from the Jehoiarib, the first of the twenty-four orders of the Temple priests in Jerusalem. He is a direct descendant of the Jonathon who governed Judea before the Romans arrived. But there is more to him than that. At fourteen, he was recognized for his understanding of Jewish law, with leaders in Jerusalem consulting him on legal matters. At sixteen, he stepped away from his wealth and lineage to live in the desert in a spiritual search with the Jewish Sadducees and Essenes. As you can imagine, when he returned to Jerusalem and decided to align himself with the Pharisees, he quickly became someone of influence."

Vitas remembered the man's quiet confidence in the darkness of the prison cell. It made sense, knowing the man's background.

"He is a man," Vitas said to lead Ruso onward, "in the same circles as Bernice."

"Yes. He was chosen five years ago to visit Rome and negotiate the release of Jewish priests imprisoned by Nero. On his way here, he was shipwrecked and among six hundred aboard was one of a handful of survivors. It would appear that God smiled upon him.

Even more remarkably, he was successful in Rome. He gained the favor of Poppaea, Nero's first wife, who convinced Nero to release the prisoners."

"And during his time in Rome, he met you? Or Titus?"

"Three of us are concerned about the Jews," Ruso said. "Bernice, Ben-Matthias, and I. When we arranged your escape, Titus was only involved because of his connections in Rome and how he could facilitate saving your life. He has less to do with this than you imagine."

"Perhaps not." Vitas smiled. "He is now intimate with Bernice and has considerably more interest in helping the Jews. And I'm still withholding the news Titus asked me to deliver."

"Let me say then that I developed a friendship with Ben-Matthias during his time in Rome. I was on a spiritual search, one that in the end led me to the Christos, through his last disciple, John. Before that, through Ben-Matthias, I learned much about the God of the Jews. And much about politics in Rome. I believe, however, it was a fair exchange. Through me, Ben-Matthias learned much about Rome. He is convinced that the Jews are fools to rebel and has always been an advocate against war. The irony, as I'm guessing you know, is that because of his leadership skills, he was elected to lead those rebels in the same war he believes the Jews cannot win. Apparently he is a great military leader."

"Jotapata," Vitas said. "Ben-Matthias was the one who managed to keep Vespasian at bay so long. But there is much more to the story than that. And you'll learn it, once you've satisfied my curiosity about my involvement."

"Titus and Vespasian are in control of the fate of the Jews. Bernice is connected to Titus and to Joseph. You are connected to Titus and Vespasian and, from what I understand, to Bernice. You are in a position to help Titus and to help the Jews. Small circles, really."

"Except I'm not clear what Joseph Ben-Matthias wants from me."

"You are a man he can trust. You are married to a Jew. You have no military ambitions. You are trusted by Titus."

"That doesn't tell me what Ben-Matthias wants from me."

"I don't know what he wants," Ruso said. "You will have to believe me. When you were in prison, Titus approached me to help protect you. He said he had highly placed friends who wished to ensure you would live. I sent word to Joseph and Bernice that if they helped us protect you, it would serve their cause too. I confess, much of my motivation was to make sure John, the last disciple, was able to escape Rome with you."

Ruso sat back. "That is as much as I can tell. Now it's your decision whether you will honor Titus's request to pass along the news of Joseph Ben-Matthias that Nero and the rest of Rome does not know. News, I would guess, important enough not to be put into a scroll or trusted to anyone else but a friend like you."

"Ben-Matthias retreated to Jotapata in late spring, knowing it would draw Vespasian and the legions. Jerusalem is the great prize, as you know, and as long as Vespasian was elsewhere, Jerusalem was safe. As for Ben-Matthias's counsel against war, you are correct, Senator. From Jotapata, he sent a stream of letters to Jerusalem, imploring the leaders of the Jews to negotiate a peace with Rome."

Ruso sighed. "The Jews, as Ben-Matthias explained when he was in Rome, believe that God will protect them until their Messiah arrives. They believe not even Rome can conquer their Temple."

"That is another matter," Vitas said.

"It is all intertwined, is it not?"

Vitas ignored the comment. "I was not there at Jotapata, of course, but you can imagine the siege as the legion set up around the city walls."

"I can imagine," Ruso said. "The great battering rams. The flaming arrows and javelins."

"Titus tells me he has never faced fiercer fighters than the Jews, who would rally furiously at all attacks. Vespasian decided simply to hold the city in a prolonged siege, rather than add to the casualties. Ben-Matthias? He responded with water."

"Water?"

Vitas couldn't help but smile, picturing the scene presented to Vespasian by the effective but unorthodox tactics of the Jewish aristocrat who did not want to be a leader in a war he did not want to fight against an enemy he did not believe he could defeat.

Vitas described it to Ruso as Titus had described it to him.

Ben-Matthias had commanded that his men soak their garments in water and hang them from the top of the walls to let the water drip down. It was such a flagrant waste of precious liquid, in front of besiegers who could barely keep their own water in supply in the desert heat, that it sent a strong message to Vespasian: the city would never yield for lack of food and drink. It also sent a message that the Jews would sooner die by sword than hunger or thirst.

Vespasian had no choice but to renew the attack against the city walls with his battering rams, knowing how many soldiers' lives it would cost.

Yet Ben-Matthias had found a way to hinder the great battering rams of the Romans. Each ram was a massive beam, one end shod with iron. The beam was hung from another beam by ropes, then swung back and forth by an entire company of soldiers.

Ben-Matthias had noted how the ram, fixed in position, would pound a single spot on the city walls. So he had his own men fill sacks with straw and drop them in front of the ram to pad the city walls just before each strike. This tactic delayed the destruction of the walls for days, if not weeks.

In the end, however, the city fell.

Vitas paused in his description. "All of what I've told you about the battle can be reported by any of the soldiers involved. What comes next, however, is something that Titus knows will put Vespasian in danger if Nero discovers it, and the reason it has not been committed to a letter or scroll."

The senator had been listening intently without interrupting and indicated with an impatient flick of his hand for Vitas to continue.

"When the city fell," Vitas said, "Ben-Matthias managed to

escape into an empty water cistern, where forty other prominent citizens had fled. Suicide, to them, would be a sin against God. So it was decided that each would kill another, and they drew lots to determine the order. One man would be drawn to die first, a second drawn to kill him, then a third man to kill the second man, and so on. Ben-Matthias was one of the last two men. He convinced the other man that enough blood had been spilled and neither should turn on the other."

"He is alive then."

"According to him, it's because he was chosen by God to deliver a prophecy to Vespasian. And this is where secrecy is crucial."

Another impatient wave by Ruso.

"Upon surrender, Ben-Matthias was brought to Vespasian," Vitas said. "All were curious to see the man who had caused them so much trouble. Vespasian wanted to send Ben-Matthias to Nero to be paraded in Rome before death, but Ben-Matthias asked for a private audience to deliver his prophecy."

Now Vitas paused because of the significance of what he was about to say. "Ben-Matthias told Vespasian that the God of the Jews had destined Vespasian to be the ruler of land and sea and the whole human race. Titus entreated Vespasian to spare Ben-Matthias's life."

Vitas watched Ruso carefully and was surprised to see no surprise. Neither at the prophecy nor at the intervention of Titus. Much could be speculated about the extent to which Titus had been motivated by Bernice to ensure Ben-Matthias's safety.

Instead, Ruso spoke softly. "The fall of Jotapata was nearly a year ago, wasn't it."

This amount of time was significant. In a year, Ben-Matthias's prediction had not reached Rome or Nero. But this wasn't the most significant factor.

Vitas thought of that night when Ben-Matthias appeared and gave him the token. Only a matter of months later had Ben-Matthias surrendered to Vespasian. "Yes. Almost a year. Ben-Matthias made this prediction long before Vindex and Galba."

This was the crux of why Vitas was in Rome now. Nero's reign was tottering. If Nero survived a revolt, his reign of terror would continue. But Titus and Vespasian wanted Vitas in Rome to help nudge the revolt to completion.

"'This calls for a mind with wisdom,'" Ruso said, almost in a whisper, looking at the ground. "'The seven heads are seven hills on which the woman sits. They are also seven kings. Five have fallen, one is, the other has not yet come; but when he does come, he must remain for a little while. The beast who once was, and now is not, is an eighth king. He belongs to the seven and is going to his destruction.'"

Ruso lifted his head and offered an explanation for his cryptic words. "The head of the Beast will be severed. From the vision of the last disciple, the Revelation. You know the kings referenced in this prophecy, don't you?"

As would any person in the world. Over a century earlier, by crossing the Rubicon with his army and taking leadership of the republic, Julius Caesar had become the de facto first ruler of the new empire, followed by the formally acknowledged emperors Augustus, Tiberius, Caligula, and Claudius. These five kings had ruled from the seven hills of Rome, including the Capitoline, where Ruso's estate overlooked the Tiber. Nero was obviously the sixth king, clearly identified in the Revelation by the number of the Beast. And if a king was yet to come, then Nero must first die.

"To the Jews, our Nero is the Beast, and thus our empire is the Beast—as is any king that follows." Vitas spoke softly. "The seventh king. Vespasian?"

"Or the eighth," Ruso said. "I suspect Vespasian wants to see what unfolds with the other generals. But if he believes the prophecy of this Jew, surely he does have ambitions."

"Then you and I have arrived in conversation at our true business," Vitas said. "The final days, perhaps, of Nero. Tell me, then, what you expect of me."

Ruso became even more intense. "Understand what is at stake.

The longer Nero lives, the greater the danger to those who follow the Christos, who as a whole are a tiny sapling, persecuted by Rome on one hand and by the religious establishment of Jerusalem on the other. The Revelation was written as a letter of hope to them, a promise that they would survive the tribulation upon them. The longer Nero is alive, the greater the chance that this tiny sapling will be uprooted and destroyed. If this generation of followers is destroyed, the hope of the Christos will not be shared beyond this lifetime."

"Nero is also a danger to the empire," Vitas said dryly. "You need not convince me that his lunacy and depravities must be stopped. What is it you want from me?"

"We need to find something in the archives," Ruso said. "Something of great danger to Nero and therefore of great value to us."

So the circle was complete for Vitas. Ruso had initiated the message Vitas received in the dungeons of the arena. "The archives have decades and decades of gathered scrolls," Vitas said. "It is not enough just to walk into the Tabularium and begin to search."

"You will meet someone," Ruso answered. "He's one of the most learned Jewish scholars in Rome and a friend of Joseph Ben-Matthias. An old man named Hezron."

"Hezron!"

"You know him?" Ruso asked.

"Only by reputation. A friend of mine—another respected Jew in Jerusalem—sent his son here to Rome a few years ago on behalf of Queen Bernice and wants to be reassured that his son is well. I have a letter from this friend to present to Hezron to inquire about his son."

"The circles are small," Ruso said. "I will send word to Hezron to expect you. Listen to his story, and when you return, you and I will continue this conversation."

HORA SEPTINA

HEZRON, THE OLD MAN across from Vitas, had two dull caves—
long healed with wrinkled flesh—where his eyes used to be. The
man's blindness had not been an accident; parallel thin white scars
at the tops and bottoms of each eye socket showed where a knife
had cut away the eyelids before his eyes had been gouged.

The man leaned on a cane at the base of a rickety tenement in
one of the slums of Rome. His other hand rested on the shoulder
of a small boy, maybe six or seven years old, of ferret-like thinness
and with dark hair specked with lice eggs.

"Greetings from Ben-Aryeh," Vitas said. "He inquires about his
son, Chayim."

"Tell me what you see," Hezron prompted the boy, speaking
Greek in a thick accent that betrayed his Jewish roots.

"He looks like a soldier, but he is wearing a toga," the boy said.

Vitas lifted his right hand and opened it to show the boy.

"And he has a marking on his palm," the boy continued. "The
symbol."

At Ruso's instructions, Vitas had permitted a slave to use a quill
to inscribe his palm with a mixture of soot and octopus ink. The
symbol consisted of three Greek letters. The first letter was the
initial letter of the name Christos. The last letter was the one that
began the Greek word for "cross"—*stauros*. The middle letter, with
the appearance of a writing serpent, represented its hissing sound.

The symbol of the Beast. Six hundred and sixty-six. It was not meant here as an indication that Vitas served Nero, but simply as an identifier for Hezron, for the followers of the Christos well knew what it meant.

"Thank you," Hezron said to the boy. "He is the one I am expecting. Go to the other side of the street and wait until he leaves."

"He is a good man," the boy told Vitas in a fierce voice. "If anything happens to him because of you, I will find you in the night and cut your throat as you sleep. I'll pull your tongue through the hole in your throat and—"

"Enough," the old man said. "Leave us now."

Still glaring, the boy retreated.

"No parents and no family," Hezron said. "I need him to lead me, and he needs me because all boys need someone to love them and discipline them. Forgive him for worrying about me."

"Forgiven."

They were standing near the wall, giving passersby plenty of room. It would have been conspicuous if anyone stopped. This place gave no risk of the conversation being overheard.

"I'm aware of your friendship with Ben-Aryeh," Hezron said. "He is an old friend. It is with sadness that I tell you his son Chayim was murdered by pirates."

Vitas closed his eyes and dropped his head. It would break Ben-Aryeh to hear of this. Chayim was reckless, and his lifestyle in Rome had scandalized Ben-Aryeh in his priestly circles in Jerusalem, but the young man was still Ben-Aryeh's son.

"You seek something in the Senate archives," Hezron said, unable to see Vitas's reaction.

"I do. Ruso told me to come to you."

"Ruso has sent you on a wasted journey, unless you have something that I seek too. You understand that?"

"I do."

Hezron held out a hand expectantly.

Vitas reached inside his clothing for the heavy token that hung from a silver chain—the token that Ben-Matthias had given him that night in Caesarea, telling him that someday, someone would show him a matching token and call upon Vitas to repay a debt. The token was like a coin, except larger and heavier, with symbols that Vitas had studied for hours with no closer understanding of their meaning.

He placed it upon Hezron's hand.

The old man felt the coin on both sides until he was satisfied, then handed it back to Vitas. He put it around his neck again.

"You have great responsibility," Hezron said. "Don't lose it."

Vitas expected Hezron to show him an identical one. When the old man cocked his head and waited for an answer, Vitas could not help but ask, "You have the other?"

Hezron's sharp laugh was like a bark. "No! You are far from the day and place when the person sent by Ben-Matthias will reach out to you with its twin."

"Who sent Ben-Matthias to me with the token?" This question was something Vitas pondered often. Ben-Matthias, it seemed, had merely been a messenger.

Another sharp laugh. "Your curiosity is natural. When Ben-Matthias was in Rome, we discussed how best to use the tokens. But I did not choose you. Nor did Ben-Matthias."

"You have conspired with Ben-Matthias and another Jew, placing me in the center of your plans."

"You are in a unique position, Vitas. You are trusted by men with power in Rome, and you are a friend to the Jews. It has been foreseen that someday you might be able to help us, but I pray that someday it won't be necessary."

"You won't tell me how?"

"If the need doesn't arrive, it is much better that you don't know. It is my prayer, and that of Ben-Matthias, that you will never see the matching token."

"I'm weary of cryptic answers," Vitas said.

"I've lost my sons and had my eyes taken from me," Hezron said. "My people face destruction at the hands of Rome. How badly do you think I'd prefer to have cryptic answers along with my vision and my family?"

Vitas took a deep, deep breath. So frustrating to be at the center of a web—Titus and Bernice and Ben-Matthias and now this old man, Hezron—that felt more like a labyrinth.

"You have no matching token," Vitas said. "But you will tell me about a certain scroll in the archives."

"Yes."

"Why will you tell me?" Vitas said. "Why not Ruso?"

"For the same reason you have been given the token and Ruso was not. You are in a unique position, trusted by men with power in Rome and by us."

"You do not trust Ruso?"

"He did not marry into the Jews as you did."

Vitas exhaled noisily. "Send me to the scroll in the archives, then."

"Without learning about its importance?"

"Why ask questions when the answers are riddles within riddles?" Vitas said. "Unless you are prepared to speak without riddles."

"I am," Hezron said. "So listen. I have a daughter, but both of my sons are dead. Nathan became a follower of the Christos. He died in the arena."

It was said calmly, but the old man's face was contorted with pain.

"The scroll in the archives," Vitas prompted the man gently. "What can you tell me about it?"

"Caleb was employed in the Tabularium. He found it by accident and immediately knew its significance. He moved it to a spot where he knew it would not be easily found."

"Do you know why it was significant?"

"Only that it would undermine Nero when the time was right." Again, the old man's face twisted with pain. "Helius murdered Caleb to keep the scroll and its contents from reaching Nero. Then, to learn more about the scroll, he imprisoned my daughter to force me to help in not only the search for the scroll, but to interpret a seditious letter that has been circulating among followers of the Christos."

Vitas nodded. "The revelation of the last disciple."

"Yes," Hezron said. "You would know of it."

The old man tilted his face briefly to the sunshine that managed to squeeze through a gap in the buildings on the opposite side of the street. Strangely, he smiled before resuming. "Nathan died because he was a follower of the Christos. His unshakable faith led my daughter, Leah, to faith, which in turn led to her imprisonment. For that alone, I hated the very mention of the Christos. And as a Jew, I found it ridiculous that anyone would claim he was the long-awaited Messiah. Can you imagine what it would take for me to become a follower myself? Yet the chain of events that has put my family into such suffering has led me to become a follower myself, for as I interpreted the Revelation for Helius, I marveled that the prophecies within were being fulfilled, and I had no choice but to accept the Revelation as divine. And if divine, then so was the Christos."

"You told this to Helius?"

Hezron touched his empty eye sockets. "Yes. His rage when I informed him that it foretold the death of Nero led to this. For if Nero dies, the enemies that Helius has made will tear him apart. It does not serve his purposes to kill me or my daughter, but Helius made sure I would never see her again."

Another smile, this one sad. "Yet Helius cannot rob me of my memories of her face, so I see her every day, even though she is imprisoned. Nor can he rob me of the hope that sustains me because of the Christos."

He lost his smile, and his jaw tightened. "It is time for Nero's reign to end. A year ago, no amount of pushing would have toppled it. But now—as he totters and threatens to regain control, as the men of influence in this city decide his fate—now is the time to reveal the scroll that Caleb was killed to keep hidden."

"Where is it?" Vitas asked.

"Only my daughter knows. Since she's been taken prisoner, she's not been allowed any visitors." The old man shook his head. "Worse, Helius has hidden her somewhere in the imperial palace."

HORA NONANA

VITAS FACED A YOUNG male slave at the entrance of a large villa, well up in the hills and away from the stench and noise of the slums where he'd left Hezron.

"No," the slave said. "Alypia will not see you."

The slave balanced a cudgel in his hands. He was obviously a bodyguard, meant to deter visitors.

"So she is here."

"I have been instructed that she is taking no visitors, no matter how urgent their business." The slave kept his face placid. He was Parthian, probably captured in battle and sold at an auction.

Alypia had a reputation for enjoying her male slaves in all manners, and Vitas guessed this one, too, had been purchased for his youth and appearance.

"No visitors at all?"

The slave did not answer, sending a clear message that Vitas had been given all the information allowed.

Vitas had come to Rome on more than one errand, each of varying importance. He had taken an hour to walk here and would spend another hour returning to the core of Rome.

Vitas clenched and unclenched his fists in a vain effort to force himself to relax. He did not have the luxury of moving at a slow pace. What if Nerva decided the political odds would be bettered by informing Nero of Vitas's return to Rome? What if a passerby had recognized him and sent for imperial guards? At any time, he could be arrested.

"Tomorrow perhaps?" Vitas asked.

"I have been instructed that she is taking no visitors, no matter how urgent their business."

Vitas was acutely aware of the pressures of time for another reason. Any moment, Nero might regain enough support and once again feel safe to travel from the imperial palace and resume duties in the Senate. If that happened, Vitas and his family would be destroyed, for if Nero regained the upper hand, Nerva would sacrifice Vitas to restore whatever favor he might have lost by not fully backing Nero during these dangerous times. And if Vespasian ever had to choose between keeping Nero happy and giving up Vitas, Vitas was practical enough to understand that Vespasian would invite Vitas to suicide.

Vitas also understood that in hushed chambers and quiet gardens all across the city, men of wealth and influence were discussing a decision between two evils—the continued reign of Nero or accepting a general in the provinces ambitious enough to declare himself emperor. All of the empire groaned under the capricious rule of Nero, the immense tax burdens placed upon citizens by his debauched lifestyle and personal spending, and the all-too-frequent murders that Nero ordered to confiscate estates. Yet if precedent were set—that a new emperor could be declared outside of Rome—the implications and long-term consequences could well be worse for Rome than all the horrors of Nero. If it were established that the general with the most might could take the throne at any time, then Rome would always be holding a snake with a poisonous bite at either end. Keeping generals weak to preserve the throne left Rome open to attack. Giving a general enough power to shield Rome would also give the general enough power to attack Rome.

Augustus had proven that a dynasty worked best. The previous three emperors—Caligula, Claudius, and Nero—had proven that a dynasty was only functional if the ruler was competent, instead of self-serving and unjust.

And so the empire had come to this point. As Galba waited in

Spain and verged on committing suicide and effectively ending the
rebellion, Nero verged on losing support within Rome. The victor
would be decided in days, if not hours.

Vitas could not waste time by attempting to return on a different day. While this task was not as important as serving Vespasian
or finding the mysterious letter that threatened Nero, it was a matter of life and death.

Vitas made his decision. He stepped forward, carefully watching
the center of the young slave's chest.

If indeed the slave had been captured in battle, he could be
physically dangerous. And it was going to come down to a physical
confrontation. Inexperienced fighters looked for the hands to move.
But a punch began much earlier, from the core of the body.

"Step aside," Vitas said.

"What?" The slave lifted the cudgel and began to poke it at
Vitas's chest.

Vitas gave no warning. With a quick, rotating move of his
upper body, he threw an elbow outward and upward. Not a fist.
The human skull was built far stronger than the fragile bones of
the hand, and the force that Vitas put into his blow would have
crushed his own fingers with solid contact against the slave's head.

His elbow caught the slave across the upper cheekbone. The
slave opened his eyes wide but was too stunned to manage a sound.
He slid to the side, and Vitas caught him as he was falling, kept
him from crashing onto the marble floor. He pulled the slave inside
and behind a couch, out of obvious sight.

Vitas picked up the cudgel and pushed through the doorway.

He needed to accomplish this next mission before the slave
regained consciousness or anyone noticed him missing.

✛ ✛ ✛

On their previous occasion together—in Jerusalem, in the summer
when the Jewish revolt began—even while her husband's body had
yet to grow cold, Alypia had tried to seduce Vitas.

His memory was of an extremely attractive woman only thirty years old, wearing a blonde wig made from the hair of slaves from northern Gaul, her arms and wrists decorated with gold trinkets—a woman with extreme confidence in her looks, where those looks had taken her, and where those looks could continue to take her in the Roman world.

Vitas found Alypia slumped in a chair that overlooked a garden, wrapped in a blanket despite the day's heat.

She caught his movement and spoke without fully looking. "I have given instructions. No visitors."

"And I have ignored those instructions," he said.

As she turned her gaze fully upon him, he coughed to hide his shock and a shiver of revulsion. The skin of her face had sagged with two decades of aging, although only two years had passed since their last meeting. Pustules marred the skin, and she was nearly bald. What disease had ravaged her?

By her reaction, she was equally shocked, but for a different reason.

She found her voice first. "Vitas? You . . . you . . . you . . . died in the arena. I was there that day."

"I am back," he answered. "And I am not dead."

Her smile was a rictus, showing gaps where teeth had fallen out. "Too bad. We could have met on the other side of the Styx, if a person believes in that sort of nonsense."

Vitas was prepared to believe in divine judgment. No punishment suited Alypia better than taking away the one thing she valued most.

She touched her balding head. "But would one corpse desire another?" Another rictus of a smile as she continued to speak. "It's obvious why I don't take visitors, but now that you are here, I'm not going to pretend to be something I'm not. I spent a lot of years doing that, and it was too much work. Tell me, what do you want? Certainly not me."

Vitas felt guilt for his continued revulsion. He should have had compassion for the woman, but he wanted only to leave. "Valeria and Quintus did not die in Jerusalem. I'm here to instruct you to begin the process of reverting their estate to them."

"Do you think I care enough about anything to actually take orders from someone?"

"I think you did your best to make sure both were killed," Vitas answered. "I'm here to tell you that if either is harmed, you will face reprisals from powerful men in Rome."

He said this because it was what he'd come prepared to say on behalf of Valeria and Quintus, but in saying it, he knew how hollow the threat was.

She began to laugh, but it ended in a choking spasm. When she recovered her breath, she said, "And what will these powerful men do as punishment to me? Send in more doctors to poke and prod? Or extend me mercy by chopping off my head?"

Pain crossed her face, and she shuddered until the spasm was over.

"It seems to me," she said, "that I'm the one who can harm you instead. Won't Helius and Tigellinus love to have you delivered to them. I may be dying, but I can still send a message that you've reappeared in Rome."

Vitas held her gaze, difficult as it was to look into a once-lovely face, now hideous. Knowing that Alypia would perceive him as a threat, he fully expected she would get word to Helius. And that was the second purpose of his visit. Vitas wanted Helius on edge, aware that he had returned, but with no idea where to look for him.

"Perhaps you should strangle me now to make sure your secret is safe," she said. "Do it. Place your fingers around my throat and squeeze."

"See to it that you begin the process of ensuring Valeria and Quintus inherit this estate," he said. "I am finished speaking."

There truly was little more to say. It was obvious that Alypia did not have long to live. It didn't even make much difference if she helped Valeria and Quintus with the legal process before she died. One way or another, the children would receive their rightful inheritance. And one way or another, Alypia was no longer a threat.

"Please," she said. "I mean it. Strangle me. My slaves won't kill me. They know they'll be executed for it. I don't have the courage to commit suicide. Please. If not your hands on my neck, then a knife. Strike quickly."

Vitas left her there, wrapped in her blanket, shivering from cold on a hot summer day.

HORA DECIMA

VITAS SLIPPED INTO the tavern where he'd met Nerva, near the forum. This time, he truly was tempted to drink beer, even knowing the quality was questionable. It had been a hard, fast march to get here from the villa, and his feet hurt. During those delightful months in Alexandria with Sophia and his new child, his excursions had been limited to chasing the baby around a shadow-dappled garden.

Drinking beer would take time, however, and he felt like he couldn't even spare the leisure to gulp any down. Instead, he inquired whether a letter had been delivered for Sophia.

The woman who answered his question was huge, with a face smeared with paint in an attempt to pass herself off as someone a decade or two younger. "You don't look like a Sophia to me."

"See if this has any resemblance to the woman who sent me," Vitas said. He opened his hands to show a glint of gold. "If there is enough similarity, you'll get this in exchange for the letter."

The woman cackled. "For that, I'll swear you look like Nero himself, if you were suicidal enough to want that. And I'd be happy to throw in a little extra. Plenty extra, if large women are your taste."

"Sophia's a jealous woman," Vitas said, putting a rueful grin on his face. "And she wants me to return with her letter as soon as possible."

"Pity."

✛ ✛ ✛

On the street once more, Vitas ducked into a gap between the buildings, knowing it led into a warren of alleys. He walked slowly without looking behind, as if he knew his destination.

The alley stank of human excrement, and rats scattered from some garbage ahead. A dozen steps later, when the alley turned, the street behind him was no longer in sight.

He stopped and waited thirty seconds, then stepped back around the turn.

He wasn't surprised when he saw a dark-haired man halfway between him and the street.

Their eyes locked briefly.

While the man was probably only in his twenties, he looked older, for he was thin, his face gaunt in an unhealthy way that suggested too many days without food. His clothes betrayed the same poverty.

Vitas didn't hesitate but advanced on the man, who turned and began to flee, only to stop abruptly when Jerome's large figure filled the space at the end of the alley and began moving toward him.

Wildly, the man looked at Vitas and back at Jerome, realizing he was trapped. He tried to leap upward, to climb the wall. He fell, then tried again. It reminded Vitas of a rat fleeing a fire. Except rats were better fed.

Jerome reached the man first and grabbed him by the shoulder, then put a massive arm around the man's neck and held him in a choke hold for Vitas. The man briefly yanked down on Jerome's arm but only succeeded in lifting himself off the ground.

Vitas moved in slowly.

The man kicked at Vitas, who smiled and stepped just out of range.

"Why are you following me?" Vitas asked mildly. "Who sent you?"

It would have been a simple guess if this man had followed

from the tavern. That would have told Vitas that he'd been sent by Nerva. But Nerva had not betrayed Vitas, at least not yet. This man had followed Vitas to Alypia's villa and back again.

Who else knew that Vitas was in Rome? Only Hezron and Ruso, and neither of them had reason to follow Vitas.

"Who sent you?" Vitas repeated.

In response to Vitas's question, the man simply closed his eyes and sagged backward against Jerome, as if his efforts to escape had drained all his energy.

"Shall we nick his nostrils?" Vitas asked Jerome in a conversational tone. "Nothing serious, of course. But painful. The cuts will bleed for days and hurt even longer."

Jerome grunted agreement.

Vitas lifted his lower garments and pulled out a knife he'd strapped against his outer thigh.

He put the tip of the knife inside the man's nostril, and the point shocked him into opening his eyes again.

"I'll ask once more," Vitas said. He pulled a little with the knife—not enough to cut into the delicate inside of the nostril, but enough to give a sense of the pain that would come when Vitas sliced it open. "Who sent you?"

The young man finally spoke. "Do what you must. I'll die before telling you anything."

Vitas saw certainty and determination in his eyes.

It was one thing to incapacitate a fit slave warrior threatening with a cudgel as he'd done earlier in the morning. Another to torture a man so weak from hunger he could barely stand. The man wouldn't have anything to report to the person who sent him except that Vitas had visited Alypia and then a tavern.

"I'm getting soft," Vitas told Jerome with a regretful sigh. "Let him go."

HORA UNDECIMA

"YOU'VE COME TO TAUNT ME?" Alypia croaked from her chair in the sun. "Go away."

Quintus and Valeria had insisted that Vitas take them to the dying woman. He'd mentally measured the risk. Had Alypia sent word to Helius about his visit to her? If she had, would Helius have sent men to watch for his possible return?

He'd weighed the likelihood of those risks against the possible danger of Quintus and Valeria's going unaccompanied to visit the woman who wanted them dead. When Valeria had informed Vitas that unless he chained them to the gates of Damian's estate, they would find a way to visit Alypia with or without his permission, he'd realized he had little choice.

And now they were here, with Valeria and Quintus sitting across from her, Vitas standing watch at the entrance to the garden, within earshot of the conversation.

"We are not here to taunt you," Valeria said quietly.

Vitas knew that even before the murder of Valeria's father, she and Alypia had been two proud and spiteful women, each grating on the other in the confines of their household. With all he knew of Valeria's past as the spoiled daughter of a rich man, he now marveled at the gentleness in her reply.

"I want to tell you about Jerusalem," Quintus said in his usual earnest and straightforward manner. "When the Romans were forced out, I lived with an old woman—Malka. A Jew. With no money or any other family."

"I hate the mention of Jerusalem," Alypia spat. "Leave me. I want to be alone."

Vitas had warned Quintus that Alypia might treat them with foulness. Quintus pressed forward anyway.

"She was a follower of the Christos," Quintus said.

"Then throw her to the lions," Alypia answered.

"There is something to these followers," Valeria said. "You must listen."

Alypia looked past them but said nothing to interrupt when Quintus began again.

"She taught me about the Christos," Quintus said. "About his teachings. About his death on the cross. And how some alive today witnessed his resurrection. Malka said he was the long-awaited Messiah."

Vitas thought of Titus and Vespasian, commanding their legions in a tumultuous land split by contention over this figure—the Messiah.

When Vespasian withdrew his legions from Jerusalem to await the outcome of the pending Roman civil war, the Jews who rejected the Christos as Messiah had proudly proclaimed this as evidence of God's miraculous intervention to save Jerusalem and the Jews to ensure the coming of the Messiah he had promised.

The followers of the Christos had interpreted the action in the opposite way. They'd recounted one of the warnings of the Christos, when he'd proclaimed that during the Tribulation, the days would be shortened for the sake of the elect. Those on the housetop should not take anything from the house, and those in the field should not return to take clothes, but all should flee into the hills.

And believing that Jerusalem would face destruction for rejecting him as Messiah and crucifying him, the followers of the Christos had used the time of Vespasian's retreat to flee the city, leaving behind their homes and much of their wealth.

If civil war killed the empire, Jerusalem was safe. But if the empire survived, it would return to Jerusalem, for it could not afford defiance from any province.

What Vitas knew for sure was the chill of the remainder of this prophecy, which Sophia had taught him. Immediately after the Tribulation of those days, the sun would be darkened and the moon would fail to give her light; the stars would fall from heaven, and the powers of the heavens would be shaken. Then the sign of the Son of Man would appear in heaven, and all the tribes of the earth would mourn, and they would see the Son of Man coming on the clouds of heaven with power and great glory. The Christos had prophesied that this generation would not pass until all these things were fulfilled.

Were Jerusalem to be destroyed, Vitas realized, it would be a confirmation of this horrible prophecy. But this horror was impossible.

He was pulled from his thoughts by Alypia's screeching nastiness. "Is there a purpose to all of this drivel?"

Valeria knelt at her feet and held one of Alypia's hands, ignoring the festering wounds on the skin. "Quintus and I have become followers of the Christos," Valeria said. "We know his teachings. And we know the hope that he offers."

"We are here because we are your children," Quintus said. "We are here because we want to help you and keep you company."

"Is this a cruel joke?" Alypia said. "You don't need to be nice to me to get this estate. I'm sure your lawyers have told you that it will be yours, no matter what I try to do to you."

"It's the farthest thing possible from a cruel joke," Valeria answered. "Whatever has happened in the past doesn't matter. Vitas told us that you are afraid to die. Learn about the Christos from us. Learn that he has prepared a room for you."

"I don't believe you," Alypia said. "You must want something."

Valeria straightened and smiled. She spoke to Quintus. "We need water. Warm water in a bowl. And a towel. Let's start by washing her feet."

VESPERA

AT DUSK, VITAS RECLINED across a table from Ruso as the senator gave thanks to God for the lavish spread of food in front of them. Vitas had bathed and been tended to by slaves, and he'd felt guilty about it, then felt vaguely un-Roman for this guilt.

He knew the source of his guilt. It had begun in the previous months in Alexandria, where he and Sophia had lived a very simple life in a small circle that included only Jerome, Arella, Quintus and Valeria, Ben-Aryeh, and their own son.

Many hours Vitas and Sophia had discussed faith and what it meant to be a follower of the Christos, with Sophia fully committed and Vitas curious but still reserved.

The teachings of the Christos were radical. To follow him, one had to crucify oneself. "It is no longer I who live," Sophia had once told Vitas, "but the Christos who lives in me."

Vitas knew that Sophia ached for her husband to share her faith. She'd told him that one must give up not just part but all of oneself. One could no longer be a rugged individualist. Following the Christos involved being baptized into a body of believers who considered everyone equal—indeed, as fellow slaves of the Christos, each was to consider others better than himself. Sophia explained with crystal clarity that there was no room for compromise on this central point. She had quoted the apostle Paul's writing in a letter to the church in Philippi: "'Make my joy complete by being like-minded, having the same love, being one in spirit and purpose. Do nothing out of selfish ambition or vain conceit, but in humility consider others better than yourselves. Each of you should look not only to your own interests, but also to the interests of others.'"

Vitas had freely admitted to Sophia that he too ached for the freedom that came with this kind of submission but said that every time he came close to it, something within him balked at the notion.

"Well," Ruso said, breaking into Vitas's thoughts. "I presume the day was eventful?"

"I had a conversation with Alypia. Her health is poor. All her strivings, it appears, will be of no use to her."

Ruso nodded. "A castle of sand. Washed away by rain. We need always remember the surest foundation and where our efforts should be directed."

It almost felt like Ruso was lecturing Vitas, and it mildly irritated him, so he abruptly changed the subject.

"I was followed," Vitas said.

"What?" Ruso lost his relaxed pose and sat upright, shifting his weight onto his feet, ready to rise. "Who? Where?"

Both understood the terrible consequences of discovery. The key to Vitas's activities in Rome was that he not be found by Nero or by Nero's closest men, Helius and Tigellinus. Not only would it end Vitas's life; Ruso would be ordered to commit suicide, and his property would be confiscated by Nero.

Vitas waved him back. "I was not followed here. It was near the tavern. You can trust that I took as many evasive steps as possible to lose any other followers before returning here. Jerome is always behind me. He's the one who first let me know about the young man who pursued me to Alypia's villa, and he helped me trap the follower."

"You don't know who sent the man?"

"I have no guesses." Which wasn't true. But the stakes were too high to speak candidly. "It wasn't Nerva."

"How can you be certain?"

"I was followed long before going to the tavern. If Nerva were involved, he would have had someone waiting when I picked up the letter."

Ruso leaned forward again. "Nerva has sent you a message."

"He has chosen a place and time for me to meet tonight with those who oppose Nero, to deliver what Vespasian has instructed me. There could not be a better chance than this. I have the scroll from the archives."

This time, Ruso did stand in a swift move of excitement that could not be contained. "Where?"

"I have hidden it again," Vitas said. "Tonight, at the meeting, I'll have it with me."

"What does the scroll hold?"

"I haven't broken the seal. Not until the meeting with Nerva and Vespasian's supporters. Tomorrow, it is yours, I promise, for I understand your curiosity."

Ruso began to pace. "Of course. Of course." He stopped. "Tonight. I'll send you with a retinue of my slaves as protection."

"That won't be necessary," Vitas said. "I'll have Jerome."

"You understand, don't you, how dangerous this is? Helius and Tigellinus."

Though Nero was emperor, Helius and Tigellinus were the two men who made sure each of Nero's whims was immediately granted, from hiring assassins to supplying young men and women for Nero's depravities. Their continued power depended on Nero's.

When Vitas nodded, Ruso continued. "Helius and Tigellinus, it is rumored, have promised freedom and immense reward to any slave who alerts them to a gathering of seditious men. If Helius and Tigellinus can imprison in one fell swoop those they can prove are conspiring against Nero, the revolt is over. Galba commits suicide, and the generals at the heads of other legions will once again meekly do Rome's bidding."

"If I travel with Jerome, there is far less chance that I will draw attention to myself."

"You must be careful. Helius and Tigellinus would give half a kingdom for the capture of the conspirators and another half a kingdom for that scroll." Ruso finished with a grim smile. "And they want you dead too."

PRIMA FAX

FULL MOON. An evening still and hot, with sheet lightning flickering above the seven hills of Rome.

The thickness of the air and sense of a gathering storm brought Vitas back to the night when he'd first defied Nero and begun the chain of events that had expelled him from Nero's inner circle.

Two and a half years earlier, Vitas had stalked Nero on a night just like this, following the emperor through the royal gardens. Nero was wearing an elaborate costume made of skins pieced together from animals imported to the arenas: leopard skin over his body; arms and legs covered by skin from a bear's legs, complete with claws at his feet and hands; two pairs of eagle's wings sewn onto the back; and a lion's head covering Nero's own.

Vitas had followed Nero that evening because back then, Vitas was the single man in Nero's inner circle whom the Senate trusted, and he felt like a thin string holding the Senate and the emperor together. Vitas had to know what the emperor was doing in the garden.

As Nero began attacking prisoners in the guise of this beast, Vitas could endure the emperor's madness no more. He'd stepped in to stop it, and the only thing that had saved Vitas from the emperor's wrath that night was a miraculous earthquake.

Since then, Nero's evils had worsened on a scale unseen by the Romans, even after enduring Caligula. Nero, the man who had slept with his own mother and then assassinated her, who had castrated a slave because the boy reminded him of the wife he had kicked to death and in a public ceremony had then wed the boy. In the arenas, he'd tortured thousands of followers of the Christos, clapping in glee at their horrible deaths. He'd ordered statues of himself placed in temples across the empire, commanding his citizens to treat him as a god.

Tonight, in a way, Vitas again stalked the emperor. With the same tension in the heat of a similar evening, Vitas was completing another circle. If things went wrong, however, he doubted an earthquake would save him this time.

He felt the way he did just before battle. Coiled. The difference was that here he needed to compress the rage that boiled inside of him when he thought of Nero and all that Nero had inflicted on Sophia. If Vitas allowed his emotion to reign, he would lose his effectiveness as a warrior.

Still, he could not escape the thought. Vitas was in Rome. Either Nero would die. Or Vitas would die.

Jerome walked beside him through the streets that led to a mansion only hundreds of yards away from the royal gardens. And Vitas, holding a scroll that Helius feared could undermine the emperor, was to meet the small circle of men who would determine Nero's fate.

And the fate of an empire.

✦ ✦ ✦

At the ten-foot-high wall that surrounded the grounds of the mansion, Jerome pushed at a gate. It opened on silent hinges.

Any other night, the gate would have been locked and guarded. Tonight, those invited inside the walls had been told it would be open for a specific period of time.

Vitas followed Jerome inside. They walked down a path between shrubs, lit by torches set strategically along either side.

Almost as if materializing from the darkness, soldiers stepped out from the shrubs in full armor, swords drawn, completely surrounding Vitas and Jerome.

Vitas drew his own sword. With a massive blow, Jerome knocked it loose from his hand.

"Stop!" a voice barked from behind the soldiers. The man who had given the command stepped through and tossed a rope toward Jerome.

"Search him for the scroll," the man said. "And bind his hands."

Vitas well knew who spoke.

Helius. The man who had ruled Rome while Nero was in Greece. The man who had gone to Greece to bring Nero back to keep power. The man who hated Vitas with as much depth as the ocean.

Daylight would have shown the feminine features of a face as sleek as a leopard's, the almost-orange eyes, and the twisted smile of a man in love with himself. Torchlight threw his face into shadows but could not conceal the gleam of the triumphant smile.

Lightning flickered, briefly filling the far sky.

None of the soldiers moved forward to obey Helius's command.

Instead, Jerome patted Vitas until he found the scroll and tossed it to Helius. Jerome spun Vitas and quickly wrapped the rope around his wrists, tying his hands behind his back.

When that was complete, Helius nodded at the soldiers nearest him; they swarmed Jerome and knocked him to the ground unconscious, then used more rope to bind the giant.

When this was complete and there was no danger for Helius, he stepped toward Vitas and used the side of a dagger to stroke his enemy's cheek.

"Usually I don't enjoy blood on my hands," Helius said. "But I'm going to make an exception for you, Vitas."

"Could you share the pleasure with me?" This came from another man stepping into the torchlight, with the wolfish grin that had for years terrified all but the richest and most powerful in Rome.

Tigellinus closed the distance to Vitas and savagely kicked him in the belly. Vitas fell to the ground, retching.

"Enough," Helius spoke to Tigellinus. "We had agreed that it would serve our purpose to butcher him alive in front of those inside. Once they see how we deal with him, they'll fight each other to be the first to name all the others who support their cause."

"I know, I know," Tigellinus said, breathing heavily. "But sometimes a man needs to give in to temptation. You of all people would understand."

Helius laughed softly.

Vitas was still on the ground, trying to wipe the edges of his mouth on his shoulder. He expected another brutal kick, but there was a commotion instead at the rear of the soldiers.

"Found another!" one soldier reported. "He sneaked in through the gate behind them."

There was a dragging sound.

"Who is this?" Helius demanded.

Vitas took another kick in the ribs and realized the question had been directed at him.

"Who is this?" Helius hissed, leaning down toward Vitas. He grabbed Vitas by the hair and twisted his head to look at the man captured by the soldiers.

A soldier was holding a torch near the face of the new prisoner. Vitas saw clearly it was the same man who had followed him into the alley by the tavern. The stranger's face showed no fear, only resolution.

"Ask him yourself," Vitas said.

"We'll see how long your defiance lasts when I begin to open you with a knife," Helius said, then turned to Tigellinus. "Take all of them with you to make the arrests." He pointed at the intruder. "Keep him with you too. We'll get all of them in one room to watch what happens to Vitas. By dawn, Rome will be Nero's again."

Tigellinus waved the soldiers to follow him, and even before the sound of their footsteps had receded, Helius knelt beside the unconscious Jerome. A flash of lightning showed the dagger in his hand.

"Sideways through the ribs," Helius said. "Straight into the heart. You'll wish you died this quickly."

"Let him live." On his feet, Vitas pulled his hands out from behind his back and withdrew the short sword he'd concealed under his toga. "And I promise you'll make it through the night too."

If Helius was surprised that Vitas had loosened his bonds, he didn't show it. Instead, Helius countered by placing the point of the dagger beneath Jerome's chin. "Step closer, and I'll drive this into the roof of his mouth."

"You are safe as long as he is safe," Vitas said.

"And I only need to stay safe until Tigellinus returns with the soldiers," Helius responded. "Run while you can."

"You held Jerome's family hostage," Vitas said. "You told him to find me and kill me and return with my insignia, or his family would be dead. I'm guessing only you and Tigellinus and Jerome have knowledge of this. So ask yourself, which one passed it along to me? Either way, this evening is not going to end as you expected."

Helius continued kneeling, holding the dagger loosely under Jerome's throat. "I'll humor you," he said. "Let's continue this conversation."

Another sheet of lightning flickered silently above the hills. The approaching storm was so distant that the rumbling would barely reach them in the next thirty seconds.

"You pretend it's about amusement," Vitas said. "But you are asking yourself right now: Which one told? If Tigellinus, then how else has he betrayed you? If Jerome, then what else do I know?"

"Tigellinus has as much to lose as I do if Nero is deposed. He betrays me, he betrays himself."

"But," Vitas said, "Jerome is mute. How could he tell anyone? And wasn't that the beauty of threatening to kill his family? Ask yourself, though. Why would I care to protect him from your knife if I believed he had betrayed me?"

Helius glanced backward, obviously waiting for Tigellinus and his soldiers to appear.

"You won't be rescued," Vitas said. "You'll find the scroll to be

nothing but empty parchment. And the men in togas you watched
enter this garden to meet inside? Tigellinus is about to attempt to
arrest hand-chosen soldiers, loyal not to Nero but to the empire.
The meeting you are trying to prevent is taking place halfway
across the city."

"Liar." But the word rang with a hint of desperation.

"How do you get a mute to talk?" Vitas said. "You give him
a voice."

Vitas had spent a lot of time in contemplation over this. His
heart had ached for Jerome, who so obviously loved his family but
had only the simplest of gestures to respond to his children.

"The man does not speak," Helius said.

"But he writes," Vitas said.

In the months in Alexandria, Vitas had found a way to give purpose to Arella and solve the mystery of why Jerome had nearly murdered him in the market in the aftermath of the camel stampede.

When at last Jerome learned to write, he'd put into letter what
he could not speak aloud, describing how his children had been
kidnapped and how Helius had threatened the entire family if
Jerome did not find a way to kill Vitas.

But Helius and Tigellinus had not counted on the anguish
Jerome faced at the prospect, and that when finally given the
chance, Jerome would be unable to betray his masters but would
choose instead for Vitas to kill him.

"I came to Rome," Vitas said, "knowing that once Jerome
returned to his family, you would seize the opportunity to again get
at me through him. I expected you here tonight because he let me
know how he'd led you here earlier and, through gestures, given you
an idea of what was happening tonight."

The storm was closer now, and the rumbling of distant thunder
louder.

Vitas looked over his own shoulder, then back to Helius, and
raised his voice to be heard clearly. "You would be wise to drop
that dagger," Vitas said. "See the torches coming onto the grounds?

Soldiers from the Praetorian Guard. It means they've abandoned the palace because Nero's fate has been decided. He no longer rules the empire. Galba has been declared."

Helius shrieked rage.

"Drop the knife or die," Vitas said. "Drop the knife and take your chances that Galba lets you live."

Helius didn't hesitate.

Coward that he was, he dropped the knife.

CONCUBIA

SOLDIERS BROUGHT Tigellinus forward, his hands chained.

"You," Tigellinus spat at Vitas. "You expected this."

Vitas nodded.

"It was remarkable," said the young man whom Vitas had caught following him. "We entered the room, and all those other soldiers raised their swords in defense. Their leader said the imperial guard no longer served Nero, and that if Tigellinus didn't surrender, all would be guilty of treason against Galba."

Again Vitas nodded.

"We have a new emperor," the young man said, almost in disbelief.

"We have a new emperor," Vitas said. "Unless he has committed suicide. Messengers have been dispatched to bring him the news that Nero is now considered a fugitive."

"And you were part of this?"

"I was."

"Then please help me," the young man said. "You have the authority to order soldiers to go with us to the palace. To rescue Hezron's daughter."

"Not without answers," Vitas said. "Who are you, and why have you been following me?"

The man pulled on his arm. "As we walk, please. If the palace is empty, we don't have time to waste. Who knows what Nero will do once he finds himself abandoned. Hezron's daughter, Leah. She's there, among others."

Vitas waved over the commander. "You'll give me some men as guards?"

"Without hesitation," he said. He pointed at four men. "You, go with him. Do as he orders. Understand?"

The soldiers, carrying swords and wearing breastplates, nodded.

The young man pulled on Vitas's arm and hurried him forward, down the path toward the street on the other side of the wall that protected the gardens.

"You know my father," the young man said as they walked. "Ben-Aryeh."

"Chayim? You are Chayim? But Hezron said you were dead."

"To protect me," Chayim said. "To protect Leah."

They reached the gate. The first rain spatters hit them, and both quickened their pace, striding into a growing wind. The edge of the storm had arrived.

"More than a year ago," Chayim said, "Helius and Tigellinus sent me in pursuit of an old man and the woman he was protecting. I was told that if I didn't return with the woman, Leah would be killed. I had no inkling it was your wife they wanted. Or that the old man was my father."

"You found them," Vitas said. "On the island of Patmos. Your father had been jailed."

"You know what happened there," Chayim said. "At least from his point of view."

Already Chayim was panting. Vitas had no doubt it was because of his unnatural thinness. The man needed food, and Vitas could guess as to why.

"Your father told me that you had a chance to identify Sophia as the woman you'd been sent to find. And that you denied it was her." Vitas put a hand on Chayim's shoulder. "For that, you have my eternal gratitude. You gave her freedom and allowed her to find me."

"I wasn't doing it for you," Chayim said. "It was for my father. You can't imagine how I felt when he looked up at me from the jail cell. In his eyes, I had become a Roman persecutor of Jews and of Christians. Worse, he was right."

Vitas did not tell Chayim of the long conversations in Alexandria, with Ben-Aryeh describing that same moment, wondering where he had gone wrong as a father, what he could have done differently. Part of Ben-Aryeh's anguish was in not knowing where Chayim had gone from Patmos, not knowing if Chayim still served Helius and Nero.

"So," Vitas said, "you did not return to Helius."

"Without the woman they wanted, Leah would be killed. I spent months wandering Greece aimlessly, pretending I was still looking for the woman. I sent reports describing my feigned pursuit, terrified that Helius would somehow discover I had defied him. During those months, I used my letter from the emperor, granting me as much money as I needed for room and board wherever I traveled. I was in need of nothing. But my soul had been hollowed in the moment I faced my father in jail."

The rain grew harder, and Vitas leaned in to hear Chayim's words.

"I found myself attending meetings of the followers of the Christos," Chayim said. "I told myself I was doing this to put it in my reports to Helius, to make them seem more legitimate. After all, he knew your wife was a follower too. After a while, I couldn't fool myself. I knew I was among them because of the peace I felt in their presence. I realized that starving in Rome, near Leah and her father, would fill me much more than eating and drinking well in solitude. So I staged my own death and returned to help Hezron. Without work—for I dared not risk being found here—it's been difficult."

Chayim was jogging now, despite his exhaustion. The palace loomed ahead, occasionally lit by flashes of lightning.

"When you met with Hezron, we couldn't know if you were to be trusted," Chayim said, panting harder. "So I began to follow you, trying to learn who your friends were."

Now Vitas understood why the threat of torture had not worked against Chayim in the alley by the tavern. Chayim wasn't going to risk revealing who he was—and in so doing, risk Leah's life—without knowing whether Vitas was an agent for Helius.

They reached the entrance to the grounds of the imperial palace.

"Stop," Vitas told Chayim. Vitas had to wipe rain from his face. "Do you know where Leah is?"

"Yes. Bribes. Never enough to visit her, only enough to learn where she has been moved and to get food to her."

"And you are familiar with the palace grounds."

"I regret all the hours I spent here, believing the luxury and power had value."

"Then," Vitas said, "lead us there."

✠ ✠ ✠

The walk was eerily familiar, especially as Chayim led them past the artificial lake that Nero had spent a fortune to create in the grounds. They were retracing the steps Vitas had taken on that night when it all began for him, when he'd followed Nero to the imprisoned followers of the Christos.

The rain came in sideways gusts, then suddenly stopped. By the time they'd moved halfway along the path beside the lake, the waters were still.

Vitas glanced at the imperial palace and saw no lights anywhere.

He was torn between the bloodlust of the hunt and the need to protect Leah. Vitas felt deep compassion for Chayim's frantic worry; he'd felt it too when he believed all was lost with Sophia.

Yet that same compassion only reminded Vitas of how badly he wanted to stare down the man who'd threatened Sophia in the same way as Leah.

The cold soldier's mind of Vitas had only one question: Where was Nero? Certainly by now the deposed emperor had learned that the imperial guard abandoned the palace.

His thoughts were interrupted by a hoarse, low shout from Chayim. "There!"

Ahead was the same small building that Vitas had followed Nero

into, little more than a hut. The night he'd stopped Nero, there had
been four followers inside. Vitas had not known it at the time, but
one of them had been John, the last living disciple of the Christos.

Chayim broke into a jog again, and Vitas stayed with him. As
did the soldiers, the leather straps of their breastplates creaking in
the silence that had fallen with the passing of the storm.

Except another sound broke the silence.

A woman's voice, crying out in protest.

Chayim burst into a sprint, leading all of them to the hut.

The woman's voice rose in pain.

Chayim pushed at the door. It didn't move.

"Imperial guards," Vitas shouted. "Open up!"

"We are imperial guards," came a voice from inside. "Go away."

Vitas threw his shoulder at the door and it popped open.

A candle set on a small table showed it all. Four soldiers. One
woman prisoner. Swords and shields were scattered on the straw.

The woman was backed against the wall, and the intentions of
the soldiers were obvious.

One of the soldiers dove for his weapon, but Vitas stepped forward and, with one foot, put his entire weight on the man's arm.
He placed the tip of his own sword against the man's neck.

The other soldiers inside froze in their positions; unarmed,
they were helpless against trained military with drawn swords.

Chayim made a move to rush forward.

"No," Vitas commanded sharply. "Don't get in the middle."

"Take them," Vitas ordered his own men, without taking his
eyes off the three remaining soldiers near the woman. "Take them
to Nerva and keep them under guard. Tell Nerva that Vitas sent
them. He and I will deal with them tomorrow."

In less than thirty seconds, all the soldiers were gone. Then the
woman said a single word. "Chayim." She held out her arms. He
sobbed and embraced her.

Vitas said nothing as he left them together and moved back
into the still of the night.

Somewhere in the empty corridors of the vast palace was the man who had ordered Vitas to be torn apart in the arena, who had commanded Vitas's wife to commit suicide.

Vitas had vowed revenge.

Now was the time.

INTEMPESTA

VITAS STOOD IN an empty banquet hall of the imperial palace. There was no escaping the memory—or the emotions—of the evening he'd last been here. With Sophia, among dozens of Rome's wealthiest elite, reclining at tables piled with opulent food.

Nero, half-drunk, had swaggeringly stood and stunned the room into silence when he loudly invited Sophia to his bedchamber, fully expecting her to comply, fully expecting Vitas to allow her to accompany him, fully expecting Vitas to remain among the guests until Nero returned to announce whether Sophia had satisfied him.

It had put Vitas in an impossible situation. Defending his wife's honor would cost him his life. But letting Nero take her by the hand to his bedchamber would have cost him everything that mattered to him.

The dilemma had been brilliantly suggested to Nero by Helius, who openly smiled at Vitas while Nero extended the invitation to Sophia.

Vitas had chosen death, rushing forward to attack Nero, knowing the consequences and the futility of his actions. He'd been knocked unconscious and later woken in the bowels of the arena, condemned to die on the sand in front of the crowds.

He stood again in the same banquet hall. Sophia awaited him in Alexandria. He had his wife again and their young child; all that remained was the restoration of his property now that Nero had been deposed.

For some, it would have been enough. But the rage that had sustained Vitas pushed him forward now. He would find Nero; he would explain exactly how he had been so instrumental in tipping the power balance away from Nero and toward Galba. He would watch with satisfaction as Nero understood the extent of Vitas's revenge. And he would rejoice in throttling the man to near unconsciousness, then taking him as prisoner back to Nerva and all the others who were baying for Nero's death.

Vitas stepped through the banquet hall and continued his hunt.

✠ ✠ ✠

"Who knows and who cares where the pig has gone."

Vitas had confronted two young male slaves in a hallway just beyond the library and had demanded, sword in hand, that they tell him the whereabouts of Nero.

The first slave had his arms full of bed linens. The second cradled a small golden box to his belly. Neither seemed concerned that Vitas had threatened to kill them.

"Gone," Vitas repeated, feeling stupid for echoing the slave. "That is all you can tell me?"

One giggled. Vitas realized both were drunk.

"See this?" The second one lifted the box. "Poison. From his bedchamber."

"His bed linens," the first said. "He'll return to an empty room."

If Vitas had wanted confirmation of the complete end of Nero's power, this was it. Slaves stripping Nero of his possessions with impunity.

"Where did you last see him?" Vitas asked.

"Dinner. Last night," the other slave answered. "He read a dispatch with news and tore it up, smashing his cups of wine and weeping; then he demanded a box of poison delivered to his bed-chamber. He spent all day with it, obviously afraid to use it."

Suicide, Vitas thought. But a failed suicide, if these two slaves were to be believed.

"Today, I heard he ran to the Servilian Gardens to beg his most faithful officers to flee with him. Already, some had gone ahead to equip a fleet at Ostia."

The first jumped in, giggling louder. "None would serve him. One even shouted out, 'Is it so terrible a thing to die?'"

The second slave was gleeful. "Tonight, only a short while ago, he heard about a Senate decision against him and leaped out of bed and gathered some servants to find his friends here at the palace. But all the doors were locked and none answered."

The first one picked up on the other's glee. "If you only understood how much we all hated him. While he was searching the palace, we decided that when he returned for his poison, he would find nothing."

The second slave shook the golden box. "We hid down the hall on his return and heard him in the bedchamber shouting for Spiculus, the gladiator, to put an end to him. But nearly all have abandoned him. He'll have to use a dagger to kill himself. But such a man wouldn't have the courage. Let him suffer the way he made us suffer."

Vitas heard the last words over his shoulder. He was already running to the last place where Nero had been seen. The bedchamber where Nero had once wanted to take Vitas's wife.

✠ ✠ ✠

The bedchamber was empty except for an elderly woman who sat on the stripped mattress of Nero's bed. The mahogany bed frame was decorated with shells and ivory and gold. Colorful damask cloths covered the mattress.

"Such evil has been perpetrated here," she said, as if speaking to herself, lost in reverie. "Men gathered around him to plot horrible injustices, often unwilling to engage in what pleased him but unable to deny him. It's a wonderful night for the empire that such a man is gone from the palace. A wonderful night that an old woman like me can sit on this bed and enjoy the thought of how the Senate has declared him a public enemy. He'll be floating in the Tiber soon enough."

"You know where he's gone?"

"There's a letter on his desk," she said. "He was working on it earlier."

Vitas grabbed a candle and hurried to the desk. As he read through what was obviously a speech, he noted with grim satisfaction the ramblings of a desperate and terrified man. Nero had first considered throwing himself at the mercy of Rome's longtime enemies, the Parthians. Or failing that, begging Galba for mercy. Nero was considering dressing in black and appearing on the Rostra to plead with the people of Rome for forgiveness, asking to be sent to Egypt to serve as a prefect there.

Another paper showed equally desperate schemes. Execute all army commanders and provincial governors. Poison all of the Senate at a banquet. Set fire to the city again, and let the wild beasts of the arena roam at large to prevent citizens from fighting the fire.

There was a note detailing Nero's military preparations, showing his major concerns were finding enough wagons to carry his stage equipment and arranging for his concubines to have male haircuts.

But nothing showed where he might have fled.

Vitas turned to the old woman on the bed again. She was reclining on the stripped mattress and smiling at him.

"History may never record this," she said. "But let it be said that I was the last to command the bed of Nero! Me, an old woman Nero never once noticed because I had no value."

Vitas snorted at the woman's humor.

She continued. "He didn't notice me, but I have eyes and ears and watched him all the time. I saw him in this room only fifteen minutes ago."

Vitas realized that she was hinting at something. "Help me search for him. I'll ensure you are rewarded."

"Took you long enough," she said. She sat up and spoke more seriously. "What's my reward?"

"Speak to Nerva tomorrow. I'll arrange your freedom."

"You have the power?" Before Vitas could speak, she waved away his answer. "If you don't, you won't be the first man who lied to me. I risk nothing to tell you anyway. I would look for Nero at the villa of the imperial freedman, Phaon. That's who he left with when he discovered his poison gone, when Spiculus and all the other trained executioners were ignoring his demands for someone to kill him."

"Phaon." Vitas knew exactly where the villa was. About four miles away. Between the Nomentan and Salarian Ways.

"Phaon," she repeated. "They spoke as if I didn't exist, as if I hadn't been summoned to tell Nero where his poison was. All Nero took was a tunic. He fled without even putting on sandals."

"Thank you. Tell Nerva that you were sent by Vitas. He'll honor my promise."

"Vitas!" She put her hand to her mouth. "Yes. You are! Good things are happening to Rome if you are still alive!"

As Vitas hurried away, she called out two words: *"Neca eum."*

Kill him.

✝ ✝ ✝

Vitas knew he was only minutes behind Nero and ran through the imperial garden toward the stable, for he'd made the decision to take a horse. Not only would it help him move quickly, but sitting astride the beast would afford some protection.

A hundred yards away, however, Vitas saw the shadows of a half-dozen men leading horses from the stable by bridles. He slowed and moved off the path, wanting to observe before choosing a course of action.

Above the wind, he heard one man plaintively call out. "I've never been on a horse before."

"Then hang on to his neck," came the snappish reply. "The horse will follow."

Nero!

Six men. Should Vitas attack? Could Vitas attack?

Closer now, he saw four were clumsy with the horses. Servants, most likely, the final few still faithful to Nero, and so lowly they had never been taught to ride.

Who was the fifth?

A flash of lightning.

The horses danced on the spot, slightly spooked.

There'd been enough light to show the fifth man, more comfortable on horseback than the others. It was Sporus, the slave boy whose elegant features had reminded Nero of his dead wife.

Nero urged his horse forward at a trot. If Vitas were to attack the man he hated, this was the moment.

Vitas held his sword at the ready and tensed to leap forward.

Yet even now, he was unable to defeat the soldier's discipline that had served him so well all these years. Much as he boiled with rage, he could not set aside the fact that given the situation and how it had unfolded, it would be of crucial importance to learn if Nero had any significant allies left in Rome. Vespasian and Titus would want to know of it, and Vitas owed them his life and the lives of his family. Much as Vitas wanted to serve himself in this moment by exacting a blood revenge, he was obligated to put that aside and serve them instead.

The horses trotted past Vitas where he remained hidden in the bushes.

In another flash of lightning, Vitas saw that Nero was barefoot, wearing a cloak over his tunic, holding a handkerchief over his face.

As soon as the final horse passed, Vitas sprinted to the stables and found a horse for himself.

✠ ✠ ✠

With the flickering lightning, it was easy to keep them in sight, about a hundred yards ahead as they moved along the road. Vitas clung to the neck of his horse to keep his profile as low as possible.

As the six men on horses passed a soldiers' camp, one man

yelled from the darkness, loud enough to reach Vitas. "Look, someone is out to chase the emperor!"

Another soldier called out, "What's the latest news? Is he
dead yet?"

A minute later, when Vitas passed as a lone horseman, he heard
the same question again from men standing beside a fire. They were
passing drinks back and forth, celebrating. Undoubtedly, when
Galba finally arrived in Rome, they expected him to follow tradition and give them a fine reward for swearing loyalty to him.

Vitas wondered if Nero, for the first time in his life, understood the gut-clenching fear he'd so callously inflicted on thousands and thousands, often for no other reason than a whim.
Thinking of this gave Vitas a cold satisfaction. It occurred to him
that perhaps the real reason he hadn't stepped out and attacked
Nero with the sword was because the longer Nero lived, the longer Nero would endure terror.

Ahead, one of the servants fell off the back of his horse.

Nero cursed at the man. "Stay with us!"

The servant found his feet and hobbled along, pathetically
trying to keep pace.

It forced Vitas to drop back slightly, and he kept the increased
distance between them for the next couple of miles, which passed
without incident except for the growing pressure as the storm
regathered.

As the procession neared Phaon's villa, Vitas began to worry
that Nero would make it inside the estate too soon. Vitas was
almost at the point of urging his horse forward when he heard
hooves on the cobblestones, coming toward him.

Had Nero changed his mind?

Vitas slipped off his horse and drew it to the side of the road,
hoping lightning wouldn't expose him.

It was a needless worry.

The horses were all riderless.

Nero and his servants and Sporus must have dismounted. The

horses would have been nervous because of the storm and simply wanted to return to the stables.

Vitas began to run down the road.

When he reached the lane to Phaon's villa, he turned without hesitation but then stopped short at seeing six figures on the lane. He darted behind a tree and watched to see if he'd been noticed. Nothing in the movement of the six men indicated they knew he was following.

Again, he felt grim satisfaction.

The man who had held the fates of millions of men in the empire, who had been served by tens of thousands of warriors, had been reduced to four servants and a slave boy.

Vitas trotted forward down the lane, ready to freeze if any turned.

They did, but not in the direction he expected.

"Here!" one of the four said.

"Phaon, I can't," Nero replied. "It's nothing but a hole between briars."

"We have to hide," Phaon replied. "None of my own servants can know you are here. This path will take us to the rear of the house."

"Then spread your cloaks," Nero said. "I will not dirty my feet."

The image that Vitas had conjured of a terrified man immediately disappeared. Nero still had his haughtiness, and Vitas felt his rage rising again. He put a hand on the hilt of his sword and eased forward.

Now he only had to give them a ten-yard lead down the path to stay out of sight. Phaon's insistence that none of his servants could know of Nero's presence indicated there was no gathering of men still loyal to Nero. It meant Vitas could have attacked immediately, bringing Nero's body back to Nerva for the reward that most surely had been placed on Nero's head. But that would have been too merciful a death for the tyrant, and now Vitas stayed his sword not because of an obligation to Vespasian or Titus, but because he wanted to watch Nero suffer in the way he'd imagined earlier that Nero was suffering.

Vitas remained far enough back that he was confident none of
the men ahead could hear him above their own noisy progress, yet
close enough to clearly hear conversation.

The men had stopped at the edge of a pool.

"There is a gravel pit just beyond the water," Phaon said. "You
could lie low there while I prepare the house. I'm expecting a letter
with news from the Senate."

"I refuse to hide in a pit before I die," Nero snarled.

"Then I will clear the entrance to a tunnel that goes beneath
the wall to my villa." Phaon ran ahead.

Nero knelt beside the water and spoke bitterly as he scooped
it into his hands. "This is Nero's own special brew."

He gulped at the water, then busied himself with his cloak.
It took Vitas several moments to realize that Nero was pluck-
ing thorns, cursing at the small pinpricks he must have felt as
he struggled in the darkness.

Moments later, Phaon returned and gestured them toward
the entrance.

Vitas waited until he no longer heard their voices, then crawled
through the same tunnel.

INCLINATIO

RISING FROM THE TUNNEL on the other side of the wall, Vitas kept his hand on the hilt of his sword. He didn't fear Nero or any of his men, but he was wary of bodyguards that Phaon must surely keep at his villa.

He realized shortly, however, another benefit of Phaon's secrecy. By not announcing his arrival in advance, Phaon had no one stationed at the rear of the estate to guard him.

Vitas didn't have to move far to find Nero and the servants. They had stopped at the first room, and only a few feet outside, he heard Nero complain, "Look at this poor mattress! And we have nothing better than this coarse bread? I'll have none of it."

"We can't stay here," Sporus said. "This must not be your fate, to die in such a pitiful room, wearing an old cape."

Nero's voice cracked. "If I am found and killed, we need a grave. Dig one outside that will fit my body. Look for pieces of marble to decorate it."

There was murmured agreement inside the room, and Vitas made his decision. He would let the servants go forth as ordered, then capture Nero at sword point. This would ensure the man would not be killed by anyone else but reach the Senate alive and face their decision.

"Dead," Nero said, now crying. "And so great an artist!"

Vitas moved back some, ducking into an alcove as he waited for the servants to leave. Before that could happen, however, he heard the slap of sandals somewhere down the corridor. From his hiding spot, he watched as a runner passed him and disappeared into the room.

"A note from Phaon," came the words from inside.

This was significant. Phaon had left them and sent a messenger rather than meeting Nero in person. Phaon had washed his hands of Nero.

"What is it!" Nero said sharply. "Give it to me."

A pause. Then a sob. "I have been declared a public enemy by the Senate and will be punished in ancient style when arrested."

The response to Nero's statement was silence. Vitas imagined Nero looking from the face of one man to another, gauging their reactions.

It was Nero who broke the silence. "Tell me, I demand—what is the ancient style of punishment?"

A shaky voice answered him. "Executioners strip the victim naked in a public place and put his head in a wooden fork so he cannot move. Then he is flogged to death with rods."

Nero began to wail. "No! No! That cannot be my final hour! Suicide! That is my only option. Where are my daggers?"

Again silence. Again broken by Nero. "These points are dull!"

Vitas heard the clanging of metal against stone, as if Nero had thrown them down.

"Weep for me, Sporus. Mourn for me!" Nero continued, barely understandable above his own wailing. "And you others. One of you must set an example for me by committing suicide first. Please! No, I'm not begging—I'm commanding. Who shall it be?"

In the next silence, Vitas again imagined each of the men looking at the others, none willing to die for a man who was now a public enemy of Rome, no longer emperor.

And in that silence came another sound. At first, like thunder. But then, more recognizable as galloping cavalry.

"How ugly and vulgar my life has become," Nero cried. Then

in Greek, "This is certainly no credit to Nero. No credit at all. Come, pull yourself together."

Vitas stood from his crouch in the alcove. Now was the time.

Just as he reached the room, Nero hissed, "Epaphroditus, help me with this."

Vitas knew that name. It told him one of the servants was Nero's secretary.

Vitas turned the corner and saw in candlelight that Nero had a dagger to his throat and was attempting to push it in.

"Epaphroditus! Now, while I have courage!"

Later Vitas would wonder, had he reached Nero in time, would he have tried stopping the man?

But he wasn't given the opportunity to choose.

The dagger plunged into Nero's soft flesh, and he pulled it out and gazed, stupefied, at the blood. It gushed onto his cloak.

Vitas knelt beside Nero, and Nero's eyes widened in recognition. But he was too weak to say anything.

He clutched at Vitas's arm and tried to force him to stanch the wound with the edge of his cloak.

Nero muttered, "Too late. But, ah, what fidelity."

Whether Nero meant the events of the evening or that seeing Vitas alive revealed that he'd been betrayed long before this evening, there would never be a certain answer.

Eyes bulging, Nero died.

Vitas stepped outside the room, raised his forearm against the wall, and leaned his head against his arm.

Rage and revenge had driven him for so long; now that Nero was gone, Vitas was spent, barely able to register the emotions that had drained him.

Before he could stop, choking sobs overwhelmed him.

He was free to go home again.

❧ SATURN ❧

HORA NONANA

TWO DAYS LATER, in the middle of the afternoon, escorted by a servant, Vitas joined Ruso in the senator's garden. The sky held wispy clouds, and the leaves of the trees moved with barely more than a rustle in the light breeze.

Ruso did not rise to greet Vitas but remained sitting with his right hand on a goblet filled with dark liquid.

The servant departed, and Vitas waited for Ruso to invite him to sit.

Ruso pointed at the nearest chair, about ten paces away.

"You behave like a worried man," Vitas said, taking the chair. "First, your servants search me for weapons. And now you make sure to keep some distance between us."

"I'm sure you're not surprised at my precautions," Ruso said. "Let's not fool ourselves. I know why you arranged this appointment."

"If we are not going to fool ourselves," Vitas said, "then you tell me why I am here."

"As judge and executioner."

"Hardly."

"You should not lie to yourself," Ruso said. He lifted the goblet and smiled with false brightness. "Helius is in chains until Galba arrives, but he is permitted to receive visitors. He told me the scroll you carried the night of Nero's death was blank. You knew already, then, not to trust me."

"It was merely caution," Vitas said. "But when Helius demanded that someone search me for the scroll, I knew. Only one person could have told him I would be carrying it with me that night. You. And in betraying me, you betrayed Vespasian and Titus."

In saying this, Vitas shivered with a premonition. The letter of Revelation had predicted the Beast would reign for forty-two months against the followers of the Christos. It was eerie. Nero had died forty-two months after beginning the persecutions, ending the reign of the first beast. And if the reign of the second beast had begun with Rome's entry into war against Judea, could Vitas believe that at the end of the second forty-two months, with the power that Vespasian and Titus held as commanders of the legions in Judea, they would become the ax of God's destruction against the Jews?

He fought against the premonition and focused on the conversation. For there was no doubt Vespasian and Titus would ensure Ruso paid the price for choosing to side against them while pretending to support them.

"I was right, then, about the reason for your visit." Ruso drank deeply from the goblet. He grimaced at the taste. "You are judge and executioner."

"I will repeat myself. Hardly. I'm obliged to report what happened to Vespasian and Titus. Your fate, in that regard, is up to them."

They both had no doubt of that fate. This was Rome. Losers in politics rarely survived.

"Why are you here?" Ruso asked.

"Naturally, they will be curious about your betrayal. Are there others among the group who helped you?"

"Where are your heated brands? If you are trying to unravel a conspiracy against the original conspirators, isn't that the usual method?"

"Again, that decision is theirs, not mine." Vitas stood. "Thank you for your time. A ship waits for me in Ostia. Jerome and his family will travel back to Alexandria with me. Rome is a dangerous place in these times."

Ruso lost his composure, and his voice came out as a groan. "Wait."

"Of course." Vitas relaxed in the chair again.

"Does it help that I hate myself for it?"

"I am not your judge. Nor do I want to be."

Ruso's face contorted. "I had so little time to make my decision." He held the goblet up and examined it as if looking for cracks in the glaze. He set it down beside him and spoke earnestly. "Helius learned of your return and that you were here. All I can guess is that a servant overheard and betrayed me. Helius came to me and gave me a choice. I could face interrogation—those heated brands and the pincers and the whips—until I divulged the extent of the conspiracy, and then die in the arena. Or I could work for Helius and keep my life and my property and be rewarded with substantial gold from the treasury."

Tremors went through Ruso's body. "I wish I'd had your courage. When Nero demanded your wife as a partner, you decided to face death instead. Me, I agreed to what Helius wanted."

"What did Helius ask you?" Vitas reminded himself that he wasn't there to judge and didn't want any introspection on the justifications Ruso used.

Ruso reached down and tapped his foot, a strange action that Vitas noted but chose not to express any curiosity about.

"First, the names of the conspirators. I told him I only knew two: Vespasian and Titus."

At this, Vitas felt more of the cold anger that had driven him for the previous months. Ruso had betrayed Titus, knowing it put a death sentence not only on Titus, but probably Vespasian.

Ruso went on. "Helius wanted to use you to lure all the conspirators together. He thought he'd finally triumph and squash all of Nero's enemies at once."

"Did you tell Helius that Ben-Matthias predicted Vespasian would be an emperor?"

Ruso countered that with another question. "Does it matter? Galba is going to execute Helius."

"Did you tell him?"

Ruso tapped one knee, then the other. He grimaced.

Peculiar, Vitas thought, but he repeated his question. "Did you tell Helius?"

"No," Ruso said. "Think of the situation. If Nero survived these revolts, his next target would have been Vespasian. And my treachery would have been exposed. I was trying to survive. I only gave Helius what he demanded, nothing more."

"Hoping that if Nero did not survive, no one would know of your actions."

Ruso shrugged. "Obviously, I'm not a man of honor. And all my life, I'd believed I was. Until I was tested."

Vitas was simply not interested in the man's self-pity. "What else did he want? You said first the names. What was second?"

"The scroll from the archives."

Vitas reached inside his cloak and pulled out parchment, rolled into a tube. "This scroll?"

Ruso's face arched with surprise. "You did have it!"

"Not until this morning," Vitas said. "The night Helius searched me for it, it was still hidden somewhere in the archives. The only person who knew where to look was Leah. It was something she knew she must keep secret, and only after her release from the palace did she retrieve it."

"Let me read it," Ruso said.

Vitas laid the scroll casually in his lap. "The night I escaped from the arena, I was told this might someday save my family. If I'd found it sooner, that might have been the case. Though, in a way, it was an accurate prediction."

"You didn't find it until after Nero was dead," Ruso said. "Ah, the irony. This is the scroll that drove Helius to desperation, and in the end, because of you, it didn't make a difference."

"To me it did," Vitas answered. "Because of this scroll, I first suspected you. That suspicion kept me alive and set the bait that trapped Helius."

"Indulge me then," Ruso said. He pinched the tops of his thighs. "Explain how you suspected me because of that scroll. Time is getting shorter."

"I began to wonder how you knew Helius wanted it so badly," Vitas said. "And the only answer I could come up with was that you knew this from Helius himself."

"Let me read the scroll, I beg of you. I've spent countless hours wondering why Helius was so afraid of it. What could it possibly contain that would have been dangerous to Nero?"

"Helius was afraid because Nero said he was god," Vitas answered. "Because Nero used the followers of the Christos as a scapegoat for the great fire. Helius was terrified because this scroll gives the Christos a legitimacy in Rome that would hurt Nero badly. It is a scroll that would lend credence to John's revelation as a divinely inspired prophecy. And if divinely inspired, the predictions about the death of the Beast would soon come to pass."

"It gives the Christos a legitimacy in Rome? What is in it?" Ruso was so frustrated that he tried to push himself out of his chair. But strangely he fell backward. "Tell me!"

In that moment, Vitas understood why Ruso insisted his time was short. The man was slowly becoming paralyzed. The tapping of his feet and knees, the pinching of his thighs. Ruso had been evaluating the progress of the numbness that was creeping up his body.

"Hemlock?" Vitas asked Ruso, remembering how deeply Ruso had drunk from the goblet. Very soon, the poison would numb and paralyze the muscles that controlled Ruso's breathing.

"What choice did I have?" he answered. "From prison, Helius has been blackmailing me to pay for food and other comforts. Any day he could let the world know of my treachery. And when you confirmed what I feared—that you already knew—it was a death sentence. I'm too cowardly to die by branding irons. Or tied in a sack with a badger and thrown in the Tiber.

"Please," Ruso said. "What was on the scroll? Grant me that before I'm gone."

"You once believed and followed the Christos," Vitas said. "Wasn't that why you wanted John spared?"

"I believed," Ruso said. He was beginning to gasp. "Until my faith was tested. Until Helius threatened my life because of it. Now I have only shame." Ruso's mouth tightened. "The scroll!"

Vitas finally succumbed to emotion. Not the cold anger he'd arrived with. But pity.

He walked over and put the scroll in Ruso's lap.

Ruso opened it with trembling hands.

Vitas watched Ruso's eyes scan the contents. "This cannot be. Tiberius?"

Vitas nodded confirmation. Few emperors were as revered as Tiberius.

"Tiberius!" Ruso repeated.

Vitas understood Ruso's surprise. He had reacted the same way himself upon reading the scroll.

Because of the miracles performed by the Christos and the tales of his resurrection that circulated through the empire, the great emperor Tiberius had gone to the Senate, asking the members to approve a decree that the Christos was divine. The Senate had refused to do as requested, and this once-minor Senate matter had been noted and archived.

But in light of the letter of the Revelation and how Nero would have reacted to any suggestion that the followers he persecuted had legitimacy to serve any other god but him, decades later this minor Senate matter would have been a major political blow.

"Had I but known," Ruso said. He could hardly breathe. The potion of hemlock must have been barely diluted with wine.

In sudden rage and with the last of his strength, he ripped the parchment in half. Vitas took a step toward Ruso, but it was too late. With flashing hands, Ruso shredded the document and threw the pieces into the water beside him.

"In the end, I served the false god," Ruso said. "Now I am finished."

He tried gasping for more air, but his lungs were failing him. His face contorted with terror and his tongue fell from his mouth. Then, slowly, the light left his eyes.

JERUSALEM

Province of Judea

Look, he is coming with the clouds, and every eye will see him,

even those who pierced him; and all the peoples of the earth

will mourn because of him. So shall it be! Amen.

REVELATION 1:7

From the Revelation, given to John on the island of Patmos in AD 63

❧ MERCURY ❧

HORA DUODECIMA

WITH DUSK APPROACHING, Vitas was perched on a large boulder, on the west side of the upper slope of the Mount of Olives, overlooking Jerusalem on the other side of the valley. Nearly three hundred feet higher than the city, this position had afforded a panoramic view of events as they slowly and tragically unfolded over the course of the summer.

Yet he was not thinking about the violence and bloodshed.

He was trying to grapple with an unfamiliar emotion. Homesickness. After three months away from Alexandria, he was becoming increasingly aware that memories of his family were no longer bringing him joy, but a melancholy that he could not shake.

Following his return to Alexandria after the suicide of Nero, he'd cherished nearly two years of domestic peace and joy with Sophia. They'd welcomed another child into the world.

Alexandria.

The perfect place for a man to live during the hazards of near civil war across the empire following the death of Nero. Far enough away from the deceits and treacheries of Rome, but far from being a dusty, obscure province.

The memory of something as simple and meaningless as a child at play or an infant's nap was enough to make Vitas ache with this homesickness. Tutillus was a strong and sturdy three-year-old, already happy to play with a wooden sword and duel any vertical objects that would serve as suitable opponents—chair legs, unsuspecting tree trunks.

Little Marcella loved to snuggle with Vitas. Not as much, however, as he loved to snuggle with her.

In long, hot, lazy afternoons, Vitas would retire to a shaded room, carrying Marcella as she reached up and played with his hair. Then he would lie on a bed with her on his chest.

He knew what made her drowsy.

His soft singing.

She would squirm at first, but as he sang, her movements would begin to slow. Then, like a cat settling into a blanket, she would shift and turn her body into the most comfortable position and begin to sleep. Unfailingly, her right hand would reach upward and clutch his hair, as if the reassurance of his presence was all she needed to feel safe.

Only then would Vitas permit sleep to fall upon him, contentment filling him. Often, when he woke, he would find his own hand upon his daughter's, where it was intertwined with his hair.

And upon waking, he would stare upward for long, long minutes, grateful for what he had but always afraid that someday it might be taken from him.

Yet perfect as it had been in the tranquility of the balmy sea breezes beneath the palm trees of Alexandria, all it had taken was a rumor for Vitas to board a ship for Caesarea immediately, to travel the road from that port to Jerusalem, where his longtime friend Titus, now the son of an emperor, was encamped in the hills around the city.

The rumor had come directly from Titus, delivered by letter.

Word has reached me that Damian has been held prisoner within the walls of Jerusalem since your time in Caesarea. I cannot promise this is true, for as you have undoubtedly heard, the city is not receptive to Roman visitors. However, I promise I will do my best to find your brother once we break through the walls.

Typical of Titus, the dry understatement. The city not receptive to Roman visitors? Jerusalem was under siege, the violence of one side against the other almost beyond comprehension.

His brother, Damian, alive?

His brother, Damian, alive!

Vitas would do everything in his power to help rescue his brother. The strong friendship between Vitas and Titus meant that he could expect any and all resources possible from Titus.

Thus far, both men had been unable to do anything.

Not for the first time did Vitas contemplate the city from his vantage point, wondering how he could get inside and search for Damian.

A crunch of sandals against stone drew Vitas.

When he turned his head toward the noise, he expected to see a soldier sent by Titus. The entire Tenth Legion was camped on one of the lower slopes of the Mount of Olives. Titus would know where to send the soldier to find Vitas, for it was Titus who often sent Vitas up to the perch to ponder the military situation for any advice Vitas might offer in the evenings when both of them met at a fire in the center of camp.

But it wasn't a soldier.

It was an older man, picking up his pace as he neared Vitas.

"Ben-Aryeh!" Vitas said, rising quickly. Alarm rose in his heart. He'd left Ben-Aryeh in Alexandria to watch over Sophia and the children. What had gone wrong? What had been taken from Vitas?

"All is well," Ben-Aryeh said, correctly reading the emotion that Vitas could not help but show. "I am not here to deliver bad news. All is well with your family."

"And with yours?" Vitas asked. "Chayim and Leah?"

"All is well. Daily, I rejoice that my son was returned to me. Much thanks to you for it." Ben-Aryeh held open his arms.

Vitas took a deep breath and stepped forward to accept an embrace. He wryly thought that at the least, Ben-Aryeh had managed to dispel the melancholy.

They stepped back from the embrace, and each took measure of the other.

"I've just arrived," Ben-Aryeh said. "Titus said I would find you here. Any word of Damian?"

"None," Vitas said.

Now that his alarm had subsided, Vitas felt the familiar return of constant dread for the safety of his brother. Was it possible that Damian had survived these years and lived somewhere inside the walls of Jerusalem, when every Jew seethed with hatred against the Romans?

Yet buffering that emotion, Vitas sensed the warmth of his affection for Ben-Aryeh. During the years in Alexandria, with Ben-Aryeh exiled from Jerusalem, the older man had become a family member.

"Your travels were unremarkable, I hope," Vitas replied. No man wanted adventure during travel, especially here in Judea. Titus and the legions had cleared resistance in all directions from Jerusalem, but there were still no guarantees of safety.

"Bah," Ben-Aryeh answered. "I had an escort of Roman soldiers along the entire road from Caesarea. How do you think I liked that?" Ben-Aryeh had been among the priests of the Temple, as staunchly nationalistic as any Jew. "As I passed through the town where I was sent to wait for you," he continued, "I could not help but think of how much I hated you when we first met, before the revolt. You, a despicable Roman."

"You were a cantankerous old man then," Vitas said, recalling that day in the market, where Queen Bernice had sent Ben-Aryeh to meet him. His personal mission had been to get to Jerusalem to search for a woman he could not put out of his mind, a Jewish slave girl he'd met in Greece. Sophia.

"And," Vitas added, "nothing has changed about you."

"But these changes . . ." Ben-Aryeh swept an arm toward the city below and the earthworks and ramparts arrayed along the wall. "Four years ago, this was unthinkable. But observe the mighty Roman war machine. That is the reason I should hate you again."

Ben-Aryeh sighed, still facing the city. "But Rome is not entirely at fault in this. And it is painful to admit that. My heart broke at the news that reached Alexandria, and it has fully shattered to behold what is before us. I could hardly bear to look over as I climbed up here to find you."

"I can hardly bear it myself," Vitas answered. "And I only see what happens at the walls. I don't let myself think of what it is like inside. Time and again, Titus has offered good terms for surrender. Yet they refuse. Prophets inside tell the people that God will smite us down."

"The second and third walls of the city, gone," Ben-Aryeh said. "I can see it from here. Jerusalem's suburb destroyed."

Jerusalem consisted of four parts, clearly visible from their location. Directly opposite them, on the east side of Jerusalem, was the Temple Mount, protected by the most massive walls, with the Antonia Fortress looking down on the Temple proper and the altar.

To their left—south of the Temple—was the lower city, where most of the poor lived; behind it, the upper city with its mansions of the rich.

To their right—north of the Temple—the new city had been built, its suburb once protected by a third wall. Well inside this third wall was a second wall, now destroyed, that separated the new city from the original upper and lower cities.

Jerusalem was down to its remnants—the upper and lower cities and the Temple Mount. Its glory had been cut in half, but the remaining half was also protected by rugged geography that put its massive walls in the most difficult position to assail.

"Titus is not entirely to blame for the destruction that you see," Vitas said. "Again and again he has offered to spare the people if they give up the fight. Instead, they hurl arrows and spears at him when he speaks. There is something else—something you can't see in the valley below from this angle. A wall built by the Romans to keep the Jews from breaking out of the city to fight."

"That doesn't sound effective. There are miles and miles of hills on the other side of the city, where the Jews can disperse beyond reach of the wall and regroup over here."

"You don't understand. Titus has put up his own walls around the entire city. Through the valley of Cedron, to Siloam, around the north, and back here again."

"Impossible."

"Titus had it built in three days. With thirteen towers filled with garrisons, dispersed around the perimeter to guard against any breach. Such is the power of Rome that a hundred thousand men can work together in unity and discipline and accomplish this."

Silence. Ben-Aryeh must have been contemplating the scope of that task and what it meant. Jerusalem was still solidly protected on its mount, yet now the entire mount was encircled by a new wall, ringed by soldiers.

"How can the Temple survive?" Ben-Aryeh asked.

"Take comfort," Vitas said. "Titus has repeatedly said he will protect the Temple."

"I pray that it is so," Ben-Aryeh said softly. "But I have journeyed here in case he fails to protect it. First tell me: Is it over for the people of Jerusalem?"

"I have journeyed here in case he fails to protect it." Vitas wanted badly to know what Ben-Aryeh had meant by that ambiguous statement, but instead of countering Ben-Aryeh's question with a question of his own, Vitas chose patience and answered Ben-Aryeh. "It is only a matter of time."

"How long?"

"Days, perhaps, until the Antonia tower is breached."

This was Titus's next military goal. With the second and third walls gone, Antonia, at the northwest corner of the Temple Mount, was the most reachable. If he could breach Antonia, which before the revolt had held Roman garrisons but now gave protection to the Jewish defenders, the Temple itself would be vulnerable. And once the Temple was taken, the rest of the upper and lower cities could be breached as well.

"Surely he can't take Antonia," Ben-Aryeh said. "Speak to me as if I were another general, just arrived. Tell me the advantages held by the rebels and the advantages held by the Romans."

Vitas furrowed his eyebrows, surprised by the request. "You've never seemed interested in the logistics of battle before."

"Will you trust me? I have good reason to ask."

"You never need ask for my trust," Vitas said, thinking of how Ben-Aryeh had saved Sophia by helping stage her death, then taking her to Patmos and Caesarea. He owed Ben-Aryeh for Sophia's life.

Vitas spent the next minutes explaining. In January—after nearly a year without any action against the Jewish rebels—Titus had returned with his legions and resumed war. It had taken him until April to subdue the entire countryside, with tens of thousands of Jews fleeing for the unassailable sanctuary of Jerusalem.

The larger issue, however, had resulted because of Nero's suicide. With Vespasian's retreat, it appeared as if the new state of Judea were secure and independent. Because of that, the Jews began to fight among themselves for rulership.

At first, it pitted Zealots against moderates. The Zealots wanted to be totally independent of Rome; the moderates believed Rome would return and looked for a way to ensure peace with the empire. The Zealots, who had control of the Temple, executed all Jewish nobles, calling them Roman conspirators. The moderates managed to drive all the Zealots into the Temple area.

A stalemate resulted, until the Zealots brought in Idumeans as extra warriors and, with the leadership of a man named John of Gischala, broke out of the Temple walls and penned the moderates in the upper city.

The moderates fought back, allowing a man named Simon Ben-Gioras and all his warriors into the city. More fragmentation occurred; once the Zealots were driven back into the Temple, John turned against the high priests. This meant three factions were battling for control and straining the city's resources.

During Passover, the priests, who still controlled the inner

Temple, allowed citizens in to worship. John took advantage of this and sent his own men in with hidden weapons, finally ending the priests' control.

Down to only two warring factions, Simon held the upper and lower cities, while John held the Temple.

Worse, as Vitas explained, in John's battle against Simon, John set fire to the supply warehouses outside the Temple, burning nearly the entire grain supply. What would have otherwise fed the city for years was now gone, driving it into famine.

Ben-Aryeh could not help but break in. "All the grain!"

Vitas nodded grimly. "Without that act, Titus would have expected the siege to last years. Finally John and Simon are working together to defend the walls. They have twenty thousand men. Even with Titus outnumbering them four to one, the defenders would have been unassailable, but every day they are weakened more by the deaths from starvation, and the survivors have less and less energy to fight."

"It's like God himself has smitten the Jews," Ben-Aryeh said.

Both men surveyed the valley in silence, unable to shake a shared sense of awe at the meeting below of an immovable object and an irresistible force.

By all accounts, Jerusalem was truly beyond conquering, for the walls of the city made it impossible for any force to breach.

Faintly gleaming as the last of the day's sun fell across the city, the stone of the wall was white marble, cut with such precision that the wall looked like one piece—sheer luminous limestone, reaching to the crowning glory of glistening gold that fashioned the Temple roof.

Every monstrous stone block was ten paces long, five paces wide, and five paces high, and the wall was four blocks high. It would take twelve men, each standing on the shoulders of the man below him, just for the man at the top to be able to put his hands on the upper edge of the wall.

But for added defense, Jerusalem was built on a high hill, and the valley was at its steepest below the wall. Thus, the geography made it impossible to stand level at the base of the wall; an arrow shot from the bottom of the valley could barely reach the wall itself.

To add to the impossibility of conquering this city, huge towers dominated the wall, where defenders could wait and pour forth at any attack.

This was the immovable object.

But the irresistible force was the Roman army. Tens of thousands of the most highly trained and disciplined soldiers had gathered in camps to surround the city.

Despite being under constant attack from spears and arrows, over the previous months they had moved thousands and thousands of tons of dirt to build the bottom of the valley upward toward the walls.

And once they had sufficiently elevated the ground, they had begun to build ramparts of wooden beams, again under hostile attack, losing hundreds of soldiers each day to the defenders, who had the tremendous advantage of height.

Slowly and inexorably, the ramparts had been completed. And this was where the genius of Roman engineering became so fearful. The great battering rams were finally in place, day after day pounding against the walls. The men who moved the rams were covered in leather shields against the boiling oil flung down upon them and given the protection of soldiers who were finally close enough to the top of the walls to fire arrows back with a degree of effectiveness.

"I would not have believed this unless I had seen it for myself," Ben-Aryeh said, breaking the silence between them. "Indeed, that's the reason I'm here. Because I had to see it for myself."

Vitas had not yet spoken the obvious. Ben-Aryeh's wife was still in Jerusalem. If she was still alive. But he believed now was the time to broach the subject. "I will do everything in my power to help you find her," Vitas said. "And Titus himself will give us both assistance."

"I pray daily that she will be spared," Ben-Aryeh said. "As you know, I was not able to reach her by letter."

Ben-Aryeh had been unable to look for her himself. Not with three factions inside the city engaged in civil war behind the walls for the previous eighteen months.

"Soon enough," Vitas said, "the city will be in Roman hands. You will have every escort needed to search."

"That is not the primary reason I am here. I had to see for myself that Rome is on the verge of taking the city that all the world had once believed was impossible to conquer. And now that I have no doubt of its fate, I have no choice but to do what is necessary for my people."

Ben-Aryeh reached into his tunic and pulled out a small object. He handed it to Vitas, who stared at it in disbelief, recalling the words he'd heard just after being taken down from a cross in Caesarea.

"Wear this around your neck, and keep it safe. If someone comes to you with its twin, you will know that I have sent him. And when that person sees you with the same token, he will know you are the one to trust with the obligations put upon you. Until then, keep this portion of our conversation secret. From everyone. Not even Bernice or Titus or Ruso should know of it."

"I trust," Ben-Aryeh said, taking back the token, "that you have its twin?"

VESPERA

AFTER SLOWLY PICKING their way down the Mount of Olives in the deepening purple that settled on the valley, Vitas and Ben-Aryeh reached the outer wall of the Tenth Legion in near dark. Beyond the sentries, the lights of fires were plainly visible.

Vitas gave the day's password to the sentries, and Ben-Aryeh followed Vitas through the camp to a tent pitched at the center, near the general's tent that belonged to Titus.

A lone man—Joseph Ben-Matthias—sat near a small fire, gazing at the flames. He stood as soon as he recognized Vitas and Ben-Aryeh in the flickering light.

"Welcome back from exile," Ben-Matthias said, holding his arms out to embrace Ben-Aryeh. "I wish circumstances were different."

Vitas had had the half-hour journey down the mountain to absorb the knowledge that Ben-Aryeh held the other token, but that was all he knew about the situation. After showing the token to Vitas, Ben-Aryeh had refused to answer any other questions, stating the next discussions would take place only when they'd met with Ben-Matthias.

Jerusalem, Vitas had pondered in the silence of their trek, was not much different from Rome. At the top, those in power formed a small circle. He should not have been surprised that Ben-Aryeh, formerly among the high priests and a confidant of Bernice, had been the one chosen by Ben-Matthias, also among the high priests and also a confidant of Bernice.

Vitas, accordingly, had expected a cordial meeting between Ben-Aryeh and Ben-Matthias and had been looking forward to satisfying his curiosity about the strange tokens.

Instead, Ben-Aryeh's actions and answer to Ben-Matthias startled Vitas.

"I am only here because of these circumstances," Ben-Aryeh snapped with vehemence, refusing to step forward to accept Ben-Matthias's embrace. "The impossible is now possible. The Temple is in danger of falling to the Romans. Vitas is one of the few Romans I trust, and he has confirmed for me that the military situation demands final and desperate measures."

Ben-Aryeh gave a bitter laugh as he continued addressing Ben-Matthias. "You, on the other hand, don't seem to have any problems trusting the heathens. From prison to the emperor's most valued Jew. Life is more precious to you than honor?"

And Ben-Matthias's answer was equally startling to Vitas. "You self-righteous old Jew. I'm not the one who fled Jerusalem."

"Fled? You well know I'd been accused, falsely, of rape. Should a man accept that punishment?"

"If honor was so important, why not stay to protect it? Instead, all of Jerusalem now remembers you only for the crime you committed."

"The crime I was accused of committing," Ben-Aryeh said. "You know as well as I do that Annas needed me gone to grasp at the power he wanted."

"Does it matter to those still in the city whether you committed the crime? Perception is their reality. You fled. They assume you are guilty. And a coward."

"And they shout your name with adulation from the city walls as you parade back and forth with the Romans?" Ben-Aryeh sneered at Ben-Matthias. "Do you sleep well in camp, fed by the Romans like a lapdog?"

"And did you sleep well in the household of your Roman benefactor in Alexandria?"

Vitas finally stepped between them. "Let me tell you something about Vespasian."

They gave him silence to continue.

"Just before the revolt against Nero," Vitas said, "Vespasian had the city surrounded. He was urged to attack Jerusalem. His reply was that it was easier to let the Jews fight among themselves inside the city and do his work for him. Even after he withdrew because of the events in Rome, the Jews continued to fight. Watching just two of you together, I can now guess what it's like when there are thousands of you."

"How dare you—" Ben-Matthias began.

"You cannot speak to us like that," Ben-Aryeh said, interrupting. "Ben-Matthias comes from a distinguished family, and—"

"And Ben-Aryeh is known far and wide for his devotion to God," Ben-Matthias said.

Vitas held his ground. "There. You prove another point. Vespasian said that if he attacked Jerusalem, it would only serve to unite them against him. Like you two turning your anger upon me."

Silence. Some of the embers in the brazier crackled. Like the tension among all three men. Then Ben-Aryeh began to laugh. Ben-Matthias joined in, and the tension was broken.

When the laughter subsided, Ben-Matthias apologized to Ben-Aryeh. "My anger was misplaced. Yes, abuse is shouted at me from the walls of the city. A few weeks ago, a spear hit me in the shoulder. Too many believe I am a traitor, and you were the one I could lash out against. Let me tell you, at least, why I walk around the city every day with Titus."

"My own anger is not against you, either," Ben-Aryeh said. "Seeing the city and the earthworks and ramparts fills me with rage and frustration. You are an easier target than the soldiers."

Ben-Aryeh held out his arms, and they embraced for long moments.

"Perhaps a kiss or two while you are so close?" Vitas asked.

Ben-Aryeh pushed away and growled at Vitas. "Don't push it."

He turned to Ben-Matthias. "I had heard that after you were captured at Jotapata, Vespasian brought you forward, and you told him
of a prophecy—that he would be emperor."

"A cynic would think I was currying favor," Ben-Matthias said.
"But I did have the vision. He believed me because he learned that
well before Jotapata fell, I had predicted the siege would last forty-
seven days. And it had been correct."

"Still, he put you in chains."

"Two years," Ben-Matthias said.

Two years. After conquering Jotapata, Vespasian had easily taken
city after city, moving unobstructed to put his legions in place
around Jerusalem. He'd retreated with those legions when the first
news of impending civil war reached him.

With Nero's death, the head had been cut off the empire
that the Jews called the great beast. Galba had become emperor,
marching into Rome and parading Helius in chains before having him thrown into the Tiber. But Galba's arrogance and refusal
to pay his soldiers resulted in rebellion again, and Galba's reign
was short. He'd proven that emperors could be declared outside
of Rome, and the sword he'd used to take the throne was the
same sword that destroyed him. German legions proclaimed
Vitellius emperor. In Rome, Otho bribed the Praetorian Guard
to murder Galba, and the Senate proclaimed Otho emperor,
commissioning him to defeat the German legions and end the
civil war.

Instead, it had worsened. The great beast went into death
throes, as legions once used to defend the empire turned on each
other. The army of Vitellius won the battle, leading Otho to suicide. Vitellius now had the power to march on Rome, and the
Senate quickly recognized him as the new emperor.

Yet other legions refused to accept the Senate's decision, meaning the civil war had been on the verge of totally destroying the
empire. In Egypt and Syria, the legions favored Vespasian, who
had cautiously waited in Alexandria, effectively holding Rome's

grain supply hostage. The legions once loyal to Otho declared for Vespasian, who was reluctant to pit legions against legions.

This wisdom and caution saved the empire from destruction. Troops loyal to Vespasian caught and killed Vitellius, and Vespasian's popularity, strength, and reputation restored the peace. Vespasian remained in Rome and charged his son Titus to end the revolt in Judea.

"When the legions declared Vespasian emperor, he remembered my prediction," Ben-Matthias continued. "Titus pleaded my case before his father, and I was given freedom."

"Titus pleaded your case?" Ben-Aryeh asked. Then chuckled. "Or Queen Bernice?"

War, Vitas thought, was much more than military machines. War was about the generals who controlled the machines. While wars had been declared for practical purposes such as appropriating resources or defending borders, wars had also been declared by these men for other reasons: ego, passion, insults, or perceived insults.

The situation here reflected that reality. While Titus had the massive military power of Rome in his control, he was making some decisions because of the woman he loved. Bernice favored Ben-Matthias, and thus so did Titus.

"Given my freedom," Ben-Matthias answered, avoiding Ben-Aryeh's comment, "I returned to giving the same counsel to our people that I had from the beginning. You'll recall at the beginning of the revolt, I took the stand that it was useless to fight Rome. It's even more apparent now. Yes, I stand by the side of Titus. But it is simply to plead for our people and Jerusalem. Ask anyone. Titus has repeatedly offered generous terms of surrender. But within the city, there are those who continuously give prophecies that God will save the Jews because he has promised us the Messiah. My own mother is in a prison inside the city; I implore the people to live at peace with Rome."

"'People will see the Son of Man coming in clouds with

great power and glory,'" Ben-Aryeh said. He paused, knowing Ben-Matthias understood the significance. "I am coming closer and closer to believing that perhaps the Nazarene was the Messiah. He called down this punishment on Jerusalem the night he was condemned."

"Some might say," Ben-Matthias replied, "it was easy to predict that the arrogance and hard-heartedness of the religious leaders would eventually bring down the wrath of Rome."

"But to see Jerusalem actually fall," Ben-Aryeh countered. "The walls, the water, the food. Tiny Jotapata withstood three legions for forty-seven days. Jerusalem should have lasted a decade. Could any man have foreseen that civil war inside the city would result in one faction burning the food supply to starve out the other?"

Ben-Matthias spoke quietly. "I will make no judgment on this, but Titus has told me privately that he believes the Romans have had divine help to bring Jerusalem to the edge of destruction."

"That's what I fear most," Ben-Aryeh said. "And that's why I'm here."

"I was wondering," Ben-Matthias said. "I knew you wouldn't tell me until you were ready."

Without further words, Ben-Aryeh held out the token for Ben-Matthias. The younger Jew squatted at the fire to examine it.

"You?" Ben-Matthias said to Ben-Aryeh. "You are the one behind the messages?"

And once again, Vitas was surprised, for he assumed Ben-Aryeh had been sent to him by Ben-Matthias.

"I," Ben-Aryeh said. "And those with me who feared that someday Jerusalem might fall."

"Finally I can learn what this is all about," Ben-Matthias said.

Vitas absorbed this and the implications. Ben-Aryeh did not serve Ben-Matthias. Instead, Ben-Matthias served Ben-Aryeh, and Ben-Matthias was as unaware of the reasons as Vitas was.

This was confirmed immediately as the older Jew answered the younger one.

"No," Ben-Aryeh replied. "Too much is at stake for you to ever know more than you already do. Instead, I expect that you will give me your full loyalty and all the help that I require to get back into the city. Without any questions about my purpose."

Ben-Aryeh turned to Vitas. "And you, my friend, will have an opportunity to search inside for your brother if you give the same loyalty and help."

⚜ JUPITER ⚜

HORA PRIMA

"I'M TIRED OF ALL THIS DEATH." Titus pinched the bridge of his nose between thumb and forefinger for a few seconds, but a pained expression remained on his face. "Last night, about two thousand women and children and old men were killed. It's like their own God is punishing them in the worst way possible."

Although Mount Olivet kept the camp in the shadow of the sun's first rising, dawn's early light spread fingers of pink clouds above them. Vitas stood at ease in front of Titus, as was usual each day, for Titus liked having a person he could trust for honest opinions.

"I am as tired of death as you are," Vitas said. "The smell of it hangs over the city like a cloud. But if they won't surrender, we can't prevent them from killing themselves."

"The two thousand did not die in the city," Titus said. "Our own men—Arabians and Syrians—were responsible."

Titus rubbed his face with both hands. He sighed. "You know I've made it a policy that any deserters who are not fighters may slip past our walls."

Vitas nodded. Famine was sending them out in droves. They risked their lives to escape Jerusalem and flee through the open zone to the Roman walls that surrounded the city, for Jewish defenders would try to kill them for deserting.

Once through the Roman enclosure, they were provided food. Some of them, unable to restrain themselves, took in food so quickly that their near-starved bodies and tightened bellies did not survive.

"I'm told that some of the Syrians noticed an old woman digging through her own excrement," Titus continued. "They realized she was looking for gold coins she had swallowed for safety before leaving Jerusalem."

Vitas rubbed his own face. He could guess what happened next, and Titus confirmed it.

"Word immediately went through the other camps that every Jew was full of gold. The Syrians and Arabians have a natural enmity for the Jews, and they spent the entire night killing them and slitting their bellies open to search for more gold."

Vitas groaned.

"Unfortunately, Rome will take the blame for this," Titus said. "What I would like to do is surround those Syrians and Arabians with horses, then shoot them dead with arrows. But there are too many of them. We'd end up warring among ourselves, and at this point in the siege, that would do me more harm than good. I see no choice but to put practicality over justice."

"By choosing practicality, you are also choosing a different justice," Vitas said. "The longer the siege continues, the more women and children will die. The sooner you get through the walls and destroy the fighting force inside, the more women and children you will spare. Thus, you bring justice to those still alive. Anyone would understand that. Bernice included."

"I do not make my decisions based on keeping her happy," Titus snapped.

"Don't fool yourself." Vitas knew that Titus intended to return to Rome with Bernice and marry her. "You are also motivated by a promise to help her people where possible."

"I am motivated by the realization that Rome functions by destroying enemies and helping allies. When this war is over, we still want taxes from Judea."

"That rationalization will sound good in Rome when you return for a triumph."

Titus suddenly grinned. "Trust me, that's not what I tell Bernice."

The grin just as quickly disappeared. "But this problem is bigger than the slaughter of women and children. Right?"

"If you continue to let any segment of your army loot and plunder at will, you risk losing your authority."

"Exactly."

"Are you asking my advice?"

Titus nodded.

"I will answer you as a soldier, but keep in mind, I am also a brother to a man who may still be alive inside the city," Vitas said. "So I have a personal stake here."

Once again, Titus nodded.

"Call the auxiliary commanders together and tell them that Rome will not permit a foreign army to indulge in unauthorized looting," Vitas said. "Warn them that anyone who does so again will be executed. Send our soldiers among the Syrians and Arabians to confiscate the gold. They will fight us to protect their lives, but they won't risk death to protect gold, especially if they are promised a fair share in the gold from Jerusalem when it falls. You keep peace among all the armies here, and your authority is not compromised."

"Wise words," Titus said. "Thank you."

"You won't consider me wise when I make a request. I'd like permission to enter the city."

"That's not unreasonable," Titus told him. "In a day or two, we'll break through the first wall. I can give you an escort."

"I don't want to wait," Vitas said. "I need to get in before your soldiers. If Damian is alive . . ."

"You have lost your sanity," Titus said. "Every male over the age of fifteen in that city is armed and ready to kill any foreigners. Allowing you inside too early is like sending you to your death."

Any other man would have decided not to argue. Titus, after all, was the son of the emperor. But they were friends first, soldiers second, and Vitas knew that Titus would not consider him insubordinate for arguing. "As you know, I am obligated to Ben-Aryeh for protecting Sophia. Ben-Aryeh's wife is in the city. Ben-Aryeh wants my help to get inside. In return, he can keep me safe. He is a man of great influence among the Jews of Jerusalem."

Titus shook his head. "No. I'm not going to give you permission."

Vitas nodded. "Anything else to discuss?"

"No," Titus said.

Vitas turned to walk out of the tent.

"Wait," Titus said. Vitas stopped and looked at his friend. "You'll go anyway, won't you?"

"That would be insubordination."

"That's a truthful response, but it doesn't answer my question."

Vitas kept a level gaze on his friend.

"I've put you in the position of choosing between serving one obligation to me and another obligation to Ben-Aryeh," Titus said. "Am I reading this correctly?"

"Yes."

Titus repeated his earlier gesture of pinching the bridge of his nose between thumb and forefinger. He closed his eyes and did not open them as he spoke.

"Today, I make one final offer for surrender," Titus said. "I'd like you to accompany me. I believe what the Jews hear will be enough to get them to accept surrender."

"You've offered it before to no avail. Even with the city racked by famine."

Titus opened his eyes. "What drives these people, Vitas? I'll tell you. Worship of their God. And the most sacred object in the world to them is the Temple, where their God resides. Every one of them—soldier or not—will fight to the death to protect their Temple. Today, I will tell them what they want to hear. I expect by tomorrow we will have peace, and then you can move through the city freely, with an escort of soldiers."

"If today's offer fails?"

"Tomorrow is the day that I begin the final push to break through the Antonia's wall. That should draw the bulk of Jerusalem's fighters to the ramparts and provide enough of a distraction for you and Ben-Aryeh to get inside unnoticed. I will expect help from Ben-Aryeh later, in return."

"Thank you."

"That decision was made for my benefit," Titus rejoined. There was no hint of a smile. "You and I have been through too much together. I don't ever want to have to choose between duty to Rome and executing you."

HORA SECUNDA

VITAS FOUND BEN-ARYEH at the tent they now shared. Ben-Aryeh was on his knees, his head bowed in prayer.

Vitas retreated to give his friend privacy. Through worship and sacrifices, the Romans did their best to make their gods serve them. He'd learned from Sophia and Ben-Aryeh that for the Jews, it was the opposite: their worship was because their one and true God was worthy of it.

There were moments—many of them—when Vitas wanted to surrender himself to the same worship, to the same sense that an invisible and all-powerful God was in control not only of mankind's destiny, but of each man's destiny. He was too much a Roman to believe without sufficient evidence, however, and every time his heart came close to this surrender, his intellect demanded proof.

Vitas returned about ten minutes later to find Ben-Aryeh standing outside, staring sightlessly at the rocks atop Mount Olivet.

Tears streamed down the older man's face.

Ben-Aryeh did not turn to Vitas as he spoke. "While you were gone, Ben-Matthias told me enough so that I truly understand how bad it has become for our people. I don't want to believe what he relayed to me. A hundred and fifteen thousand?"

A week earlier, reports had come to Titus that this was the total of the dead carried through the gate. The dead bodies of the poor had been laid in heaps in large houses. Other bodies were simply thrown over the city walls into the valleys, in such numbers that in Titus's rounds along the valleys, he had groaned and spread his hands skyward, calling to God to witness that this was not Titus's doing. War and death Titus had seen in plentitude, but this was so tragic that even an experienced general like him felt anguish.

Vitas knelt and took some dust from the ground. He threw it upward and watched as the breeze took it away. The wind was coming from the west, over the city and toward the Mount of Olives.

"I have a vial of oil of myrrh," Vitas said. This was common, and many soldiers used it as a salve on light wounds. "My advice is to rub some of it on a cloth and keep it nearby to hold over your face if the wind continues to blow in this direction."

"A hundred and fifteen thousand?"

"You will be grateful for the myrrh," Vitas said. "All of those dead and more. As the heat strikes the dead, the stench is almost unbearable."

✦ ✦ ✦

Later that morning, Vitas rode at a stately walk alongside Ben-Matthias and Titus, who'd had a black stallion saddled.

They were near the bottom of the valley and had to look upward at the walls of Jerusalem. The sun was high enough now that when Vitas turned his eyes toward the Temple, it seemed to burn. The outward facing of the Temple was covered with burnished plates of gold, and the fiery splendor glimmered like a mirage but was far too painful on the eyes for more than momentary admiration. Later, when the sun's angle shifted, it would no longer be like staring directly into the sun, but still so breathtakingly beautiful that often a man looked away for fear of being hypnotized.

The soldiers had begun their day's activities, and the sounds only served to remind Vitas of the fate of this beautiful city and the hundreds of thousands still behind the walls.

The methodical windings of the *ballistae*—the great catapults—prepared for the daily barrage of stones sometimes double the weight of a man's body. The *doctores ballistarum*—the commanders of the weapons—would take pride in their ability to aim and pick off single defenders. The whirring sound of the stones struck terror into all who heard, each stone chiseled to make it as round as possible.

In the weeks earlier, the Roman soldiers had realized the brightness of the stones made them as obvious as hail. Watchmen in Jerusalem would see the stones against the sky and call warning. Now the stones were painted black and were devastatingly effective.

The monotonous thumping of the siege engines began to form the rhythm of a heartbeat, a sound that never failed to chill Vitas. Not only did the *arietes*—battering rams—break down walls, but morale. Roman law dictated that defenders could surrender and be given full rights, until the moment before the first ram touched the wall.

Each ram was protected by a *testudo*—tortoise—with a steeply angled roof so that any objects hurled upon it simply slid down the sides. It was covered with uncured hides, and fiery oil flung upon it would slide to the ground before the flames could get through. As for the beam beneath, it was drawn back by dozens of men, who then pushed it forward in unison, letting go just before the iron head made impact with the wall. Not once in Roman history had any wall survived repeated blows, and often, in Vitas's experience, a thick stone wall would collapse at the first blow.

Here, Titus had needed to send tens of thousands of men to bring in dirt and stone from dozens of miles away, just to be able to fill the valleys with earthworks. At the same time, Titus had sent thousands more men to dig beneath the city walls. The tunnels were filled with wood and resin and sulfur, then lit so the fire would undermine the walls even further.

And behind all of these engines were the dreaded *scorpiones*, crossbow devices smaller than the ballistae, firing arrows capable of piercing any armor.

Day after day for weeks now, these tens of thousands of disciplined men had steadily applied pressure on Jerusalem.

What had once been the immovable object was finally about to give way to the irresistible force.

HORA OCTAVA

FOR THE NEXT HOUR, Ben-Matthias and Vitas remained with
Titus, who rode from camp to camp, giving instructions. No clouds
weakened the sun's heat, and Vitas was grateful for the skins of water
they carried.

They completed the entire circumference of the Roman wall,
staying out of range of arrows or stones. It was a grim ride for Vitas.
Many of the bodies thrown down from the Jerusalem walls had
begun to putrefy. He tried not to imagine what it was like within
the city among the gaunt and starving. He tried not to imagine the
horrors that Damian faced, if his brother was still alive.

As they returned to the Mount of Olives, Titus rode to a position
directly opposite the Temple Mount and looked upward, remaining
on horseback. Vitas and Ben-Matthias flanked him on their horses.

Immediately defenders on the walls jeered and hurled rocks and
debris, all of it falling short of Titus. His safe position had been easy
to choose, for the perimeter was well established by previous detri-
tus already scattered in front of him.

Titus continued to gaze imperiously upward, saying nothing. He
remained immobile in the heat, until his inaction drew the curiosity
of the Jewish defenders, and this curiosity, in turn, silenced them.

Only then, with their full attention on him, did Titus raise his
right arm.

Because each of his auxiliary commanders had been instructed to watch for that signal, all movement on the Roman side stopped—the winching of the ballistae, the battering of the arietes, the constant rain of arrows from the scorpiones.

Except for the squawking of vultures among the bodies between Jerusalem and Titus, silence descended on the valley.

Titus dropped his arm, but he continued to gaze upward with no expression on his face.

Within minutes, more faces appeared above him at the walls of Jerusalem. Citizens had been drawn forward by the silence after weeks and weeks of the constant sound of warfare.

Still, Titus said nothing.

And minutes after that, a new sound broke into the silence. A distant but constant sound, unidentifiable at first, but slowly growing in volume.

Vitas knew what the sound was. He'd been prepared for it because he'd been alongside Titus as the general gave his instructions. Even so, the eeriness gave him shivers.

He expected it was a sound no person here had ever experienced—the sound of feet against ground, sandals against rock and pebble, as thousands and thousands of soldiers marched in unison, not one man uttering a single word.

Titus had given very clear instructions. He wanted the entire Roman army to assemble along the Mount of Olives, behind the Roman wall—safe from any attack by Jewish defenders but clearly visible to all in Jerusalem.

It took nearly an hour for every Roman soldier in all the legions to gather on the slope of the Mount of Olives. In that hour, no man spoke. In that hour, more and more citizens within Jerusalem moved to the secure walls above the valley, staring down at the spectacle of power.

When it was complete, more than sixty thousand soldiers, all in armor, all carrying weapons, spread across the hillside, hundreds of men deep, hundreds of men wide.

The entire time, Titus did not move but held his gaze upward.

A messenger ran up to Titus's horse and said a single word. "Ready."

Titus raised his arm again. Every soldier, in unison, shouted three Latin words, repeating them again and again and again.

"Veni, vidi, vaporavi. Veni, vidi, vaporavi. Veni, vidi, vaporavi. Veni, vidi, vaporavi."

I came, I saw, I burned.

The words rolled like thunder through the valley, echoing as they bounced off the smooth city walls and back at the soldiers.

I came, I saw, I burned.

Never had Vitas been assailed by such a mighty noise. It continued for ten minutes as Titus held his arm in the air.

I came, I saw, I burned.

Then Titus dropped his arm, and instantly the shouting ceased.

His plan had been to put on display the entire might arrayed against the people of the city, to let them see that Rome would not and could not be stopped.

Such was the effect of the renewed silence that when Titus addressed the thousands of people on the wall above him, his voice carried clearly across the steep valley.

"I am Titus, heir to the throne of Rome, the right hand of my father, who has commanded me to put an end to this rebellion. I freely acknowledge that your God is a mighty God and that his house, your Temple, is the most holy sanctuary. Neither my father nor I, when I someday inherit the throne, will ever attempt to desecrate this holy place."

Titus drew a breath. "In front of your God and all of us assembled, I pledge that I will protect the holy house of your God with all my power. You should now see that it is inevitable that your city will fall if you do not surrender, yet I do not want to burn your city. John of Gischala, I appeal to you."

As Titus had expected, jeering and catcalls began from some of the Jewish defenders.

He raised his arm again, and the soldiers behind him began to shout once more.

I came, I saw, I burned. I came, I saw, I burned. I came, I saw, I burned.

Titus dropped his hand, and the shouting stopped.

Before he could speak again, jeering began immediately. Titus responded by raising his arm, and the thunderous noise again overwhelmed any catcalls from the Jewish defenders.

I came, I saw, I burned. I came, I saw, I burned. I came, I saw, I burned.

This time, when he dropped his arm, none above him interrupted.

Titus began to speak, knowing he would be clearly heard. "As for the Zealots among you, why do you pollute this holy house with the blood both of foreigners and Jews? Why do you yourself allow the abomination and desolation in the holy Temple of your God?

"I appeal to the gods of my own country," Titus continued, "and to every god that ever had any regard to this place. I also appeal to my own army, to those Jews who are now with me, and even to you yourselves, that I do not force you to defile this sanctuary. Citizens, now is the time to surrender to save your holy Temple. If you do not surrender, I promise you this."

He paused, but no jeers broke his pause. If the citizens of Jerusalem expected further threats, Titus surprised them.

"My legions have the power to break through the Antonia tower at any moment, but I promise if you move the place of fighting away from your holy sanctuary, no Roman shall go near it or offer any affront to it. No! I will endeavor to preserve your holy house, whether you will or will not surrender. Let us not battle in the holy place."

Titus nodded at Ben-Matthias. Word for word, Ben-Matthias translated into Aramaic the promise Titus had made so that every citizen understood.

Ben-Matthias added his own words too, pleading with his people, telling them that was how Titus intended to secure the peace. If they battled because of their God, he would not make it a battle any longer. They were starving to the point of death, and the wall to Antonia would fall in days, if not hours. Could they not see that fighting Rome was useless? And if Rome promised them the Temple would be secure forever, was that not enough of a victory? The women and children would be allowed safety and the military men sent to Rome as part of a triumph. Was this not better than the surety that nearly all would die without surrender? And he exhorted them to remember that Caesar would preserve the Temple and give the Jews the freedom to worship as God intended.

Vitas, like Titus, believed this might be enough to avert full-scale tragedy. If the soldiers struck, blood would flow, as the saying went, to the height of a horse's bridle at the death of thousands upon thousands by the sword. By promising them the Temple, how could they not accept his terms?

A man stepped forward on the wall and held up his own hand as if he had the power of Caesar.

It was an obvious mockery of Titus, who could have silenced the man with the renewed shouting of all his soldiers. Instead, Titus ignored the insult and let the man speak.

"We have been promised a Messiah, and God is faithful to his people," the man shouted. He was John of Gischala, as recognizable as Titus, large and bearded, exuding the strength and ferocity of a bear.

"You speak as if you have power, and you assemble your men as if you can destroy the Temple, but God would preserve us even if your army were a hundredfold its current size." John of Gischala held a spear and waved it as he spoke. "You ask us to move our fight away from the Temple, but that is because you know that the Temple will protect us and that your only hope of victory is if we give up the Temple. I say this in front of God and in front of man: by offering to fight anywhere but the Temple, you expose your fear of defeat. My promise to you is this. If you bring your fight to the Temple, the one and only God will strike you down and send you away, just as he defeated a hundred thousand Assyrians to preserve his people. Return to Rome, and leave us with the land God gave us."

With a final act of defiance, John of Gischala hurled the spear toward Titus. It landed well short and stuck hard in the ground.

Even before it stopped quivering, Titus had turned his horse to ride away.

HORA DUODECIMA

"TOMORROW, WITH THE blessing of Titus, Vitas and I go into the city," Ben-Aryeh said to Ben-Matthias. "I am not naive enough to believe that it will be entirely successful. I don't want to be dramatic, but I want to thank you both for your help in all of this."

"You have nothing to thank me for," Vitas growled. "You are giving me a chance to see if my brother is still alive, something not even the mighty Titus is capable of doing."

The three of them were at a fire in the camp of the Tenth Legion, eating drumsticks of chicken. At each meal, Vitas could not help but think of the hundreds of thousands trapped in Jerusalem, starving, perhaps with Damian among them. And at each meal, Vitas thought of the many times Titus had implored them to work out terms of surrender so the women and children would be spared.

"Thank me by finally telling me the reasons that I have helped," Ben-Matthias answered. "I am a man of great curiosity, and I began writing about the war during my time in prison, as I intend to chronicle it for future generations. I promise whatever you tell me won't be revealed until the need for secrecy is long gone. I also promise you will be portrayed in a flattering, heroic manner, unlike Simon Ben-Gioras and John of Gischala, who are directly responsible for this horror."

"I am going to ask you the fates of twenty prominent men in Jerusalem," Ben-Aryeh said in response. "I want to know if they are alive and, if so, among the moderates or the Zealots."

"Then you will answer me?"

Ben-Aryeh gave Ben-Matthias a name instead of responding to that question. "Annas."

This was the name of the priest who had threatened to execute Ben-Aryeh for false charges of rape, causing Ben-Aryeh to flee Jerusalem with Vitas.

"Dead," Ben-Matthias said. "Executed by John of Gischala."

"Eleazar."

"Dead. Executed by Simon Ben-Gioras."

When Ben-Aryeh finished his list of names, he learned that most had been killed. Two were moderates. Two were Zealots.

"Now," Ben-Matthias said, "you'll tell me what brings you here and why it was so important that Bernice and Titus protect Vitas on your behalf? Was it a conspiracy that involved all those men?"

"Some whom I asked about were involved," Ben-Aryeh said. "I added other names so that you will never know which were involved and which were not, but I had to know if the few are still alive."

"I trust the ones you need are not dead."

"You will get no answer from me in that regard. Let me simply say that these men have been called to a duty that goes back genera-tions and is of utmost importance to our people. Vitas was chosen by these men and will learn his role tomorrow."

"What!" Vitas was startled. Chosen? By a secret circle of Jews he did not know?

The old man rubbed his face, then gave a weary smile. "My friend, I have borne much guilt over these last few years, hiding from you that I am, in a sense, an infiltrator."

"Our friendship has been false?"

"No," Ben-Aryeh said. "Otherwise, I would not carry the bur-den of guilt. Otherwise, I would not be making this confession now, asking forgiveness."

"You protected Sophia and brought her back to me. Don't ask forgiveness."

"I must. From the beginning, once I learned who you are and

of your love for Sophia, I realized you were the one person who could help should this day ever arrive, with the fall of Jerusalem so imminent."

"Then explain," Vitas said.

"You were chosen because you are a Roman with influence and a man the Jews can trust. I was given the task of becoming close to you. At first, it was a role, gladly accepted because of how it might help my people. But I have come to love you as a father loves a son."

"Forgiven," Vitas said softly.

"If I die tomorrow," Ben-Aryeh said, "I die in peace. Thank you."

"Let's not die," Vitas said lightly, looking for a way to break the mood. "Instead, tell me more about why we enter the city."

"Aside from my promise to help you look for Damian," Ben-Aryeh said, "I must keep my silence."

"Surely," Ben-Matthias protested, "you can tell more than that? If it is this important that you enter the city while it is on the verge of destruction, then it is important enough for future generations of Jews to know."

"I promise you it truly is this important," Ben-Aryeh said with finality. "And such is the importance that it must never be known to history."

❖ VENUS ❖

HORA PRIMA

THE ROMANS HAD long conquered the outer walls of the northern part of the city, moved into the suburbs, and gathered assaults at the base of the Antonia tower at the corner of the Temple Mount.

It was all that stood between Rome and the Temple itself.

At dawn, under a sky streaked with red, Titus stood on a hastily constructed platform and addressed the legions. They were men in polished breastplates that reflected the reddish gleam in the sky, men with spears and swords, standing in organized columns, utterly silent, as not a single man shifted from one hobnailed boot to another.

"Fellow soldiers," Titus began. It was said that a commander needed more than a grasp of military strategy to succeed. He also needed to be a skilled orator, one who knew not only how to assemble words but how to project them. The great Greek orator Demosthenes, as legend had it, practiced his speeches by delivering them with pebbles in his mouth, at the waves of the sea to be heard above the water. Skilled orators learned to speak above the disrespectful crowds at the forum; here, Titus had the focused attention of every man, and his words carried clearly. Vitas sat on the back of a donkey at the rear of all the massed soldiers and heard his friend Titus as well as if they were having a conversation in a quiet courtyard.

"I am fully of the same opinion as you," Titus said, "that it is a difficult task to go up this wall. But it is proper that those who

268 THE LAST TEMPLE

desire reputation for their valor should struggle with difficulties like this, and I have particularly shown that it is a brave thing to die with glory."

Titus scanned all the soldiers to see the impact of his words. When command of a legion was a political appointment only, oration like this was hollow. But Titus was a fighting man, and every soldier knew it. They would die for him because they knew he would die for them.

"Listen as I say this. The courage here necessary shall not go unrewarded for those who first begin the attempt."

Those words reverberated. Titus truly was a good orator. He did not speak until he knew every soldier had absorbed his promise. The Temple held untold riches. Titus would share the spoils according to each man's bravery.

"It is unbecoming to you—who are Romans and my soldiers, who have in peace been taught how to make wars, and who have also been used to conquer in those wars—to be inferior to Jews, either in action of the hand or in courage of the soul," Titus said.

Vitas smiled. Titus had offered the carrot first, and now he was showing the stick.

"And this especially when you are at the conclusion of your victory," Titus continued, "and are assisted by God himself. Our misfortunes have been owing to the madness of the Jews, while their sufferings have been owing to your valor and to the assistance God has afforded you. The seditions they have faced, the famine they are under, the siege they now endure, and the fall of their walls to our engines—what can they all be but demonstrations of God's anger against them, and of his assistance on our behalf? If we go up to this tower of Antonia, we gain the city." Titus let excitement and fervor build in his voice. "Pull up your courage, set about this work, and mutually encourage and assist one another—and your bravery will soon break the hearts of your enemies."

He drew a breath and raised a fist to the sky. "As for that person who first mounts the wall, I should blush for shame if I did not make him the envy of others by those rewards I will bestow upon him. If such a one escape with his life, he shall have the command of others who are now his equals. Step forward and be that man!"

Titus surveyed the soldiers.

Collectively, the soldiers seemed to hold their breath. And then movement. One man strode down the line between the columns and stood in front of Titus.

"Who are you?" Titus asked.

"I am Sabinus. Syrian by birth."

From the vantage point of the donkey's back, Vitas had a good view of the Syrian. His color was black, and he was lean and thin. At first glance, he appeared too small and too weak to be a soldier of any measure. But he stood with his back arched and his chest forward and spoke with a fervor that made it clear Titus had inspired him.

"I readily surrender myself up to you, General," Sabinus said. "I will first ascend the wall, and I heartily wish that my fortune may follow my courage and my resolution. And if some ill fortune deny me the success of my undertaking, remember that I choose death voluntarily for your sake."

He made a fist and touched his chest above his heart as he said this. Titus made the same gesture, and as if in a single voice, every soldier in the army roared.

Sabinus spread his shield over his head with his left hand and, with his right hand, drew his sword. He began to march up to the wall, and eleven others fell in behind him.

Titus motioned the commanders to hold back the other soldiers.

As the twelve men approached Antonia, Jewish defenders started hurling rocks and rolling stones. Some of the eleven fell, but Sabinus seemed to emerge unscathed from the hailstorm as he dashed up the ramp and clawed to the top.

The Jewish defenders, in apparent astonishment at his bravery, allowed him to stand at the top of the wall, and without hesitation, Sabinus pressed the attack with his sword. Sabinus stumbled, but even then, on his knees and covering himself with his shield, he lashed out at the men who surrounded him.

That was when Titus waved his commanders to send their men forward.

The soldiers roared again in one voice. It felt to Vitas like the rumble of thunder.

And the battle began.

✛ ✛ ✛

Leaving the battle well behind them, as planned, Vitas and Ben-Aryeh led a convoy of twenty soldiers and camels south through the Kidron Valley below the Temple Mount on the east side of Jerusalem. They kept close to the outer Roman wall, passing beneath the watchful eyes of soldiers in the staggered garrisons along that perimeter. Titus had not committed all his men to the battle; others were needed to keep the Jewish defenders penned.

While Vitas and Ben-Aryeh were far enough from the walls of the city to be safe, it was an unnecessary precaution; the defenders had left their posts for a last stand to keep Antonia out of the hands of the Romans.

In less than half an hour, moving parallel to the lower city, they reached the southeast corner of the city. The wall turned at nearly ninety degrees, and they followed it, moving directly west. Another half hour at a slow and steady upward climb took them to the southwest corner of the city, and they turned again, heading north along the walls, with the upper city now on their right. The outline of three towers farther up the wall cut cleanly against the sky. They were the towers that overlooked Herod's palace—Phasael, Hippicus, and Mariamne.

These were monstrous fortifications within the city, for in Herod's lifetime, as a king put in place by Rome, he had always needed to keep a wary eye against revolt from his own people. Now, the fortifications had served to protect the moderates and Simon Ben-Gioras, who had held the upper city in their battles against John of Gischala and his Zealots.

With the towers in sight, Vitas again wondered how they would enter the city.

✛ ✛ ✛

At the wall at the base of the Phasael tower, Ben-Aryeh held a shofar in his hands. Made of a ram's horn, it was traditionally used by priests to sound alarm or call a congregation to worship.

Ben-Aryeh blew three times through the ram's horn, paused, then three more times.

Vitas kept his gaze upward. Solid stone blocks extended so far above him that he had to tilt his head as far back as possible to see the top of the Phasael tower. It was square with ornate ramparts; the tower continued rising above the ramparts with rectangular openings just below the roof.

Again, Ben-Aryeh blew through the ram's horn, keeping the same pattern.

Behind Vitas, two hundred steps away from the wall and well out of range of anything that might be flung at them, the soldiers watched impassively. They had been given simple orders. Remain in place with the camels until ordered otherwise by the authority of Vitas or Titus. These were older soldiers, not motivated by dreams of glory. Vitas guessed they were content not to be in the forefront of battle at Antonia.

For a third time, Ben-Aryeh blew the horn, then watched expectantly.

Vitas wasn't surprised to see motion far above him—two men leaning out from one of the rectangular openings of the tower. Nor was he surprised when he realized they had begun to lower a knotted rope down the tower wall. Short of tunneling beneath the walls, the only way into the city was by climbing. He certainly wasn't surprised that the horn had called them to action, for the scenario had obviously been prearranged.

What did make him curious, however, was how they had known to expect Ben-Aryeh and what the arrangements were, for Ben-Aryeh would not have been able to get a message of any kind into the city.

Vitas knew better than to ask Ben-Aryeh, for the older man had made it clear he wasn't revealing anything until the moment any new information for Vitas was necessary.

Instead, when the bottom of the rope touched the ground, he began to climb into a city of Zealots ready to tear apart any Roman on sight.

HORA SECUNDA

FOR THE NEXT FIFTEEN MINUTES, Vitas wondered if each breath would be his last. He was exposed on the wall and a very slow-moving target. He kept waiting for a cry of alarm from somewhere along the ramparts, followed by a barrage of arrows.

Each time he looked down, Ben-Aryeh's head was just below his feet. More than once, he felt the man's hand brush against a heel. He was impressed at the older man's strength, and that spurred Vitas to climb faster, knot by solid knot.

Soon, though, Vitas stopped looking down. The height began to dizzy him, and he focused on the sensation of rough hemp against his palms and the burning in his biceps from pulling upward.

Near the top, Vitas was gasping with exhaustion, his face and forearms dripping with sweat. If he hadn't been able to support much of his body weight on the succession of thick knots in the rope, he doubted he would have made it.

When he reached the opening, men grabbed him with secure grips just below his armpits and hauled him into the coolness of the tower.

The room was a square, about ten steps wide and ten steps long. The rectangular openings gave plenty of light, but there was nothing to see inside the room. It was bare.

Vitas noted this as he was drawing deep breaths and trying to recover. Seconds later, the two men pulled Ben-Aryeh inside. They immediately began to pull up the rope, coiling it at their feet.

"Your strength put me to shame," Vitas told Ben-Aryeh, almost euphoric at surviving and glad to be in a position to joke about it. "I'm twenty years younger, but it was like you were trying to pass me as we climbed."

"Not strength," Ben-Aryeh croaked. "Terror."

Ben-Aryeh dropped to his knees and kissed the stone floor.

The two young men who had helped them into the small, bare room at the top of the tower were bearded, but even the facial hair wasn't enough to totally conceal the gauntness of their faces.

Vitas had been wondering about the sack that Ben-Aryeh had insisted on carrying over his shoulder, and his curiosity was answered almost immediately.

"Thank you," Ben-Aryeh said when he stood again. "I'm aware that you've risked your lives to help."

He reached into the sack and pulled out a loaf of bread and some cheese wrapped in a cloth. Both men stared at the food, almost in awe. Ben-Aryeh extended it to them, and one took the offering with trembling hands. Instead of immediately eating, however, he handed the bread and cheese to his companion and said, "It must be shared."

The second one nodded. Neither spoke as they moved toward the thick wooden door.

Vitas took a step to follow, but Ben-Aryeh put a warning hand on his arm, and Vitas remained.

Both men left, and Vitas heard the door lock behind them.

They were now prisoners.

"Your trust is important," Ben-Aryeh said.

"I'd rather know what is ahead of us."

"One thing at a time. I've told you that repeatedly."

"Then at least answer this," Vitas said. "How did they know to be waiting with a rope?"

Ben-Aryeh led Vitas to the opposite side of the tower. Because the tower was at the top edge of the city, the view east through the opening would have been breathtaking under any other circumstances. To the right were the expansive grounds of Herod's palace. There the Christos had been taken to face a jesting Herod during his trials before crucifixion.

Down the slope of the upper city were the mansions of the nobles, including the estate where Ben-Aryeh had lived in luxury before the false claims of rape had driven him away. Vitas remembered from his visit four years earlier that the gardens had been lush and the walls of the estates pristine and white. Now, burn marks scorched the walls, and the vegetation had been devastated by people desperate from famine.

Directly opposite, at the far end of the city, where the land rose again for the Temple Mount, white smoke rose in a straight line, mixed with dark plumes. The wood around Antonia was burning, tainted by the oil used to keep the flames as intense as possible.

Vitas now understood why the sounds of Ben-Aryeh's shofar had drawn no attention.

Below and outside of the city, the massive walls of Jerusalem had shielded him from the sound of the fighting at Antonia. Up here in the tower, the shrieks and screams and wails carried clearly. All attention in the city was focused on the battle that might continue for hours. Only someone listening for the shofar would have noticed.

Which was the question Vitas wanted answered.

"Look," Ben-Aryeh said, pointing at the top of the Mount of Olives, beyond the Temple.

Even at this distance, Vitas saw what Ben-Aryeh meant.

The top of a group of olive trees was swathed in white.

"Cloth?" Vitas asked.

"That was the signal to have someone waiting," Ben-Aryeh said.

Vitas squinted. Lost in puzzlement, the sounds of battle faded for him.

"You had no way of getting a message into the city," he told Ben-Aryeh.

"Not recently," the older man said. "This was arranged long ago."

Vitas cocked his head. "Am I to understand that for months, someone has been looking out every day at the Mount of Olives for that very signal?"

"No," Ben-Aryeh said. "Years."

The implications whirled through Vitas's mind, but he didn't have a chance to voice them.

There was a sound of a key turning in the lock.

"Give me a reason to trust you," a man said upon entering the room. He pulled the door shut, and someone outside locked it behind him.

Roughly Vitas's age, the man had a crescent-shaped scar on top of his left cheekbone, above a sparse beard. He was unarmed but stared at them with unnatural ferocity.

"No," Ben-Aryeh said. "Give me a reason to trust you."

The man barked out the semblance of a laugh. "All right then. I'll first tell you who I am. Simon Ben-Gioras."

Ben-Aryeh spit.

It didn't seem to offend Ben-Gioras, who barked his attempt at laughter again. "I see you know of me. I'm the one who captured and killed and tortured hundreds until my wife was released to me. And I'm the one who saved the upper city from destruction."

Vitas knew the story. When Roman troops first marched to Jerusalem four years earlier, Ben-Gioras, little more than a highway robber, had assembled men and helped defeat the Roman advance by attacking from behind and taking many of the beasts that carried their weapons, boosting his ragged army even more. But the Jerusalem authorities had rejected him. He was too popular as the leader of a rebellious peasantry consisting of bandits and unemployed looters. Ben-Gioras drew even more men and, inside the city, began robbing houses of the wealthy. Then he fled to Masada, where he gathered more men, promising liberty. With his army ravaging the countryside to support themselves, Zealots in Jerusalem managed to ambush and capture his wife, holding her hostage. Instead of being cowed, Ben-Gioras camped outside the walls and captured anyone exiting the city, killing some and cutting the hands off others, then sending them back inside with a message that he would do the same to all. The Zealots let his wife go, but Ben-Gioras wasn't finished with Jerusalem.

The return of the Roman army forced him again to camp outside the city walls with his own army. By then, John of Gischala, given power by the Zealots, had become a tyrant inside, and the Temple authorities invited Ben-Gioras and his army of fifteen thousand into the city to drive John and the Zealots away. They retreated into the Temple area and held ground there.

"Tell me who you are," Ben-Gioras demanded. He pointed at Vitas. "This one, I've been informed, betrayed his Roman heritage with his accent. He'll be dead within minutes unless you satisfy my questions, and you will be next. Both of you, flung from this tower."

Ben-Aryeh began to pace. "No. What I demand from you is a force of fifteen of your strongest soldiers, willing to sacrifice their lives."

Ben-Gioras reached into a pocket and flipped a coin in Ben-Aryeh's direction. "See that coin? It was minted by my authority. I am king of an independent Jewish state. You will not make demands on me."

"Who told you the significance of the olive trees in white?" Ben-Aryeh said. "Who told you that when it happened, two men must be prepared to lower a rope from this tower? It is not I who make demands, but that person."

"You have proof that you are here on his behalf?"

"I am here. That's proof enough."

"Listen, old man. In the last week, I have run a knife across the throats of friends. I've looked them in the eyes as they died. They were about to betray our cause and flee to the Romans. I control this city, and nothing happens without my authority. I will tell you what is proof enough."

"Either you understand the importance of why I am here. Or you don't. If you do, then send me the soldiers. If you don't, stop pretending and throw me out of the tower."

Ben-Gioras leaned against the wall. "You have passed my test, and I now understand why you were chosen for this. You, too, are prepared to die."

"There is nothing more important for a Jew than that," Ben-Aryeh said. "It's enough to unite sworn enemies. Am I right? Who among the Zealots told you? I need to know, or we proceed no further."

Vitas was watching and hearing but not understanding any of this. Ben-Aryeh was treating one of the most feared and ferocious men in the city as a servant. What kind of power did the older Jew have?

"You are aware of the treachery that John of Gischala used to gain control of the inner Temple?" Ben-Gioras asked.

"When Eleazar opened the gates to allow worship during the festival," Ben-Aryeh said, "John committed the ultimate abomination, spilling blood instead."

"Eleazar was hours from dying, cut down by a sword in the battle for the inner Temple. I was told about this by a woman. Please give me her name before I trust you with any more information."

"Amaris," Ben-Aryeh said.

Vitas was taken aback. That was the name of Ben-Aryeh's wife. And it echoed through Vitas's mind. *This was arranged long ago.*

"I am getting closer and closer to trusting you," Ben-Gioras said. "But I will not speak openly of the secret in front of this Roman."

"I've told him very little," Ben-Aryeh answered, "and the less he is told for now, the better."

Ben-Gioras nodded and continued. "When I learned about Eleazar's injuries, men brought him to a place where we could meet, a place hidden beneath the city. I am going to assume you know where it is, because if you don't lead me there within the hour, I will know you are not who you say you are."

Ben-Aryeh growled. "I know where it is."

"He dismissed the men who carried him there. He's the one who told me. And you are correct. He was a sworn enemy, a man I'd hunted for months. Yet the secret united us, and he knew its importance was enough that I would uphold the duty that came with it."

"You acknowledge that the time is now?"

Ben-Gioras bowed his head briefly. "Rome can't be stopped. The time is now." He raised his head again. "But this man here—what is his purpose? Surely you don't trust any Roman alive with the secret."

"As I said, he will only know when it is necessary," Ben-Aryeh said. "And without him, the plan will fail. This was decided long ago. If you defy me, you defy all of us who have sacrificed to make arrangements for this day."

Ben-Gioras gave that some thought before speaking. "We proceed, then. I will send for the soldiers."

"Not yet," Ben-Aryeh said. "If Eleazar told you to expect me, then you know what I require next. That is my test for you."

Again, that barking laugh. "No. You've passed another test. Had you not asked, I would have had you thrown from the window."

HORA TERTIANA

LEAVING BEHIND THE MEN who had been guarding the door in the upper room, Ben-Gioras led Vitas and Ben-Aryeh downward in the square tower. The stone steps skirted the inside of the outer walls, descending at forty-five degrees and bending ninety degrees at every turn. The air was cool and quiet, and it seemed unreal to Vitas that on the other side of the city, thousands of men were fighting and hacking and spearing each other in a battle to the death that would not end until one side had defeated the other in a haze of smoke and dust.

He was trying to grapple instead with all the implications of what he had heard in the conversation between Ben-Aryeh and Ben-Gioras. Obviously, the Jewish factions could unite against a common enemy. The proof was across the city: after fighting each other so fiercely that they had burned the city's grain supply and forced a famine on the people, the men of Ben-Gioras and John of Gischala were defending the Temple together against Titus.

But a deathbed secret from one enemy to the other, each knowing it was important enough that the other could be trusted? And a secret that put Ben-Aryeh at the center of it?

Vitas could guess that his own role involved the soldiers waiting outside the city with camels. This caravan would not move without his permission.

He was still pondering this when he realized they'd reached ground level. But Ben-Aryeh instructed Ben-Gioras to lead them lower, to the dungeon beneath.

"We'll move slowly," Ben-Gioras answered. "No torches remain. But your eyes adjust."

The air that had been cool and pleasant became fetid with the smell of body waste and rotten straw. Much as Vitas wanted to ask Ben-Aryeh what was ahead, he resisted. The man was stubborn, and Vitas knew he would get no answer. What was obvious, however, was that Ben-Aryeh was moving with the confidence that showed he was in control of the situation. All Vitas could do, at this point, was trust the older man.

Vitas heard coughing ahead. Prisoners. Each side of the corridor held men behind bars. It brought Vitas back to his time in the bowels of the arena, where prisoners stood and pleaded for mercy from each passing visitor.

Here, however, there was only the coughing. The prisoners were too weak to move.

"This one," Ben-Gioras said, stopping at a set of bars. "You'll have to drag them outside. Last I saw, they were barely alive. If it weren't for the woman bringing them scraps, they would already be dead."

Vitas expected Ben-Gioras to take out a key for the locks. But Ben-Gioras said to Ben-Aryeh, "You know what's next. Or both of you die instead."

There was rustling behind Vitas, and it took him a moment to realize that Ben-Aryeh was moving forward. Vitas dimly saw Ben-Aryeh reach out, and when he heard the scraping of metal on metal, he understood that it was Ben-Aryeh who had the key. And must have had it with him long before entering the city.

Ben-Aryeh stepped inside. A shadow seemed to move. Two figures became one.

Vitas heard a gagging sound. The shadow that had attacked Ben-Aryeh was choking the man.

"No fast movements," the prisoner said. "I'll snap his neck like a chicken bone."

Vitas had no doubt the man behind Ben-Aryeh was not only

capable of it but had the willpower to do so. For despite his stunned disbelief at hearing the man's threat, he recognized the voice. It belonged to a man who had killed dozens in the arena, probably the only man alive who could be starving to death in a prison and yet retain the strength and quickness to take an unwary visitor hostage.

Vitas also knew how to stop the man. He had to do nothing more than identify himself.

"Maglorius," he said. "It's Vitas. No need to kill your friends."

Yes, Maglorius. A man whose death Vitas had grieved many times. But now alive!

Could Vitas dare hope that . . .

Then he heard another voice, a voice that was barely more than a croak, but that filled him with unexpected joy.

"And you complain," the voice said, "that I'm the one who is always late?"

Damian. Vitas rushed forward and clung to his brother.

✱ ✱ ✱

When all of them reached sunlight, Vitas assisting Damian up the stairs from the dungeon prison, Vitas saw that he would not have recognized Damian but for his voice.

His last memory of his brother had been of laughter coming from a vigorous man in his prime. That had been in Caesarea, when Vitas was posing as a slave in Helva's household. Damian had been on horseback, ready to ride down the road, assuring Vitas that any worry was needless, that nothing would go wrong.

Then, Damian's hair had been just a little too long to be stylish, but perfectly suited to a man who enjoyed the attention of women for the amused devilish appearance he cultivated with so little effort. Now, it was a greasy mat, down to his shoulders.

Then, his face had been smooth, with a nose bent from a loss in a bar fight. Now, he was bearded well below his collarbone, with pieces of straw hanging from his chin.

Then, Damian had been a dashing figure in the latest fashions.

Now, he was in tattered clothing that would not have been suitable to serve as rags.

And thin. Vitas marveled that a man so gaunt could still be alive.

Maglorius, too, was much diminished, and his thinness was even more striking because of how large-boned he was. His hair and beard were equally as long and filthy as Damian's. Vitas could only conclude they had been in prison as far back as Vitas had been told of their deaths.

Three and a half years. Since Vitas and Sophia had been reunited in Caesarea. In that span, Vitas had been given more than three years of luxurious estate living in Alexandria, content to see his two children born—that span only broken in the middle by a journey to Rome at the end of Nero's life. And while Vitas had continued this domestic idyll in Alexandria after Nero's suicide, the distant empire had almost collapsed as a succession of emperors fought for power.

Three and a half years of full living for Vitas.

Three and a half years in a filthy prison for Damian.

Damian shielded his eyes from the indirect sunlight piercing through one of the tower openings.

Vitas could only imagine the death-like pallor of the skin beneath the filth that crusted Damian's bony wrists. His forearms showed open sores.

"Usually the reasons you gave for not returning on time were easily perceived lies," Vitas said. "This time, however, I'll accept the excuse you give for not returning to Caesarea and rescuing me from slavery."

He meant it as a jest, and Damian took it that way.

"It wasn't the prison that was a burden," Damian said. "It was the torture of enduring Maglorius for all that time. Have you ever heard him sing?"

Vitas swallowed against a lump of joy. Broken as Damian's body was, his spirit was still the same.

Damian scratched himself and absently examined a flea that he found. He popped it with his long fingernails, then dropped it into his mouth. A puzzled look briefly crossed his face as he realized what he'd done; then he grinned, and his teeth were startlingly white against the grime of his beard.

"I guess I won't have to worry about food now, will I? You are taking us out of this city, right?"

Ben-Aryeh finally spoke. "You have the strength to climb down a rope?"

Damian cocked his head. "What's that noise I hear?"

Vitas, totally lost in the moment of discovering his brother alive, had not consciously noted the shrieks and screams coming from across the city.

"Titus and his legions," Vitas answered. "A final push to take Antonia."

"Let's go then," Damian said, grinning again. "I've never been much of a fighter."

Vitas spoke to Ben-Gioras. "You can spare a few men to help them down the rope? Damian's always been a liar. He doesn't have the strength to even walk to the upper tower."

Ben-Gioras nodded.

"Good," Vitas said. "I'll give them the password for the soldiers I have waiting down below."

To Damian, Vitas said, "They'll have food and water. Tell them I have ordered two of them to take you directly to the medics at the Tenth Legion."

"You're not coming?" Damian said. "If the city is about to fall, what other reason could you have to stay?"

"I wish I could answer that," Vitas said dryly. "You'll have to ask this stubborn old Jew."

A shuffling of footsteps on the stones of the stairs drew attention away from Ben-Aryeh, and all of them looked toward the person approaching.

It was an older woman, dark hair streaked with gray. Vitas gaped.

That wasn't Ben-Aryeh's reaction, however. He rushed forward and threw his arms around her.

The woman was Amaris, Ben-Aryeh's wife. With her arms around him too, her face was over his shoulder, her eyes closed.

Vitas rejoiced for his old friend and did nothing to interrupt the moment. Still, he could not help but wonder. If Ben-Aryeh had known Damian and Amaris were alive, and if he had been able to make these arrangements to enter the city, why wait so long?

Vitas heard Ben-Aryeh choke out some words. "God has been faithful."

She was weeping as she said, "Truly faithful. He has spared us both."

They pulled away from each other, but Ben-Aryeh kept a protective arm around Amaris as he spoke. "You are safe now. Go with Damian. If the Lord is willing, you will see me at nightfall."

"You and Vitas are staying in the city?" Damian said, incredulous.

"We have a final task," Ben-Aryeh answered.

"Not without me," Damian said.

Vitas would have laughed if Damian hadn't been so serious. His brother was barely more than a skeleton.

"I need you to protect Amaris," Ben-Aryeh said. "Otherwise, she risks the dangers any other deserter faces. Without you, she won't be protected by Titus."

"No," Damian said.

"I've heard enough," Ben-Gioras snarled at Damian, then turned to Ben-Aryeh. "I have fulfilled my obligation to you by sparing all of them. But that is as far as I will be pushed."

Ben-Aryeh nodded. "You have done what was required."

Ben-Gioras addressed Damian. "Time is short. You escape now, by rope with the help of my men. Or be tossed from the wall. For what lies ahead only one Roman will be permitted to witness."

HORA QUARTA

THE WALLS SURROUNDING the palace that Herod the Great
had built for himself on the western hill of Jerusalem were almost
as high and wide and impregnable as the walls surrounding the
Temple across the city. While Herod had built it to protect himself
from the Jews while he lived among them, it had also served to keep
the remnants of the moderates safe from John of Gischala until they
had appealed to Ben-Gioras to help them with his own army.

Ben-Gioras led Vitas and Ben-Aryeh through the high marble
corridors of the palace with a sense of familiarity and proprietorship
as if it belonged to him—which was closer to truth than presump-
tion, for after driving the Zealots to the Temple Mount and con-
taining them there, he'd made the palace his headquarters.

"Where are your men?" Ben-Aryeh asked, his voice echoing in
the quiet of the palace.

"Waiting," Ben-Gioras answered. "I kept them back once I was
notified of your signal on the Mount of Olives."

"Do they know why?"

"Of course not," Ben-Gioras snapped. "We both know not a
whisper of this can escape."

"And the other requirement?"

"All are sons of Levi."

No more was said until they reached a room buried in the
depths of the vastness of the palace.

It was empty except for old blankets on the floor. And ten young

Jewish men, all armed with short swords on their belts. The men straightened from where they had been leaning against the walls, some of them near a luxurious decorative royal banner that hung from ceiling to floor.

Hunger had etched their bodies too, but they still appeared strong. None spoke, but all kept questioning eyes on Ben-Gioras.

"These two will join us," Ben-Gioras said with no preamble as he motioned toward Vitas and Ben-Aryeh. "If needed, you will die to protect them, because in protecting them, you are protecting all that is holy to our people."

Ben-Gioras spoke as if he fully expected total obedience, and not one of the young soldiers even flinched.

"Where is it?" Ben-Gioras asked Ben-Aryeh.

Instead of speaking, Ben-Aryeh answered by walking to the royal banner and yanking it loose from where it was attached to small spikes near the ceiling. Behind it was an elaborate mosaic of small, gleaming tiles set in a tall, rectangular pattern with the seven candles of a menorah at the center, as if the entire piece was a giant painting.

Ben-Aryeh looked at Vitas. "Now."

Vitas didn't understand at first but saw that Ben-Aryeh was fumbling with the token around his neck. Vitas did the same.

Ben-Aryeh held out his hand, and Vitas gave him the token.

The older man turned to the wall. Vitas could not help but step to the side to see what was happening.

Ben-Aryeh inserted the tokens into nearly invisible slots in the center of the mosaic, where the tiles formed a circle that represented the base of the menorah.

He pushed his palm against the circle of tiles, and with a clicking sound, the circle moved inward a couple of inches.

"I'm told by a tradition handed down only among the leading priests of my circles," Ben-Aryeh said, "that the workmen who completed this for Herod were slain so this would always remain secret. I find it fortunate that he chose stoneworkers from Egypt for the task."

Ben-Aryeh didn't wait for a reply. He moved to his left, and where the mosaic patterns ended, he leaned against the wall. Slowly, it shifted inward as the right side of the mosaic pattern moved outward.

He kept pushing until the entire piece, hinged in the center at the top and bottom, was turned ninety degrees to the main wall.

It exposed the darkness of a tunnel, a couple of paces wide and two or three hands higher than the height of a tall man.

"We have no torches," Ben-Gioras said.

Ben-Aryeh walked in a few steps, shuffled around, then came out with an armful of torches.

"The flints are on the floor," Ben-Aryeh told Ben-Gioras, who pointed at one of the young men and waved at him to get them.

Ben-Aryeh passed off his armful to another of the young Levites and kept one torch for himself. After he lit the torch, he said, "Only one torch. We'll need to keep the others with us as replacements." He stepped back inside. "I'll lead the way."

HORA QUINTA

THEY'D BEEN WALKING for five minutes when Ben-Aryeh spoke to Vitas. "Since the time of David, there have been tunnels beneath the city. Only the leading priests know about this one. Soon enough, it will take us into a larger tunnel. You need to remember the return route, as I may not come back with you."

Ben-Aryeh gripped Vitas by the wrist and squeezed tightly. "No questions, though. You'll have your answers when we get there."

The air was cool and dry, the ground beneath them hard-packed dirt. Vitas had heard rumors of the tunnels. Anyone who visited Jerusalem had. By the slight downward angle of their travels, he felt they were heading toward the lower city. He guessed the Levites were there to protect them once they left the tunnel, but beyond that, he had to bide his curiosity.

It didn't take them long to reach the end of this tunnel. Ben-Aryeh, still carrying his torch, leaned into the wall blocking them. Like the entrance, it was hinged in the center and turned at an angle to let all of them step into a larger tunnel.

"We leave this open too," Ben-Aryeh said. They had left the hinged wall open at Herod's palace as well. Two things were obvious to Vitas. They would be returning to Herod's palace. And Ben-Gioras had ceded command to Ben-Aryeh.

Ben-Aryeh's torch was nearly exhausted, and he motioned for another. Once the second torch was lit, he extinguished the first against the wall of the tunnel.

They resumed their march, no man speaking. For most of the remainder of their twisting, turning journey, the only sounds were of sandals against dirt, flames licking the oil of the torch, and breathing.

When Ben-Aryeh stopped them to light the third torch from the second, Vitas finally heard some different sounds. Faint as they were, the sounds were unmistakable.

As they resumed their journey, those sounds grew louder and louder, telling Vitas their destination—for the shrieks and screams came from the fighting for possession of Antonia.

He'd guessed wrong when he thought they would be leaving the tunnel somewhere in the lower city.

Instead, they were almost beneath the Temple.

When Ben-Aryeh stopped one more time, he pushed the torch close to the wall of the tunnel and examined the wall as he moved a few steps back and forth.

Vitas heard him grunt slightly with satisfaction.

"Take this," Ben-Aryeh said to Vitas, handing him the torch. "Hold it close for me."

Vitas did so, aware of how silent the men were behind him and equally aware of the sounds of battle that carried down to them.

He watched Ben-Aryeh use the same two tokens that had triggered the opening of the wall in Herod's palace, running his fingers over the stone until he found where the tokens fit.

This time, when a wall hinged in the center pushed to ninety degrees to permit a large opening, Vitas was not surprised. The torchlight showed that beyond, the steps upward were made of polished white marble.

"We are here," Ben-Aryeh announced to all of them. "Once we go up these steps, there is no turning back. Each of you will be committed to give up your life to protect what must never be lost to our people. Speak now if you are not prepared to do so. And until we return to this spot, not a single word must be spoken, for we are about to enter into the presence of the almighty God."

"I trust each one of these fighters with my life," Ben-Gioras growled. "Let's move. Time is short."

Vitas saw that three steps up, the wide stairs ended at a platform. It was long enough and wide enough that it could have held Ben-Aryeh, Ben-Gioras, Vitas, and the Levites, but the ceiling was so low that all of the men would have had to crouch. What looked like a wooden box rested on the platform.

Speaking to Vitas, Ben-Aryeh said, "You may go no farther. I love you as a brother or a son, but you are a Gentile. You are not permitted in the Kodesh Hakodashim. Do you understand?"

The Kodesh Hakodashim. The Holy of Holies.

Vitas knew the name from what he had learned during his marriage to Sophia. It was located at the westernmost end of the Temple building. A perfect cube: ten cubits by ten cubits by ten cubits. No one but the high priest was allowed to enter, and that but once a year to offer the blood of sacrifice and incense. It was a symbolic place, Sophia had explained, and completely empty.

"Although you must remain here, you are about to learn something that has been kept secret for centuries," Ben-Aryeh told Vitas. "Our written records state that the Ark could not be found when our people rebuilt the Temple at the time of Ezra and Zechariah. The explanation for our people was that Jeremiah hid the Ark in a cave in Mount Nebo and that its location would be revealed only when God was ready for it to be found."

He put a hand on Vitas's shoulder. "It was not a lie, only a half-truth. Where else should the Ark be but in the Holy of Holies? And that is where it was placed, without letting it be known—for the secrecy protects it, and there is nothing of greater value to our people."

"Pompey found it empty," Vitas said. When the Roman general had conquered Jerusalem over a century before, he'd demanded to be allowed into the Holy of Holies, only to come out again, puzzled that an empty room would have so much significance to the Jews.

"You think we would desecrate it by allowing our conqueror

into its presence?" Ben-Aryeh said. "We are standing below a drop door built into the floor above us, of such craftsmanship that it is seamless and invisible. It was built so no conqueror would ever find the Ark. For Pompey, we moved it here, where we stand now, before he entered. For Titus, we do the same. Except with Titus, we dare not leave it below the Holy of Holies but must find a place for it elsewhere, to protect it forever."

Vitas's curiosity intensified, and he watched closely as Ben-Aryeh walked the steps with Ben-Gioras. Using the same tokens, Ben-Aryeh found two slit openings in the low ceiling that turned another lock.

Slowly, the ceiling dropped like a lengthwise door, but because the Holy of Holies was in total darkness, not a single ray of light filtered down the steps. When the door finished moving, it hung vertically. The light of the torch showed that the side facing Ben-Aryeh had two steps. Vitas caught a glimpse of a raised platform through the opening in the room above them. He visualized that when the door was shut, it would be part of the floor, and those steps would seem a natural way to reach that platform in the room above.

Ben-Gioras waved the Levites to ascend. When the final two had entered the room above, Ben-Gioras and Ben-Aryeh handed the wooden box upward. From the ease with which they lifted it, Vitas guessed it was empty.

Ben-Aryeh held the torch, climbed the steps into the room, and stood in front of a rectangular object, about the size of the empty wooden box. There was just enough illumination for Vitas to see that this new object had the dull shine of gold.

HORA SEXTA

IN THE DAYLIGHT of the room in Herod's palace, when the Levites set down the object they had transported through the subterranean passage from the Holy of Holies, Vitas first saw clearly the clever construction of the wooden box.

The bottom portion, now resting on the tiled floor, was essentially a large, shallow tray. At each end, two half circles had been cut into the edges of this tray, as near to the sides as possible.

The upper portion of the box was like a roof, with walls that had been set upon the lower tray. Half circles had been cut out of the bottom edges, precisely matching those on the tray below.

When the rooflike structure rested on the tray, these circles allowed poles to pass through the box; the Levites had used these poles—overlaid with gold—to carry the box through the tunnel.

The top and bottom were latched together in places, forming an outer shell that protected the object inside.

All told, the rectangular box was about two paces long and barely one pace wide, and the height was the same as the width. The box itself wasn't heavy; Vitas had seen that earlier when it had gone upward into the Holy of Holies. Leaving the Holy of Holies, however, the Levites had strained under its weight.

He knew it had great value because the men around him were staring at the outer shell with awe and fascination on their faces.

Ben-Aryeh broke the silence by speaking to Ben-Gioras. "If these Levites are going to their deaths, it is only fitting that they see in full daylight the reason for their sacrifice. In the Holy of Holies, there was not light to give the Ark its glory."

Each stared at the other, and finally Ben-Gioras nodded. He stepped forward and began to open the latches. When that was finished, he spoke to the Levites. "Take your places around it, and remove the top as carefully as you added it. If any of you cause the box to touch it, or if any of you lay a hand upon it, the others will slay you."

They stepped forward, some of them sweating visibly, others with shaking hands. And when they lifted the lid, sunlight hit the sacred chest and Vitas gasped at the beauty of it. Some of the young Levites began to weep, and all of them fell to their knees.

With the upper shell removed, Vitas saw that the poles on each side ran through gold rings, two on each side, and that the poles supported the object. With the ends of the poles resting in the half circles of the shallow lower tray, no portion of the object had touched the shell.

Vitas felt a hand on his shoulder. It was Ben-Aryeh, pressing him down to his knees too, alongside Ben-Gioras, who had already knelt.

On his knees, in utter silence shared with the others, Vitas felt an incredible sense of awe. The entire object was overlaid with pure gold, and a crowning wreath of more gold served as an artistic border all around it. It had a cover of solid gold, the full length and breadth of the chest. Mounted at each end of this cover were two cherubs of hammered gold; the cherubs faced each other, heads bowed, wings extending upward and overspreading the object.

All of them remained bowing, and time seemed to stop. They only rose when Ben-Aryeh gestured for the Levites to put the lid back on this object, and it wasn't until then that Vitas became aware he'd been on the floor so long his knees hurt.

No one spoke until the Levites had secured the plain wooden cover back on the bottom tray and it was latched completely shut again. At Ben-Aryeh's direction, they wrapped the outer shell and the poles in blankets.

"You will fight to your deaths today?" Ben-Aryeh asked quietly.

Vitas saw that the faces of the Levites glowed with holy fervor. To a man, each Levite nodded. Many of them still wept, not from sorrow, but joy.

"Send for the other Levites," Ben-Aryeh told Ben-Gioras. "We are all ready."

"Not yet," Ben-Gioras said. He nodded at two of the men closest to Vitas, and they seized him before he could react. They held his arms with such strength that he was effectively pinned between them.

"The Roman must die," Ben-Gioras said. He pulled out a short dagger and advanced on Vitas. "For he has seen it too."

Ben-Aryeh reacted calmly. "If he dies, then the Ark of the Covenant is lost to us forever."

Ben-Gioras was close enough when he answered that Vitas could feel the man's breath hot against his face. "Our own Levites are commanded to die in battle today to protect this secret, and yet you say the Roman must live?"

"The only safe passage for the Ark is through him. The escort of Roman soldiers waiting with camels will not move unless he accompanies the Ark."

"They are expecting a group of our men to be with the Ark, are they not?"

Ben-Aryeh nodded.

"Our Levites will slay the Roman soldiers and take the camels themselves."

"Jerusalem is surrounded by sentries. Without Vitas and his seal of authorization from Titus, the Ark won't make it more than a mile before the camels are stopped."

"The gold," Ben-Gioras protested. "What's to stop him from ambushing our Levites and dividing it among the soldiers? What's to stop him from delivering it directly to Titus?"

298 THE LAST TEMPLE

Ben-Aryeh spoke in a conciliatory tone. "Ben-Gioras, you know the military situation. If we lose our final battle and the Ark is still here, it is most certainly lost to our people forever. It is far too late into the war against the Romans for Jews alone to accomplish the task of hiding it safely. With the city surrounded by entire legions, only someone who has influence with Titus is capable of giving safe transport."

"But how can we trust this man?"

"We have to trust someone in his position," Ben-Aryeh said. "That is inescapable. Of any Roman, he is the one. He is married to a Jew. He is not driven by greed but by justice. I've spent years with this man. He understands what is at stake, and I trust him with my life."

Ben-Gioras threw his dagger down in disgust, and to Vitas, the sound of its clattering on the tiles was the sound of life.

"Let him go," Ben-Gioras said reluctantly to the two Levites who held Vitas.

Immediately he was freed.

Ben-Gioras took a deep breath and spoke to the young men, moving his eyes from face to face. "All of you, by agreeing to help preserve the Ark until the return of our Messiah, have willingly agreed to sacrifice your lives. Not a single person alive will know of your nobleness and love for God. Each of us must someday die, and you have chosen a time and place and reason for death that surpasses the lives you give today."

Ben-Gioras paused, measuring each of the men.

When he was satisfied with what he saw, he gave them a final command. "Go. Return through the tunnel, back to the Temple. Join the defenders and throw yourselves into the thickest and most dangerous part of battle. And before you die, make sure you each take the lives of a dozen Romans with you."

HORA SEPTINA

VITAS AND BEN-ARYEH stood alone in the room in Herod's palace with the Ark covered by its wooden shell and wrapped in blankets.

"You did not know what object I was asking you to protect when you made your promise to me," Ben-Aryeh said. "And now that you've seen it, I will not ask you to assure me that you intend to keep your promises. I spoke truly to Ben-Gioras. You are the only Roman alive I would trust with this."

"The Ark," Vitas said, still barely able to comprehend. "Sophia said it had been lost during the Babylonian captivity. That in the Holy of Holies, a platform had been raised to signify where it would have rested."

"We learned from the destruction of the first Temple. The high priests decided long, long ago that the best way to protect the Ark was through secrecy. As we are doing now. Ben-Gioras will never reveal it and expects to die in battle. Those young men will die today as pledged, so no one will know of its existence. The new group of Levites who will lower it from the tower won't even see that the poles are plated with gold. They only know your task is to escort them far away from Jerusalem until it is safe for them to leave you and the soldiers. They will take it to a cave in the desert. To break that chain of knowledge, after they leave, those of us in the small circle of priests who know about it will go there and move it somewhere else until it is safe to return it to the Holy of Holies. Titus has vowed to preserve the Temple, and from everything you have told me, he means to fulfill that vow."

"I find it strange you allowed me to remain in this room while you showed the Levites the purpose of their sacrifice."

"You will never know the cave where it was placed or where we have moved it after."

"Even so, you didn't have to let me see it."

Ben-Aryeh put a hand on Vitas's shoulder. "For what you are doing, there is not enough all the Jews could do to repay you. There is no other object in the entire world as sacred, and by protecting it, you will ensure that God will always be among us. For if this Temple is destroyed, we can build another to hold the Ark."

Ben-Aryeh stepped back and moved toward the hinged wall that was still open. Standing at the opening, he continued speaking. "Vitas, we cannot repay you for this. Ever. I pray that you will live to be an old man surrounded by grandchildren. I believe if you had not seen what was inside, you would have wondered your entire life what was at stake. If I did wrong by letting you know, then I call God's wrath solely upon me."

"You did not do wrong," Vitas said. "The Ark will be safe."

"Thank you," Ben-Aryeh said. He began pushing the hinged wall back into place. "Help me move this. When Ben-Gioras returns, it would be better if the men with him did not know about this passage."

Vitas leaned into the wall with him, and it turned until it was almost parallel with the original wall. When there was just enough of a gap for Ben-Aryeh to slip into the darkness behind, he motioned for Vitas to stop.

"I can't leave without saying this," Ben-Aryeh said. He stepped into the darkness on the other side of the wall and spoke from there. "Someday you'll realize what I did. I beg that you understand the reasons for my actions and through that understanding, that you will forgive me. Nothing in my life has mattered more than preserving the Ark. Amaris understands this too. Now that my part has been accomplished, she has accepted that today is the day I die in battle."

Ben-Aryeh pushed the hinged wall completely shut. From the inside. Leaving Vitas to stare at the image of the seven candles laid in the mosaic on the outer wall.

August 30, AD 70
JERUSALEM
Province of Judea

Then I heard another voice from heaven say: "Come out of her, my people, so that you will not share in her sins, so that you will not receive any of her plagues; for her sins are piled up to heaven, and God has remembered her crimes.

"Give back to her as she has given; pay her back double for what she has done. Mix her a double portion from her own cup. Give her as much torture and grief as the glory and luxury she gave herself. In her heart she boasts, 'I sit as queen; I am not a widow, and I will never mourn.'

"Therefore in one day her plagues will overtake her: death, mourning and famine. She will be consumed by fire, for mighty is the Lord God who judges her."

REVELATION 18:4-8

From the Revelation, given to John on the island of Patmos in AD 63

JUPITER

DILUCULUM

VITAS WOKE EARLY on the day that Jerusalem would experience the culmination of its sorrows of death and mourning and famine, as the sun rose bloodred behind the haze of columns of smoke from the smoldering gates and porticoes of the outer Temple. Its early light cast an otherworldly glow over the undisturbed sanctuary of the inner courts and the crowds of refugees huddled against the chill of dawn.

From an upper balcony of the tower of Antonia, he saw that the smoke came from fires whose flames had been extinguished the day before, fires of such size that the embers were still dull orange beneath the ruins of massive beams.

Not even the slightest breeze passed through the great city of Jerusalem, perched on the mountain that protected and isolated its beauty, surrounded by massive stone walls that had resisted the siege of legions of soldiers for half a year.

The columns of smoke formed straight lines to the heavens, eerily reminiscent of the smoke that had spiraled upward from the Temple altars during daily sacrifices without cease for centuries before this, what would be the final day of the Temple's existence.

The Antonia Fortress had fallen; the massive towers and walls that had once been thought invincible had caved to the siege and determination of the most powerful military force in the history of mankind. The echoes of the screams of those who had died seemed to linger over the ruins, and still-burning heaps of homes that had been reduced to rubble added to the columns of smoke that were like sentries guarding the outer courts of the Temple.

Without a breeze, the stench of death imprisoned the city. This was a city where once, as decreed by law, bodies were not even permitted to lie waiting for a funeral overnight, lest the sacred house of God be defiled. Now, hundreds of corpses littered the streets— some savagely violated by sword or spear or fallen walls, others curled into a deceptive peacefulness that masked the torture of the final moments of bodies starved so thoroughly that the breath of life had departed in a feeble gasp.

Without a breeze to sigh through the stoneworks of the surviving buildings, it was silent in these moments after dawn, a silence unbroken by any of the waiting attackers outside the Temple or the unfortunates who still survived inside or those who lived in the upper city and waited in dread for the final walls to be broken and the soldiers to gush in for ultimate victory.

It was a mountaintop where hundreds of thousands lived. Yet now it was as hushed as if the hand of God pressed down upon it.

The priests and rebels and thousands of refugees who huddled within the inner courts of the Temple were exhausted from fear and famine and the horror of all the slaughter they'd witnessed in the previous weeks. Theirs was a silence of hopelessness, and those awake—especially the parents who held their children in numbed sorrow—prayed that those around them would remain in the oblivion of sleep for as long as possible.

On the other side of the walls, in tents gathered at the bases of the giant earthwork ramps that had finally allowed them to break through, the Roman soldiers shared that silence. Their silence was different, however; it was a silence of unexploded rage, a gathering of strength, a mixture of grimness and satisfaction that their victory was now so close.

Because of the silence and the stillness of the air, it seemed like the earth itself had paused in respect for the imminent terror that gripped the Temple and those within it.

Vitas was so lost in his feeling of melancholy that he didn't realize Titus was there until he stepped forward and leaned on the balcony. "The battle is no longer in doubt," Titus said. "Jerusalem will fall. But can I control my soldiers?"

Vitas knew what had motivated the question. Titus worried about delivering on his vow to preserve the Temple. His soldiers—professionals who were usually stolid under all circumstances—hated the Jews for their treacheries during the siege. Titus doubted he could find a way to hold them back once the inner court was breached.

Vitas didn't answer. He knew it had been a rhetorical question.

They stood together without speaking.

Moments later, when the growing light of the sun broke over the top of the Mount of Olives across the valley, it was not greeted with the trumpet calls of the priests as had been done every dawn for generations. Instead, the sound that greeted the sun was a wailing, crazed howl from a solitary figure standing on a roof overlooking six thousand women and children gathered in a courtyard, a figure barely visible against the haze.

The uncanny sound echoed clearly in the silence of the city that had not yet begun to stir to its final moments.

The man on the rooftop spoke with a singsong cadence. Each word pierced the stillness. "The time is coming when the Lord will say to the people of Jerusalem, 'A burning wind is blowing in from the desert. It is not a gentle breeze useful for winnowing grain. It is a roaring blast sent by me! Now I will pronounce your destruction!'"

Vitas wondered, had this man—insane from hunger and grief, his lungs half-destroyed by smoke—consciously known when the first heat of the day would begin to rise from the barren hilltops? For as his prophecy reached those huddled in the sanctuary of the inner Temple, so did the first winds of the morning.

"Our enemy rushes down on us like a storm wind! His chariots are like whirlwinds; his horses are swifter than eagles. How terrible it will be! Our destruction is sure!"

h the quickening breeze, the columns of smoke shifted ightly, bending around the man on the rooftop.

Below Vitas, a woman holding a baby shielded her eyes to look upward against the bloodred sun, straining to see the source of the ominous wail. The movement woke her baby, and it cried for milk. But the breasts that had once fed the child had long since been dry. The woman leaned over the baby, and her tears formed splotches on the soot that covered her child's face.

As the child continued to wail, it was as if the man on the rooftop had peered into the woman's heart. "I hear a great cry, like that of a woman giving birth to her first child. It is the cry of Jerusalem's people gasping for breath, pleading for help, prostrate before their murderers! Therefore, you prostitute, listen to this message from the Lord!"

The glow of the sun from behind the columns of smoke that had begun to dance to the wailing prophecies seemed so supernatural that none spoke above whispers.

"This is what the sovereign Lord says: Because you have worshiped detestable idols, and because you have slaughtered your children as sacrifices to your gods, this is what I am going to do. I will gather together all your allies—these lovers of yours with whom you have sinned, both those you loved and those you hated—and I will strip you naked in front of them so they can stare at you."

The figure on the roof bent in half, coughing out smoke and blood. When he rose, somehow he found the strength to add vigor to his cry. "I will punish you for your murder and adultery. I will cover you with blood in my jealous fury. Then I will give you to your lovers—those many nations—and they will destroy you. They will knock down your pagan shrines and the altars to your idols. They will strip you and take your beautiful jewels, leaving you completely naked and ashamed. They will band together in a mob to stone you and run you through with swords. They will burn your homes and punish you in front of many women. I will see to it that you stop your prostitution and—"

"Silence that man!" The roar came from an elderly Sadducee, a once-wealthy man whose upper city mansion had been plundered by starved rebels searching for grain. He needed no reminder of the Hebrew prophecies, needed no reminder that Jerusalem had become a Babylon prostitute hated by God.

The old man's roar of anger seemed to be the catalyst that shifted the earth itself from its near-reverent anticipation of the apocalypse about to fall upon the Temple and the rest of the city.

The silence was completely broken.

The winds picked up, rising from the valleys. The soldiers outside the walls began to move their armor, swords, and spears in readiness, a dull clinking sound that was ominous because of its familiarity to the people trapped inside the walls.

The high keening of the man on the roof reached one of the chambers of Antonia, where the Roman general Titus paused as he lifted water from a basin to his face. This was the son of an emperor, soon to be emperor himself, a man who was Rome personified, the Rome of seven hills, of the ten horns of the ten provinces, the Rome that was the great beast who had almost died in the civil wars after its head, Nero, was cut off.

Yet the Beast had survived, with other heads to replace Nero. Titus and his legions were ample proof that the Beast had returned—and was about to destroy its prey.

For Vitas, the words of the man on the roof and the wailing death cries below were so set apart from the cacophony of all the other death cries of the previous months that he shivered. As if the presence of the God that the Jews claimed as theirs had brushed against his soul.

Then enraged shouting drowned out the wail of the madman on the roof.

At the outer gates of the Temple, where Roman guards were posted, hundreds of Jewish men had begun a furious, desperate raid to force a way out of their trap.

Some of the soldiers were caught unawares, but most relied on instinct and years of training. They closed ranks and locked their tall shields together, forming a wall that withstood the attack.

Titus immediately dispatched a message for his elite cavalry to assist the troops.

The rest of the city was aware of the drama only from what noise of warfare reached them. It almost drowned out the solitary figure on the roof, yet in the occasional lulls of fighting, his prophecies descended from on high. "Do you see these buildings? I assure you, they will be so completely demolished that not one stone will be left upon another!"

Less than fifty yards from the man, outside the Temple's inner wall, soldiers on horses charged Jews armed with broken spears and flaming torches. The screams of the horses joined the screams of the men.

"The time will come when you will see what Daniel the prophet spoke about: the sacrilegious object that causes desecration in the holy place!"

Vitas wondered if the man spoke from divinely inspired prescience. Or was that man, like so many other Jews, so familiar with Scripture that he was simply gasping out prophecies of doom that all of them recognized but had ignored until far, far too late?

More shouting, screaming. The Jews could not withstand the disciplined charge of the Romans and retreated again to the inner court. One of the gates to the inner court had caught fire, and the Roman soldiers tried to put it out.

"How terrible it will be for pregnant women and for mothers nursing their babies in those days!"

Vitas groaned. It had been reported by refugees that the week before, a woman had roasted her own baby and devoured half of it.

"And pray that your flight will not be in winter or on the Sabbath. For that will be a time of greater horror than anything the world has ever seen or will ever see again!"

From their vantage point, Titus saw enough to be satisfied that the outer gates would hold. He motioned for his elite to withdraw.

In the quiet that followed, an archer appeared on the balcony, one Titus had sent for earlier. Titus and Vitas and the archer stared at the man on the rooftop, his silhouette a dark form against the smoke.

"And they will see the Son of Man arrive on clouds of heaven with power and great glory!" The man on the roof knew his listeners would recognize this imagery as God's way of declaring judgment; again and again their prophets had used the phrase in the centuries before.

The archer lifted his bow. Drew aim.

Titus put out a hand. "I've changed my mind. Let him speak to those gathered below."

Vitas could guess why. During the last weeks, the Jews had inflicted such degradations upon themselves that Titus had openly said on more than one occasion that the imminent fall of the city was not because of Roman power but because of divine hand. What if this man was speaking on behalf of that presence? It would invite divine disfavor to shoot the messenger.

"The sun will be darkened; the moon will not give light. The stars will fall from the sky, and the powers of heaven will be shaken!"

Shaken indeed, Vitas thought. How else to describe the indescribable? What other images to convey the horror as the foundation of the entire Jewish world began to collapse?

He understood enough of Jewish culture to know the source of those metaphors. The stars had been fixed forever. It was as unthinkable that the points of light which had been above the Jews since creation might shift without warning as it was to comprehend the sun and moon without light. And equally as unimaginable that the world's great empire would plunge into death throes and then survive as that the city once considered unassailable would be on the verge of a destruction of such utter and implacable violence.

Titus sent the archer away, and when the two of them were alone again, he spoke to Vitas not as a general but as a friend who had endured much with him.

"As Jerusalem falls, I fulfill my duty to my father and Rome," Titus said. "But I betray the woman I love."

HORA QUARTA

AS VITAS MADE HIS WAY to his tent among the legions camped in the new quarter of Jerusalem, the rebels again charged the Roman soldiers as they were occupied with the fire at the gates of the inner court.

The fighting became impassioned. The Roman soldiers did not fight as a trained unit, but with the bloodlust of men who wanted to kill other men. The rebels scattered again.

This time the soldiers did not stop pursuit. They chased the rebels to the sanctuary, to the Holy of Holies. One of the soldiers, so filled with anger that he was not awed by the sight of something no heathen had ever seen, grabbed a burning brand.

He shouted for help, and a dozen eager hands hoisted him to a better vantage point. With a cry of satisfaction, he hurled the brand through a small golden door on the north side of the chamber.

The flames caught.

This was the ultimate desecration. The exterior of the Holy of Holies on fire!

Uncaring of their lives, dozens of Jews rushed forward among the soldiers to try to stop the fire.

Despite their efforts, the flames grew. So did the fighting as hundreds more Jews joined the first few dozen.

✝ ✝ ✝

Vitas received word from a breathless messenger to join Titus outside the Temple sanctum. There, in the noise and the confusion, the s could not hear Titus's orders to stop. Or, in their bloodlust, ey chose to ignore him.

Their fury was unstoppable.

Many were trampled by other soldiers rushing forward to kill more Jews. Others fell among the burning ruins, sharing the fate of the Jews they wanted dead.

More and more soldiers hurled torches into the depths of the sanctuary. The rebels were helpless with despair and no longer fought as the soldiers butchered them.

Corpses began to heap around the altar, and streams of blood flowed down the steps, just as the blood of countless calves had done over the centuries.

The fight spilled over to the women and children and old men who had taken sanctuary there, clinging to the altar and crying to the God of Abraham for mercy. For most, the mercy was in the savage quickness of death by the sword rather than the torturous crucifixion that still waited for tens of thousands in the weeks to come. At the altar, sharpened steel cut through supplicant flesh, just as if they had been bound sheep.

Yet the very innermost place of the Holy of Holies was still untouched.

✝ ✝ ✝

Titus, Vitas, and the other commanders entered and stood as children, awed by the splendor within, by the sheen of plated gold, the draped jewels, the fine tapestries.

At the sight of the treasure, Titus rushed out again and appealed to his troops. The inner sanctum must be saved! Not just because of the woman he loved, but because of the incredible beauty and wealth, because of the prize it would be for Rome.

He even ordered a nearby centurion to club any Roman soldier who disobeyed.

But hatred for the Jews and hope of plunder made his orders useless. The soldiers were not blind. Every time they looked up from the hacking and killing, they saw the gold and assumed the interior contained vast treasure.

Even as Titus tried to restrain the troops, a soldier thrust a fire-brand into the hinges of the final gate that led to the Holy of Holies.

Unquenchable flames shot upward. And this, the last sanctuary, began to burn.

The slaughter continued. As the soldiers rampaged, they stole everything of value, stopping only to run a sword through any Jew within reach, Jews who were on their knees, begging for God's Holy Place to be saved.

✦ ✦ ✦

Within half an hour, it seemed the entire city was blazing.

The roar of fire, the shrieks of the dying, the hoarse screams of the soldiers. All made it seem as if the world were ending.

Corpses were piled so high that soldiers had to climb over them to pursue the fugitives.

The soldiers set fire to all the surrounding buildings, to the remaining porticoes and gates, and to the treasury chambers. The great fire howled, and the draft of the heat pulled upward with the force of a storm.

Only one courtyard remained untouched.

In it, six thousand women and children had taken refuge, prom-ised safety by a false prophet. This was the courtyard the man on the rooftop overlooked.

His wailing had been lost in the other noises, and even now, as he screamed to the skies, beating on his chest, no one below could hear his final repetition of all the prophecies that had warned of this day, for the cries for mercy became a united keen that would have touched the heart of any sane man.

Yet the soldiers were crazed, and one by one, they threw torches at the courtyard walls until this, too, added to the ungodly fire at the top of the mount of Jerusalem. The keening for mercy inside the courtyard became shrieks of agony.

As an afterthought, one of the soldiers hurled a spear at the man on the roof. It hit him with such force that it pinned him where he fell.

The flames began to lick toward him.

The cries of agony rose louder and louder, until one by one, each voice was snuffed by death, and there was only the crackling of flames.

Not one woman or child in the courtyard survived.

❖ VENUS ❖

HORA PRIMA

AT DAWN THE NEXT DAY, Vitas learned that Amaris had gone to the upper slope of the Mount of Olives. He found her near the rock where less than two weeks earlier, Ben-Aryeh had sat with him to overlook the Temple.

Then the building had gleamed in glory. Now it was smoking ruins.

Tears were wet on her face. He didn't know if she was mourning the death of Ben-Aryeh or the fall of the Temple or if she was overwhelmed by both.

He didn't offer any trite words of sympathy but instead waited until she was ready to speak.

Half an hour passed.

Much as he shared her grief, Vitas didn't think he could fully comprehend it and felt guilty as his thoughts shifted to his own family and the joy he would feel to be reunited. Damian was on the lower slopes among the Tenth Legion, preparing for a journey to take all of them back to Caesarea, where they could catch a ship to Alexandria. From there, all of them would go to Rome and the estate that Vitas had once lost to Nero but had been granted again by decree of Vespasian.

When Amaris spoke, her voice was almost lost in the wind. "I'm glad my husband did not live to see this," she said. She was no longer weeping but calm. "It would have broken him beyond all endurance. The Temple and serving our God were at the core of his entire being."

"In his final words to me," Vitas answered just as softly, "he said you understood how much it mattered to him to ensure the Jews did not lose the Ark."

Amaris laughed for a few moments, a reaction that Vitas did not expect. Almost immediately, however, the laughter broke into tears, and the rawness of her emotions was evident in how long it took for her to regain her composure. "Vitas," she said. "It's almost a certainty he did not succeed."

"I was there," Vitas said. "I escorted the Levites to the edge of the desert, near the Dead Sea. When I departed with the soldiers, they were safe and headed into the hills. Both the Jewish and Roman armies were gathered here. They were in a desolate area, with no band of robbers big enough to attack them, even if they were seen."

"The Ark might have been preserved," she answered, her voice becoming clearer, "but it has still been lost. Somewhere, it sits in a cave, hidden, where I'm sure it will never be found in all of history."

"I don't understand."

She shifted and faced him squarely. The sun was coming from behind her, over the top of the Mount of Olives, and her face was in shadow.

"The Levites who put it in the cave have no idea what it was and so have no reason to return," she said. "As for the ones who planned so carefully to move it into that cave to reclaim it later, they were so few, and they are gone. Dead."

"So few?"

"A man and wife cannot be closer than he and I were together," she said. "I thought neither of us had secrets from the other. I knew early that he was part of a special group of Temple priests. From generation to generation, twelve men. Only when one died would another replace him. But not until the beginning of the revolt did I learn that he had always kept from me what their service to the

Temple was. Yes, ensuring the Ark would always remain among the Jews. He told me only because of the desperation of the times, and because I was needed to help preserve the Ark if the unthinkable happened—the destruction of the Temple. Their first level of protection was the secrecy afforded by the Holy of Holies, and the second was to keep knowledge of its existence to themselves."

Vitas nodded.

"When the revolt first began—and you were here in Jerusalem that summer—my husband came to me and said it was feared the Zealots would force war against Rome, and he doubted we could win," she said. "He told me that the priests entrusted with the Ark had begun to plan for a day when the Ark might be in danger. He said they feared to try to move it while bandits roved the countryside, but if they waited too long and Rome did appear on the verge of triumph, it might be too late."

Again Vitas nodded. "He told me that I became part of that plan."

"Yes. And you know he had to flee Jerusalem or face death by stoning. What you don't know is that later I was asked to replace him to help the other eleven. Ironic. They chose me not *despite* the fact that I am a woman, but *because* I am a woman."

Vitas tilted his head slightly, expressing a silent question.

"It was becoming too dangerous for any men of power in the city. Women are invisible. My own sacrifice was to stay and help as needed. It was not our doing that Damian was captured, but once it happened, we saw how it could give you a reason to come to Jerusalem. One of my roles was to ensure that Damian did not die in prison. I fed them every day as well as possible. The others in the small circle used their influence to ensure they were not executed, contrary to the story that was falsely spread."

She smiled grimly. "And that story was spread so that you would not return to Jerusalem too early."

It came back to Vitas, the conversation he'd had with Ben-Aryeh in the tower of Phasael.

"Am I to understand that for months, someone has been looking out every day at the Mount of Olives for that very signal?"

"No. Years."

"I'm sorry to tell you this," Amaris continued. "It was important to keep Damian and Maglorius alive for the day when you would be needed to return to help. The others involved in this thought if you refused, Damian and Maglorius could be used as hostages to force you to use your influence with Titus."

Her grim smile softened. "Much as I argued against that and for the release of Damian and Maglorius, they would not believe what my husband and I already knew. That if he asked, you would freely give your help."

This had been arranged long ago.

"Vitas," she said. "You asked me last night if I would leave here and live with you and your family. I must ask you something first. Do you think it was coincidence that he spent years with you?"

"Not at all. I've wondered, in the last few days, if Ben-Aryeh arranged for those false charges to be laid against him."

She gaped. "How could you guess?"

This had been arranged long ago.

"It was the perfect excuse to join me and Sophia," Vitas said. "To earn my trust. And for me, in turn, to earn his. He himself said that I was the only one in the perfect position to be trusted and still have influence with Titus. I began to wonder how long he'd known that and realized he probably would have known it immediately upon meeting me, when Bernice sent him to be my guide."

"You are right," Amaris said. "Yet you don't look angry."

"He saved my family. You argued for the early release of Damian and Maglorius and, when that didn't happen, ensured they would survive. I'm not angry. I'm grateful. Amaris, don't stay here alone and widowed. Jerusalem is desolate. Let me honor my friend Ben-Aryeh and provide a home for you where you will be loved and cherished. I will never forgive myself if I leave you here."

"I'm afraid that someday you will resent me. That someday you'll be bitter about my husband's deceit."

"The last time I saw him, he begged me to understand the reasons for his actions. I promise you, Amaris. I do understand. If I could speak to him, I'd tell him there is nothing that needs forgiveness."

She looked at the ruins of the Temple, then back at him. "Vitas, please take me from here. Let me join you and your young family in Rome and serve you as if I were the grandmother of your children."

He nodded. "You promise not to resent me and become bitter?"

"You have done nothing wrong."

"But the Romans have. The Ark is lost, and all that Ben-Aryeh lived and died for is lost. You will be living among the people who took that hope from your husband."

Vitas remembered what Ben-Aryeh had said to him at the campfire. *I am coming closer and closer to believing that perhaps the Nazarene was the Messiah.*

"If he were alive, he would finally acknowledge what I must acknowledge. The fall of the Temple confirms that the Nazarene is our Messiah. It fell because Jerusalem—my husband among the religious leaders there—rejected him."

She laughed softly. "If my husband were here, he would shake his head. All his efforts to protect what he believed was the most important thing to our people, only to learn that God does not need the Ark preserved, nor do the Jews."

She put her hand on Vitas's. "I am now among the first generation of believers. Here is what I understand. God's people no longer need a building or sacrifices on an altar to be heard by God or to make atonement. The Christos was the Lamb. The destruction of the Temple is more than God's punishment for rejecting his Messiah; it releases us from requiring a physical place to worship."

She was smiling, and it seemed like she glowed from within. "Vitas, his words have been fulfilled within this generation as promised. His prophecies came true. He was—he is—the Messiah."

She pointed across the valley. "Vitas, that is not the last Temple. Instead, the Christos is."

Something brittle inside Vitas seemed to shatter. He'd fought so hard and so long to believe that a man lived and died on his own terms, his own honor, and he'd learned to depend on no one, to yield to no other man.

It was as if he'd built a structure around his soul based on these convictions and the principle that a man paid for his own sins and suffered for the suffering he'd caused others.

He thought of Sophia, kneeling in prayer. Of Sophia, so open and so vulnerable, yet so calm and enduring.

His mind moved inexorably to the river of the water of life described by the last disciple of the Christos in the scroll that had been so feared by the beastly Nero. The words washed over him with the force of a torrential downpour. *"Whoever is thirsty, let him come; and whoever wishes, let him take the free gift of the water of life."* He thought of a stream of pure water and how thirsty he felt, thirsty for something that was beyond his grasp and understanding.

He thought of a man lying prostrate in a pool of his own blood, a man bearing the sin and suffering of all humanity, a man accepting the burden so that others would not have to bear their own. Vitas thought of all that was helpless and hopeless in his life. That no matter how much he loved and cherished Sophia and his children, death would eventually turn his love into ashes as horrible as the ashes of the destruction before him. Unless, as the Christos had promised, there was a home with many rooms waiting for him and his family.

Vitas thought of how much he wanted to believe.

And he fell to his knees and began to pray.

To the Christos.

To the last Temple.

AFTERWORD

REVELATION RECORDS the first all-out assault of the Beast against the bride lasting approximately three and a half years. Prior to AD 64, the church was persecuted by the woman who rides the Beast (apostate Israel), but shortly after the Great Fire of Rome, the Beast unleashed its full fury against a fledgling Christian church. That Nero started the Great Fire of Rome is historically debatable.[1] That Nero used it as the catalyst for the first state assault against the emerging Christian church is not.

To quell rumors that he himself was the incendiary, the arsonist-matricide who had ignited the Great Fire that transformed Rome into a smoldering inferno, Nero purposed to make the Christians scapegoats. As the Roman historian Tacitus explains in his *Annals*, "To get rid of the report, Nero fastened the guilt and inflicted the most exquisite tortures on a class hated for their abominations, called Christians by the populace."[2]

In November AD 64, the persecution began in earnest. Dr. Paul Maier, professor of ancient history at Western Michigan University, provides gut-wrenching color commentary in a documentary novel titled *The Flames of Rome*.[3] Vast numbers of Christians were arrested, convicted, and sentenced to death. Tacitus records, "Covered with the skins of beasts, they were torn by dogs and perished, or were

---

[1] See Paul L. Maier, *The Flames of Rome* (Grand Rapids: Kregel Publications, 1981), 432-34. For ancient sources, see Tacitus, *Annals*, xv, 38ff; Suetonius, *The Lives of the Twelve Caesars: Nero*, xxxviii; Cassius Dio, *Roman History*, lxii, 16-18; Pliny, *Natural History*, xvii, 5; Seneca, *Octavia*, 831ff.

[2] Tacitus, *Annals*, xv, 44, translated by Alfred John Church and William Jackson Brodribb, eBooks@Adelaide, 2009, online at http://ebooks.adelaide.edu.au/t/tacitus/t1a/book15.html (accessed February 17, 2012). See also Suetonius, *The Lives of the Twelve Caesars: Nero*, xvi.

[3] See Maier, *The Flames of Rome*, especially pp. 317-331, 435-437.

nailed to crosses, or were doomed to the flames and burnt, to serve
as a nightly illumination, when daylight had expired. Nero offered
his gardens for the spectacle, and was exhibiting a show in the circus,
while he mingled with the people in the dress of a charioteer."[4]

Those who suggest Nero "was a wimpy emperor" who "went
down in history as the emperor who fiddled while Rome burned"[5]
do violence to the collective memories of those who suffered
valiantly in the first Roman persecution of the bride of Christ.
Nowhere in the annals of credible history is there any evidence for
the legend that Nero fiddled. He might have sung or swayed in
maniacal madness—but he did not fiddle! Indeed, the violin was
not even invented until fourteen centuries after the Great Fire.[6]

Far from the "wimpy" Nero invented by some scholars, the Nero
of history was the very personification of wickedness. The malevolent
state massacre of Christians that he instituted continued unabated
for some three and a half years. In the end, Peter and Paul themselves
were persecuted and put to death at the hands of this Beast. Indeed,
this was the only epoch in human history during which the Beast
could directly assail the foundation of the Christian church of which
Christ himself is the cornerstone. Only with Nero's death, June 9,
AD 68, did the carnage against the bride of Christ finally cease. The
"forty-two months" he was given "to make war against the saints"
(Revelation 13:5-7) corresponds to the time period in Revelation
during which the Beast wreaks havoc on the bride. Those looking
for a literalistic interpretation for the ubiquitous three and a half
years need look no further.

Moreover, it is no mere coincidence that within a year of Nero's
suicide, the Roman Empire suffered a near-fatal wound. In a
moment, in the twinkling of an eye, the century-long dynasty of
Julio-Claudian emperors disappeared from the face of the earth.

[4]Tacitus, Annals, xv, 44, translated by Church and Brodribb.
[5]Tim LaHaye, introduction: "Has Jesus Already Come?" in Tim LaHaye and Thomas Ice, eds., The End Times Controversy (Eugene, OR: Harvest House, 2003), 13.
[6]Maier, The Flames of Rome, 433-434.

Indeed, AD 69 would go down in history as the year of the four emperors—Galba, Otho, Vitellius, and Vespasian.

Nero's death not only brought an end to the Julio-Claudian dynasty but the near extinction of imperial Rome. From the perspective of a first-century historian, it appeared certain that the death of the emperor was tantamount to the death of the empire. Civil war raged in the territories as four Caesars, beginning with Nero, were felled by the sword. Galba, who reigned but a little while (seven months), was decapitated, impaled, and paraded around with grotesque and grisly gestures. Otho, rumored to have been one of Nero's lovers, stabbed himself to death. And Vitellius, engorged and inebriated, was butchered and dragged by hook into the Tiber.

The very symbols of Roman invincibility—shrines and sacred sites—collapsed in evidence of her near extinction. Says Tacitus in his *Histories*, this was

a period rich in disasters, frightful in its wars, torn by civil strife, and even in peace full of horrors. Four emperors perished by the sword. There were three civil wars; there were more with foreign enemies; there were often wars that had both characters at once. . . . Cities in Campania's richest plains were swallowed up and overwhelmed; Rome was wasted by conflagrations, its oldest temples consumed, and the Capitol itself fired by the hands of citizens. Sacred rites were profaned; there was profligacy in the highest ranks; the sea was crowded with exiles, and its rocks polluted with bloody deeds. In the capital there were yet worse horrors. . . . Besides the manifold vicissitudes of human affairs, there were prodigies in heaven and earth, the warning voices of the thunder, and other intimations of the future, auspicious or gloomy, doubtful or not to be mistaken. Never surely did more terrible calamities of the Roman People, or evidence more conclusive, prove that the

Gods take no thought for our happiness, but only for our punishment.[7]

For three and a half years, the Beast systematically ravished the persecuted bride and sought the ruin of the prostituted bride. Now the kingdom of the Caesars was itself writhing in the throes of certain death. To friend and foe alike it appeared as though the empire had suffered a mortal wound. Indeed, the imminent collapse of Rome seemed so certain that Vespasian and his son Titus lost all will to advance on Jerusalem in the Jewish wars. Just as all seemed lost, however, an empire tottering on the edge of extinction arose from its funeral dirge with renewed malevolence. General Vespasian was proclaimed emperor and not only succeeded in restoring Roman sovereignty but in rehabilitating the Roman Senate. Therefore, Vespasian "resurrected" the empire and ushered in the Flavian dynasty, which would rule Rome until AD 96.

Finally, while Revelation was inscripturated in the shadow of three and a half years of tribulation, it encompasses the year that will forever stand in infamy. With the resurrection of the Roman beast, Vespasian and his son Titus once again set their sights on Jerusalem. By spring of AD 70, Titus had besieged the city. By summertime he had surrounded it with a wall, relegating the Jews within to either starvation or surrender. The Jewish historian Josephus describes the horror that ensued. Some Jews who had failed to flee to Pella "prowled around like mad dogs, gnawing at anything: belts, shoes, and even the leather from their shields." In graphic detail he recounts stories such as that of Mary of Bethezuba. "Maddened by hunger, she seized the infant at her breast and said, 'Poor baby, why should I preserve you for war, famine, and rebellion? Come, be my food—vengeance against the rebels, and the climax of Jewish tragedy for the world.' With that, she killed her infant son, roasted his body, and devoured half of it, hid-

7Tacitus, *Histories* 1:2-3, translated by Alfred John Church and William Jackson Brodribb, eBooks@Adelaide, 2009, online at http://ebooks.adelaide.edu.au/t/tacitus/t1h/book1.html (accessed February 17, 2012).

ing the remainder."[8] Josephus's words inevitably bring to mind Jesus' warning a generation earlier: "How dreadful it will be in those days for pregnant women and nursing mothers!" (Matthew 24:19).

By August, the altar of the Temple was littered with heaps of rotting corpses, and "streams of blood flowed down the steps of the sanctuary."[9] And on August 30, the unthinkable happened. "The very day on which the former temple had been destroyed by the king of Babylon,"[10] the second Temple was set ablaze. As the Revelator had prophesied, "In one day her plagues will overtake her: death, mourning and famine. She will be consumed by fire, for mighty is the Lord God who judges her" (Revelation 18:8). "While the temple was in flames, the victors stole everything they could lay their hands on, and slaughtered all who were caught. No pity was shown to age or rank, old men or children, the laity or priests—all were massacred."[11] By September 26, all Jerusalem was in flames. "The total number of prisoners taken during the war was 97,000, and those who died during the siege 1,100,000."[12]

So great was the devastation of Jerusalem and its Temple "that there was left nothing to make those that came thither believe it had ever been inhabited."[13] As the starved and shackled survivors slumped out of the smoldering ruins, no doubt more than a few remembered the words of Jesus, "O Jerusalem, Jerusalem, you who kill the prophets and stone those sent to you, how often I have longed to gather your children together, as a hen gathers her chicks under her wings, but you were not willing. Look, your house is left to you desolate" (Matthew 23:37-38). Some might even have recalled the scene. As his words still hung in the air, Jesus had turned his back on the place that had tabernacled the Shekinah glory of the Almighty. Sensing the gravity of the moment, his

[8]Josephus, *The Jewish War*, Paul L. Maier, translator and editor, *Josephus: The Essential Works* (Grand Rapids: Kregel Publications, 1988), 369.

[9]Ibid, 371.

[10]Ibid.

[11]Ibid, 372.

[12]Ibid, 376.

[13]Josephus, *The War of the Jews* VII, 1, 1, translated by William Whiston, online at http://www.ccel.org/ccel/josephus/works/files/war-7.htm (accessed February 17, 2012).

disciples had called his attention to the majesty of the Temple and its buildings. "Do you see all these things?" he had responded. "I tell you the truth, not one stone here will be left on another; every one will be thrown down" (Matthew 24:1-2). An improbable prophecy had become a nightmarish reality.[14]

[14]Afterword adapted from Hank Hanegraaff, *The Apocalypse Code: Find Out What the Bible Really Says about the End Times . . . and Why It Matters Today* (Nashville: Thomas Nelson, 2007).

HISTORICAL RECORD OF THE FALL OF JERUSALEM

NOW AS SOON AS the army had no more people to slay or to plunder, because there remained none to be the objects of their fury, (for they would not have spared any, had there remained any other work to be done,) Caesar gave orders that they should now demolish the entire city and temple, but should leave as many of the towers standing as were of the greatest eminency; that is, Phasaelus, and Hippicus, and Mariamne; and so much of the wall as enclosed the city on the west side.

This wall was spared, in order to afford a camp for such as were to lie in garrison, as were the towers also spared, in order to demonstrate to posterity what kind of city it was, and how well fortified, which the Roman valor had subdued; but for all the rest of the wall, it was so thoroughly laid even with the ground by those that dug it up to the foundation, that there was left nothing to make those that came thither believe it had ever been inhabited.

This was the end which Jerusalem came to by the madness of those that were for innovations; a city otherwise of great magnificence, and of mighty fame among all mankind.

FROM BOOK SEVEN OF *THE WAR OF THE JEWS*,
AS RECORDED BY FLAVIUS JOSEPHUS

Jesus left the temple and was walking away when his disciples came up to him to call his attention to its buildings. "Do you see all these things?" he asked. "I tell you the truth, not one stone here will be left on another; every one will be thrown down."

MATTHEW 24:1-2

HISTORICAL NOTES

THIS FICTIONAL TRILOGY stays true to the history of the war of the Jews and the fall of the Temple, as given to us in the only first-hand account, written by Josephus.

Revelation: written before or after AD 70?

Just as it is common to describe Patmos as a barren Alcatraz, mis-identify the great prostitute as the Roman Catholic Church, or identify the 144,000 as exclusively Jewish male virgins, so too it is common to contend that the book of Revelation was written long after the destruction of the Jewish Temple in AD 70. Thus, accord-ing to modern-day prophecy pundits, Revelation describes events that will likely take place in the twenty-first century rather than the first century.

Among the reasons we can be certain that Revelation was not written twenty-five years after the destruction of Jerusalem, three tower above the rest. First, just as it is unreasonable to suppose that someone writing a history of the World Trade Center in the after-math of September 11, 2001, would fail to mention the destruc-tion of the Twin Towers, so too it stretches credulity to suggest that Revelation was written in the aftermath of the devastation of Jerusalem and the Jewish Temple and yet makes no mention of this apocalypse.

Furthermore, if John were writing in AD 95, it is incredible to suppose he would not mention the fulfillment of Christ's most improbable and apocalyptic prophecy (Matthew 24:2; Mark 13:2; Luke 21:6). As the student of Scripture well knows, New Testament writers were quick to highlight fulfilled prophecy.

Finally, New Testament documents—including the book of Revelation—speak of Jerusalem and the Jewish Temple as intact at the time they were written (for example, Revelation 11:1-2). If Revelation were written *before* AD 70, it is reasonable to assume that the vision given to John was meant to reveal the apocalyptic events surrounding the destruction of Jerusalem—events that were still in John's future but are in our past. According to Scripture, Jesus sent his angel "to show his servants what must soon take place" (Revelation 1:1). Thus, the prophecy concerns a near-future event, not one that took place twenty-five years earlier. This, of course, does not presuppose that *all* the prophecies in Revelation have already been fulfilled. Just as Christ came to earth once to bear the sins of the world, so too he will return again to gather the elect and to usher in the restoration of all things. On that day, the justified will be resurrected to eternal life and the unjustified to eternal conscious torment and separation from the love and grace of God. Paradise lost will become paradise restored, and the problem of sin and Satan will be fully and finally resolved.[1]

The letter in the Senate records regarding the divinity of Christ

The historian Eusebius reported Tertullian's earlier claims that Emperor Tiberius brought details of Christ's life before the Roman Senate, apparently for a vote of approval regarding his deity. The Senate then reportedly spurned Tiberius's own vote of approval, which engendered a warning from the emperor not to attempt actions against Christians.

---

[1]For further study, see Hank Hanegraaff, *The Apocalypse Code: Find Out What the Bible Really Says about the End Times . . . and Why It Matters Today* (Nashville: Thomas Nelson, 2007).

And when the wonderful resurrection and ascension of our Saviour were already noised abroad, in accordance with an ancient custom which prevailed among the rulers of the provinces, of reporting to the emperor the novel occurrences which took place in them, in order that nothing might escape him, Pontius Pilate informed Tiberius of the reports which were noised abroad through all Palestine concerning the resurrection of our Saviour Jesus from the dead.

He gave an account also of other wonders which he had learned of him, and how, after his death, having risen from the dead, he was now believed by many to be a God. They say that Tiberius referred the matter to the Senate, but that they rejected it, ostensibly because they had not first examined into the matter (for an ancient law prevailed that no one should be made a God by the Romans except by a vote and decree of the Senate), but in reality because the saving teaching of the divine Gospel did not need the confirmation and recommendation of men.

But although the Senate of the Romans rejected the proposition made in regard to our Saviour, Tiberius still retained the opinion which he had held at first, and contrived no hostile measures against Christ.

These things are recorded by Tertullian, a man well versed in the laws of the Romans, and in other respects of high repute, and one of those especially distinguished in Rome.

EUSEBIUS, *THE CHURCH HISTORY*

The Ark of the Covenant

In historical record, the Jewish historian Josephus does not include a description of the Ark of the Covenant as part of the spoils for the Roman soldiers. This is significant by its absence, as he describes in detail that Titus took the vessels from the Temple and brought them to Rome. There are carvings of the lampstand or menorah, the Table of Shewbread, and ritual trumpets on the Triumphant Arch of Titus in Rome. There is no carving of the Ark of the Covenant.

In *The Jewish War*, Josephus writes, "Most of the spoils that were carried were heaped up indiscriminately, but more prominent than all the rest were those captured in the Temple at Jerusalem —a golden table weighing several hundredweight, and a lampstand, similarly made of gold but differently constructed from those we normally use. . . . After these was carried the Jewish Law, the last of the spoils. . . . Vespasian made up his mind to build a temple of Peace. . . . There too he laid up the golden vessels from the Temple of the Jews, for he prided himself on them; but their Law and the crimson curtains of the Inner Sanctuary he ordered to be deposited in the Palace for safe keeping."[2]

Josephus describes the Holy of Holies as empty. He states, "The innermost chamber measured 30 feet and was similarly separated by a curtain from the outer part. Nothing at all was kept in it; it was unapproachable, inviolable, and invisible to all, and was called the Holy of Holies."[3] It seems that there was no Ark of the Covenant in the second Temple when the soldiers desecrated it.

Since its disappearance from the biblical narrative, there have been a number of claims of having discovered or having possession of the Ark, and several possible places have been suggested for its location.

Historical figures in *The Last Temple*

Joseph Ben-Matthias was captured at Jotapata under extraordinary circumstances, after a siege of forty-seven days as described in the novel. Also as described in *The Last Temple*, when brought before Vespasian and Titus, Ben-Matthias predicted that Vespasian would become emperor. He was not believed, and he spent the next two

---

[2]Josephus, *The Jewish War*, VII, V, 5-6, translated by G. A. Williamson (New York: Dorset, 1959), 385-386, cited online at http://www.bible andscience.com/archaeology/ark.htm (accessed February 17, 2012).
[3]Josephus, *The Jewish War*, V, V, 5, translated by Williamson, 304.

years in chains in the Roman camp, during which time he began to write about the war. After four emperors died in quick succession—and Vespasian became emperor himself—Ben-Matthias was freed. His actions at the fall of Jerusalem at Titus's side took place as depicted in the novel. Later, Ben-Matthias was adopted into Vespasian's family, the Flavians, and so became Flavius Josephus, the name by which we remember him for his chronicles of the history of the Jews, including *The War of the Jews*, which is the only eyewitness record of the fall of Jerusalem.

Titus and **Queen Bernice** returned to Rome and lived together as though husband and wife. When Titus became emperor after the death of his father, Vespasian, he tried to marry Bernice officially, but the decision was unpopular, and he changed his mind.

Nero's final night took place as described. Josephus reports that after Nero stabbed himself in the throat, a military man fitting the description of Vitas tried to stanch the wound and was with Nero as the emperor died.

During the latter part of Nero's reign, **Nerva** was a godfather to Vespasian's son Domitian. He later oversaw the emperorships of the Flavian dynasty—Vespasian, Titus, and Domitian—then briefly became emperor himself.

Helius was paraded in chains by the emperor Galba, then put into a bag and thrown in the Tiber River.

Simon Ben-Gioras and **John of Gischala** both fled as the Temple was conquered. They were later captured by the Romans and paraded in Rome during a triumph for Titus. Ben-Gioras was subsequently executed, and John of Gischala died in prison.

DISCUSSION QUESTIONS

What was your understanding of Revelation before beginning this series? How has that changed?

What was your reaction when Jerome refused his opportunity to murder Vitas? Why was Jerome so fiercely loyal to Vitas? Was his loyalty justified?

How does Jesus' death compare to Vitas's crucifixion experience in this novel?

Vitas conducts an elaborate deception to get to the bottom of the assassination of Helva. Were his methods acceptable? Did he make any errors in judgment or in conduct?

Why does Vitas have trouble trusting in Jesus? How can we respond to people's intellectual misgivings about Christianity? How can we respond to their emotional barriers?

Christ's prediction about the destruction of Jerusalem and the Temple came to pass. What does this say about the promises of God yet to be fulfilled in the future? What are some of those promises?

What makes Hezron a believer in the Christos? What happens to him as the result of that decision? How are Hezron's sufferings similar to what many Christians experience in the world, even to this day?

What is the significance of Valeria and Quintus's act of washing Alypia's feet?

Who were the Sicarii? How was their way of violence different from the way of Christ? How does Christ want us to deal with evil in this world?

What drives Vitas in the first section of this book (while he's in Caesarea)? What motivates him in Rome? How do these motives affect your attitude toward Vitas?

In Rome's political environment, people had to carefully weigh their words. Have you ever been in a situation when you worried that your words might betray you? How did you work through that conversation?

The politics of Rome were turbulent and dangerous. How does this compare to politics today? How should followers of Jesus interact with politics and culture?

Do you agree with Titus: that he had divine help in the destruction of Jerusalem?

Ben-Aryeh was willing to sacrifice everything to save what was most precious to him. What new perspective can we gain from Amaris's final reflections about the true Temple?

Other Books by Hank Hanegraaff

Has God Spoken? Memorable Proofs of the Bible's Divine Inspiration
The Apocalypse Code: Find Out What the Bible Really Says
   About the End Times and Why It Matters Today
The Creation Answer Book
The Complete Bible Answer Book—Collector's Edition
The Bible Answer Book, Volume 1
The Bible Answer Book, Volume 2
The Bible Answer Book for Students
Christianity in Crisis
Christianity in Crisis: 21st Century
Counterfeit Revival
The Legacy Study Bible
The Heart of Christmas
The Da Vinci Code: Fact or Fiction (coauthored with Paul L. Maier)
The Face that Demonstrates the Farce of Evolution
Fatal Flaws: What Evolutionists Don't Want You to Know
The Millennium Bug Debugged
The Prayer of Jesus: Secrets to Real Intimacy with God
The Covering: God's Plan to Protect You from Evil
The Covering—Student Edition (coauthored with Jay Strack)
Resurrection
The Third Day

Other Books by Sigmund Brouwer

Novels

The Weeping Chamber
Out of the Shadows
Crown of Thorns

The Lies of Saints
Degrees of Guilt—Tyrone's Story
Fuse of Armageddon (coauthored with Hank Hanegraaff)
The Leper
Pony Express Christmas
Wings of Dawn
Double Helix
Blood Ties
Evening Star
Silver Moon
Sun Dance
Thunder Voice
Broken Angel
Flight of Shadows
The Canary List
The Orphan King

Nonfiction

Rock & Roll Literacy
Who Made the Moon

Kids' Books

Bug's Eye View series
The Little Spider, a Christmas picture book
Watch Out for Joel series
CyberQuest
Accidental Detective series
Sports Mystery series
Lightning on Ice series
Short Cuts
Robot Wars series
The Winds of Light

CHRISTIAN RESEARCH INSTITUTE

THE CHRISTIAN RESEARCH INSTITUTE (CRI) exists to provide Christians worldwide with carefully researched information and well-reasoned answers that encourage them in their faith and equip them to intelligently represent it to people influenced by ideas and teachings that assault or undermine orthodox, biblical Christianity. In carrying out this mission, CRI's strategy is expressed in the acronym EQUIP.

The *E* in EQUIP represents the word *essentials*. CRI is committed to the maxim "In essentials unity, in nonessentials liberty, and in all things charity."

The *Q* in EQUIP represents the word *questions*. In addition to focusing on essentials, CRI answers people's questions regarding cults, culture, and Christianity.

The *U* in EQUIP represents the word *user-friendly*. As much as possible, CRI is committed to taking complex issues and making them understandable and accessible to the lay Christian.

The *I* in EQUIP represents the word *integrity*. Recall Paul's admonition: "Watch your life and doctrine closely. Persevere in them, because if you do, you will save both yourself and your hearers" (1 Timothy 4:16).

The *P* in EQUIP represents the word *para-church*. CRI is deeply committed to the local church as the God-ordained vehicle for equipping, evangelism, and education.

Contact Christian Research Institute:

By Mail:

Christian Research Institute
P.O. Box 8500
Charlotte, NC 28271-8500

In Canada:

CRI Canada
56051 Airways P.O.
Calgary, Alberta T2E 8K5

By Phone:

U.S.: 888-7000-CRI (700-0274)
Canada: 800-665-5851

On the Internet:

www.equip.org

On the Broadcast:

To contact the *Bible Answer Man* broadcast with your questions,
call toll free in the U.S. and Canada, 888-ASK HANK (275-4265).

For a list of stations airing the *Bible Answer Man* or to listen to the
broadcast via the Internet, log on to our Web site at www.equip.org.

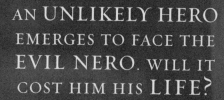